# Befor There Were Rules

a trilogy by
## David "Tank" Abbott

Book One
## Bar Brawler

Copyright © 2010 by David Abbott

Published by Full Circle Press, Inc.
www.fullcirclepressbooks.com

ISBN-13: 978-0615658605 (Full Circle Press, Inc.)
ISBN-10: 0615658601

Edited by Todd Hester

# Table of Contents

Foreword ................................................................. 1
Prologue ................................................................. 4
Kaos Rules ............................................................... 9
Heading South .......................................................... 18
Impending Doom ......................................................... 30
Boxing and Brawling .................................................... 40
East Meets West ........................................................ 52
Going Nowhere .......................................................... 61
Rock at Roller's ....................................................... 69
Lucky in War ........................................................... 80
Wannabe-Me ............................................................. 93
Road to Ruin .......................................................... 108
Liar, Liar ............................................................ 119
Fight Night ........................................................... 131
Ready, Aim, Fire ...................................................... 139
Railroad Job .......................................................... 149
Trial of Error ........................................................ 160
Truth Will Prevail .................................................... 171
Mud, Guts and Beer .................................................... 183
Delaying Destiny ...................................................... 196
The Dark Road Calls ................................................... 208
Behind the Eight Ball ................................................. 223
Lockdown Countdown .................................................... 235
A Crazy Run ........................................................... 247
Out with a Bang ....................................................... 257
Gates of Smell ........................................................ 274
Belly of the Beast .................................................... 292

# Foreword

When I started my writing adventure I promised myself it would be as true as I am, with no bullshit, and would be just as authentic as my life has been. All the posers of the world who have no claim to fame other than a predictable and boring life can talk all they want about how I was out of control and had 200 street fights before the age of 30 but that doesn't mean that they're smarter or better than me but only that they don't understand what a true warrior is really about.

I lived the life of a true warrior long before people ever started watching phony martial artists in a cage pretending they were real fighters. Now that the sport has been watered down to nothing and sanitized and commercialized for pure corporate profit, the so-called experts justify themselves by saying it's all for the good of building a sport, but that's just an excuse for their lack of historical understanding and petty jealousy that they weren't there at the very beginning and are only there now because there's money to be made.

Several years ago, when I started writing this, I was sitting outside at the Malibu Health Club, looking at the queen's necklace, sipping on a siren, and struggling with what I was going to write. While I do have a college degree in History I've spent more time living my passion than writing about it. So things like the correct format and proper grammar were holding me back from fictionalizing the story of a true warrior based on my ultimate insider's perspective.

"Hey, Tank! What are you doing?"

It was a regular at the club who's a very prominent author and director.

"I'm writing a book."

"Cool!" he said.

"Yeah, but all the spelling and grammar is holding me back."

"Tank," he shrugged, "Thomas Jefferson once said that only a fool thinks there is only one way to spell a word."

A light bulb went off – an epiphany – he really struck a chord. After that I let it fly out of my head, not worrying about anything but being true and honest to the spirit of my life. It was like when I had dinner at an anniversary party at Spago in Beverley Hills and ate with my fingers. The company was evil but the sliced New York steak looked so good that I decided who needs silverware. Besides, I was with an angel, so when all was said and done what else mattered?

The party hosts didn't understand me even though they acted like they did. *Better yet, ah!* I thought. *They'll think the same of me if I eat like an English duke or tear into it like a caveman. So let the good times roll.* While I'll admit I was having a little fun at their expense I actually didn't take it personally, because I realized it had nothing to do with me but rather their preconceived notions of who they thought I was. So judge me on the stories you've heard or the rumors that have been spread or judge me on my character and integrity. In the end, what's inside is all that really matters.

Trust me. If I wanted to write a novel that would make the norm of society happy and play one-hundred percent by their rules I could. I could also eat with silverware at Spago – but to hell with that. So read on, keep your mind open, and judge this on its own merits rather than by what you've been told to think. In the final analysis, true understanding is all on you.

-Tank Abbott

# Prologue

Gunslinger of the bars, where a duel was a fist-fight without weapons or you backed down by calling the bouncers. It was just kicking ass or getting your ass kicked. The gunslinger didn't care if he won or lost, but only about his personal integrity and being satisfied when he woke up in the morning that he had delivered justice to a deserving cockroach.

It was the early '90s in Southern California – a much different society than today. It was back in the sunset of the punk rock generation and it seemed liked bar fights just fit into the scene like a hand in a glove. It wasn't like someone cut their ex-wives head off or shotgunned their scumbag boss, but rather a fair duel. Two warriors, most likely drunk, just looking for fun in the purest form of battle: hand-to-hand combat with fists as the only weapons. Bar fights just happened – like working out on a dirty wrestling mat and waking up with ringworm on your face – they were no big deal and just part of normal nightlife.

But in modern times, good old boy fun is long gone. People can pop off and say whatever they want to then hide behind the threat of a civil lawsuit or criminal prosecution for giving them a bloody nose when they

4

damn well deserved it. I guess I lucked out because when I was around it was the last of the good hell-raising.

It would start with me picking up a friend. We'd get a twelver of cheap beer to pre-tune and then we'd hit the bars. Once we got in I'd have it in the back of my mind that I was going to stomp the hell out of some poser or scumbag who was throwing his weight around and needed to have his ass handed to him. There was always some idiot who had too much to drink and thought he could hand it to me. Oh, yeah. There were plenty in line. I didn't have an intimidating look. I varied between 200 to 300 pounds – from lightweight to fat. But either way I wasn't scary-looking until I left them lying in a pool of their own blood.

The wolf in sheep's clothing or the fat kid on the playground, they'd pick who they wanted and then get enlightened at the end of the night. It was all up to them how badly they wanted to get hurt. I would just slap them around if they said something and regretted it, but if they wanted to go hard and really try to hurt me they were going to leave in an ambulance. It was up to the fool to decide what level of punishment they wanted. After that it was a late night cheap drive-through for some burritos, then a visit to a willing girl's apartment that you'd met that night, then home to pass out.

I was going to Long Beach State pursuing a degree in history. I had no clue what I was going to do in life so I lied to myself that I would become a high school teacher and wrestling coach. I had just started boxing at the Westminster Boxing Gym and was lifting weights and going to different wrestling rooms to bang around with willing participants; then at night it was on at the bars with whoever wanted to try me. Without knowing it I

5

was doing the research for my novel and for its hero, Walter Foxx.

So when did I start this story and bring bar brawler Walter Foxx to life? The first paragraph was written on the back of a bar receipt. I wrote a decent opening but as my life would have it, I lost it in one of my drunken vodka blizzards, which seem to come around nearly every day.

You see, I've always lived my life at full throttle and I don't care what people think about me and never have. That's something that I share with Walter Foxx. In every person's life there are forks in the road upon which all their future destiny depends. Even something as mundane as deciding to run a yellow light at an intersection could be the difference between becoming a doctor or spending 10 years in prison for vehicular manslaughter. The same is true for Walter Foxx and so I focus on the intersections in his life that were his turning points.

In Walter's life, one wrong step could have meant a long prison stretch and there were many turns that could have been dark ones. I have always been attracted to the bright lights of fighting like a moth is attracted to a flame and the same is true of Walter. It has been said that you make your own luck, so you must make your own misery as well. One thing for sure is that Walter has plenty of both.

What I write here, while based on general personal experiences, is a fictionalized account of choices made and consequences earned. It is not an autobiography by any means but rather how I view the spirit of my life through the eyes of a protagonist who faces a series of difficult choices. Through it all Walter Foxx strives to stay true to who he is; which in the end is all that really matters. I can honestly say that I've been around this big blue marble a few times and I have never met anyone with experiences in bar brawling and cage fighting who can hold a candle to those I drew from in writing this novel.

I know there are legions of wannabes and posers out there who think that my life has just been an act. But to think that way just proves that they live within their own minds and can't comprehend the truth. Therefore, they're wannabes. I honestly think I'm closer to the criminally violent than I am to the joker wannabes. The criminally violent will often act on principal while posers are cowards and phonies who do things on the outside to impress people but who have no honor or courage inside.

Don't get me wrong, violence against innocent people isn't right and should never happen. But if you have it coming and it comes then so be it. I don't feel bad for you if you asked for it.

The real people of the world know that if you beg for a beating and you get it then it's your own fault. I have obliged well over 200 beggars of various degrees in my life, in and out of the cage, and it was my pleasure. No one gets over on me. If you think you have and you're still untouched then I just haven't gotten around to you yet. Trust me.

While Walter Foxx shares many of these same feelings and experiences keep in mind that this is just a novel and some of the forks that Walter takes are ones that I didn't but maybe wish I had. So strap on your seat belt and get ready to take a rocket ride because you could never dream of living the life of Walter Foxx and going from bar brawler to street warrior to cage fighter - which also just happens to be the titles of the three books in this trilogy.

To all the haters who talk about me behind my back there is only one David "Tank" Abbott to ever walk this Earth, so bring it if you dare. This is a reflection of the way I live and how I see life. I'm not some skinny moron swinging a golf club dreaming of wearing a green blazer, or a seven-foot goofball running up and down a parquet wood floor trying to put a rubber ball into a steel hoop, or an overpaid idiot with a wooden stick trying to hit a ball. I'm a warrior that nothing else matters to besides the pain they give and receive. It's about nobody knowing who you are but yourself — the only true self there is — since a true warrior stands alone.

I will not offer any further insights into who I am because it's all spelled out in the pages to follow. Walter Foxx represents how a warrior thinks so let's talk about how he became a fighter in the No-Holds-Barred Fighting Championship, or better yet how the NHB came across a real warrior in the world and not some poser who shaved his legs, dyed his hair, and made up a persona just to become known as a fighter in order to impress people. Let's talk about a man who lived solely for his passion of fighting.

-Tank Abbott

Chapter One
**Kaos Rules**

Beep! Beep! Beep!

I hit the snooze button with a loud crack. It's 8:50 A.M. and I hate waking up to the alarm clock. I look up at the ceiling with a blank stare. *What am I going to do with my life?* I shift in bed and my right hand hurts with the motion. *I must have got in a good shot last night.* As the memories come into my head I crack a smile. I was at Café Pistol in Happening Harbor yesterday evening with a group of friends. When we're together we call ourselves Kaos, which when spelled by anyone other than Agent 86 is another name for entropy, the second law of thermodynamics. It's also a name we copied from a group of pro wrestlers out of Atlanta that were on cable TV every Sunday morning. They used Kaos as a gang name when they were causing trouble together.

We were sitting outside of Café Pistol at Happening Harbor Marina, having drinks and looking over the docked boats. Our table was next to a railing that separates the walkway from the water. It was low tide and there was a ten-foot drop down to the waterline. On the other side of the table was a sidewalk that led to the Dead Grunion nightclub at the far end of the marina.

As luck would have it the Dead Grunion was having a pajama party that night where you could get in for free if you dressed in nighties. I was in an unusually quiet mood but the rest of Kaos was not. The girls in pajamas and nightgowns that walked by looked hot, but the guys all looked like nerds and were taking a lot of ribbing. Most of Kaos were wearing surfer tee-shirts or spooners and board shorts with leather Sperry Topsiders but the pajama boys had given up their dignity for a free cover charge and were fair game.

After an hour or so of drinking, a big guy walked by wearing silky, light green pajamas with dark green trim on the sleeves and a two-tone gold and stainless steel Submariner Rolex on his wrist. He had on black cowboy boots and the word "Donovan" embroidered across his chest. It looked like he could have been a regular on the pajama party circuit, if there was such a thing. The guy was clean shaven and his short black hair was perfectly groomed. He was in his mid-twenties, about the same age as me, and his silk sleeves were pulled up tight around his 20-inch arms.

From spending a lot of time in the weight room myself, I could tell he lifted. He was a giant and must have been over six feet, eight inches tall without shoes and weighed over 300 pounds. His stomach was big so it was obvious that he lifted for power and not for looks. He had "professional athlete" written all over him and I guessed he was an NFL lineman who lived in Southern California in the off-season. He was with two pretty boys about the same age who were wearing housecoats over long, baggy surfer trunks. They all sat down at a table next to us to watch the girls go by.

Since the guys and I had been there for a while it was amazing that nobody in pajamas had made it over the railing yet and into the water, which usually would have happened after four or five drinks followed by a sprint to our cars before the cops came. The big guy and his friends started throwing us dirty looks when we made too many rude comments about the pajama boys going by. After a while their presence quieted the wilder, younger kids who were part of Kaos. Their dirty looks bothered me because I don't like people dictating my environment. We were there first so if they didn't like it they just should have left.

Now that the mood had changed because of Donovan and his friends, most of the Kaos guys had started to leave, walking 20 yards to the outdoor fountain that served as an unofficial wishing well, and out of my sight towards the parking lot. As I sat there sipping my drink I suddenly heard yelling from the parking lot.

"Kaos! Kaos!"

That call meant the guys were in trouble and since they had been ribbing so many pajama boys it could have been anything. I jumped up and ran towards the fountain and turned the corner into the parking lot. Sure enough, five or six of the Kaos guys were getting into it with a similar number of pajama boys. I guessed they had waited to jump them until they were out of my sight and Kaos didn't have their big gun: me.

The fight looked evenly matched so I didn't jump in but just sat back and watched the fun unfold. The Kaos guys were doing fine without me and holding their own against the pajama boys. Two pairs were circling each other throwing wild punches and a couple more were wrestling on the ground without doing much damage.

The guy that my friend Marcus was fighting got hit with a left, didn't like it, and jumped into his topless Bronco to take off. As he tried to drive out of the lot, though, Marcus jumped in to drag him out. Two pajama boys watching from the side jumped in to get Marcus. The two guys wrestled Marcus in the back seat but the driver kept going. Outnumbered, Marcus put a chokehold on the driver and forced him to stop the car. Just then some pajama fool who wasn't even fighting pulled out a gun and fired it into the air, causing everyone to freeze.

Marcus took this break in the action to hop out of the car and run back to where the Kaos crew was so he'd have back-up. The fool with the gun had taken off running and everybody was just milling around unsurely. It seemed that the fight had ended and I was going to walk away from the wishing well but Donovan and the two surfers approached me.

They must have been there watching the fight the whole time but I didn't notice them until they walked up and put themselves in the middle of something that wasn't their business. Donovan had this arrogant look on his face that I've seen countless times and is one of the reasons I hate big guys. They think that just because they're big they can intimidate smaller people and push them around, but they just piss me off.

I was standing on the cement base of the fountain that's about a foot off the ground and he was on the walkway. With his cowboy boots, though, he had to be at least seven feet tall and so was eye to eye with me.

"Who's the ringmaster of this circus?" he said loudly in a deep voice. "Somebody is going to end up getting killed!"

"Nobody was getting killed," I said. "They're just having a little fun."

"Some fun," Donovan replied. "You're lucky I'm in a good mood tonight."

He and his pretty boy friends walked away and went down ten spaces to where a brand new white BMW convertible was parked that still had dealer plates on it. Somebody had put a beer on his trunk and it had overturned and apparently scratched the paint.

"Who the hell did this?" Donovan turned towards us, screaming. "I'm a pro athlete and I throw down with anyone who messes with me including you, fat boy!"

I was speechless for a second before I realized that the "fat boy" he was referring to was me. I felt my temper rise and made no effort to control it. I was being quiet and trying to be a good boy but he dialed the right combination to open the throw-down vault and it was on. He was a loudmouth and now he was going to get it.

Donovan got into his BMW, backed up with a screech of tires and steered towards us, gunning the motor and making everyone scatter to avoid getting hit. I tried to throw my plastic cup at him but it bounced off the side of his car. To my side I saw that Tim, another Kaos guy, was holding a bottle of beer.

"Throw it!" I screamed.

With no hesitation Tim wound up and launched his alcoholic cruise missile. It made an ominous hum as the air caught the mouth of the bottle. It flew unerringly towards the target, guided by the hand of fate, and shattered on the trunk of the brand new BMW luxury sedan with a loud splat.

Donovan slammed on the brakes and the red brake lights came on and then the white back-up lights. Slowly and deliberately he backed towards us, the new car's paper license plate coming into clear focus. I bent down quickly and tightly laced up my Doc Martins into fighting mode. The car came to a stop and then the driver's door opened and Donovan got out of his car and stepped right into Kaos.

I checked out the pretty boys who were hanging out behind him but they didn't have serious, hard looks on their faces so I knew they didn't want any part of this. I dismissed them from my mind and I knew this was just going to be between Donovan and me. All the Kaos guys backed off with scared looks on their faces. Donovan was a giant and his face was red with rage.

"I'm going to murder somebody!" Donovan screamed, looking around. "Which one of you idiots threw the bottle?"

"I did," I said.

He turned around in his black cowboy boots and saw me standing in front of the wishing well by myself. The eager audience had backed away to give us space; they wanted to see the gladiators do battle. He stepped towards me and when he was five feet away raised up his hands in a bad boxer's pose to protect his face. I'd been putting up with this guy's crap all night and now he was going to get what he'd been begging for: a beating.

I put my hands up as he got closer. He towered over me and had eight inches and seventy pounds on me. When he got within arm's reach he dropped his left shoulder and threw a looping right. Before the sloppy punch was even halfway to my head I stepped forward and blasted him with a straight right to the point of his chin. I had just started bench pressing four repetitions of 495 pounds and there was power behind my fists as I put my weight on my front foot and turned my hips into the blow. I drilled him good and he was gone, done in by a one-punch knockout. The big oaf fell back and his big body toppled over like a redwood in the forest. He hit the ground with a hard thud that only I was close enough to hear.

As soon as he was down I was on him in a split second, hitting him with three clubbing rights to the face. He was big and strong and I wanted to punish him. After the third punch his face blew up immediately like the elephant man. I glanced over at the two surfers to make sure they weren't going to jump me but they were rooted to the ground, shocked by how fast I had put down their giant. I started to speed bag Donovan's head, hitting him with lefts and rights.

Just 20 seconds had passed since I first hit him and I knew I had to end it quickly and get out of there before the gunshot brought the cops. I grabbed his hair right above each of his ears and smashed his head into the ground; it sounded like a bowling ball hitting the first pin perfectly when you throw a strike. I've perfected this move and used it in many fights to finish people quickly: *double leg, climb the rope up their body, grab their hair, then smash their head until they're out.* The key is to pull up fast to create a whiplash motion.

Only 30 seconds after Donovan threw the first punch the fight had ended. The air was now silent except for my heavy breathing. As I released his head I could hear the faint wail of sirens in the distance. His friends in the car were in shock. Their big NFL bully was lying in a pool of his own blood as I got off him. His big stomach looked like a nice big trampoline to me so I jumped on it twice, smashing his boiler into the asphalt.

"I think he killed him!" one of the surfers finally yelled. "Somebody call an ambulance!"

I knew the bouncers from Café Pistol had already called it in and it was time to jam. I had beaten up this beggar good and everyone saw my face and knew who I was. I took off towards the marina and passed the patio we'd been sitting at in full stride. My heart was pounding and my sweat was cool in the night air. I made it to the condos at end of the water and jumped over the cinderblock wall. It was six feet high but I was so pumped with adrenalin it seemed like three. I made my way to the back of the bushes where I finally started to laugh.

That idiot had it coming but I was safe for now. Johnny Law wouldn't find me here. The best part was that I could watch it all, like an artist admiring the canvas he just finished painting. This was not my first barbeque. In fact, this happens all the time.

It didn't take long for the cops to show up: five black-and-whites, an ambulance and two fire trucks. The pro athlete got what he begged for. He wanted to be the big man on campus and got his ticket punched instead. I sat in my foxhole, sweating, laughing, and breathing hard.

They loaded him onto a stretcher with a yellow oxygen mask over his face and the full attention of the paramedics on him. One of the ambulance guys had set up an IV and was feeding a tube into his arm while they wrestled the stretcher into the back. The ambulance finally left and only the cops stayed, talking to the surfers and pajama boys and taking notes. All the Kaos guys were long gone, not wanting to stick around and get questioned. I moved down the bushes and jumped back over the fence a little way down from where I was, where the cops couldn't see me.

I ran across the street and made a call on a pay phone outside the restaurant: "Rolando, come pick me up. Johnny Law is after me. I'm at Happy House Café. Leave the side door unlocked. I'll jump in so no one can see me."

As I waited for him the gravity of what just went down set in. I had crushed this moron to a pulp and put him in the hospital in front of witnesses. *He started it*, I reminded myself. *He had it coming*. Rolando pulled up and I jumped in the open side door.

"You need to get out of here, Rolando," I said, slumping down in the front seat to hide. "Fast."

## Chapter Two
## Heading South

Beep! Beep! Beep!

I hit the snooze button again and wiggle my hand. It hurts a little but once it moves around it's not that bad. No more lying around and thinking about the pro football bully I beat up last night, I've got to get to class. It's cold and I've only got 15 minutes to get to Wong Beach State College and it usually takes 20, so I'm going to have to ride hard. I shower, grab my book bag, and climb on my Interceptor 700. Duct tape holds the ragged seat together from the wear and tear of all the crazy miles it has traveled. I snake through the residential streets at an eye-watering speed and hit the freeway on-ramp. It's backed up and I can't be late so I make my way across traffic to the fast lane and twist the throttle wide open, watching as the speedometer needle passes 90.

That isn't all that fast — unless you're splitting lanes in backed-up traffic and one opened door could send you flying without a soft place to land. But I don't have time to wait like these cattle in their cars. That's why I ride a bike — for freedom.

I get to the first of my three classes for the day on time. My life at the university is juxtaposed with my life away from it. It's so strange comparing the kind of fun that went down last night with this so-called "place of higher learning." I'm hung over and as the professor's speech falls into a constant drone I drift off. I feel myself torn inside, like an adventurer without a territory to explore. Is there ever going to be a fighting sport that is authentic, with real fighting like last night?

I mean come on. The world has to know that boxing isn't real in the sense that the heavyweight champion is the baddest man on the planet. Maybe he is under Queensberry boxing rules but outside of that? No way. It's a sham. The average Joes just don't get it. They think boxing is fighting but it's really just a glorified game of tag.

I come back to reality as class ends and the students get up and pack their book bags. Now it's down the hallway to the next building. All the history buildings are old, red brick, two-story classrooms. I enter Russian History where the professor looks like the Zig-Zag man. He's wearing a traditional colorful Russian peasant shirt that goes down to his knees and looks more like a dress to me. Being that he's about six feet, three inches tall it's a painful sight for my hung-over eyes. His looks don't really bother me, though, but the clashing colors do. I don't pay attention to how people dress or act as long as they leave me alone.

He starts his lecture on Russian history and he knows the subject quite well. The last quarter of class somehow turns into a discussion of existentialism and some dude named Beaubriad. *Whatever.* I find it more interesting to close my notebook and stare at the girls outside the window. When class ends I head to an identical building across a twenty-yard-wide grassy knoll that could have come straight out of Dallas, Texas. When you're a History major you tend to make those connections.

I step into the classroom, which seems more like a theater to me, and see the professor in front of his captive audience, talking about robber baron Cornelius Vanderbilt. He then talks about locomotives and how they came to be. *Could this be any less interesting?* I like college but on the days I'm hung-over it's hard to be me. My state of mind isn't helped by the fact that my jaw is starting to ache again!

My school day finally over, I cruise home at a normal speed. The cool air feels good on my head and I park the Interceptor on the front lawn and go to the front door of my single-story rental house. As I stick the key in the lock and turn the knob I hear one of the loves of my life running to greet me. It's Adolf, my dog, an eighty-pound pit bull and of course, my best friend. He's named after a famous Colorado beer brewer whose products I quite admire. I drink a lot of Rocky Mountain cool-aid and when I got him, Coby Swapper, a friend of mine, said "Coors" should be his name. I refused to saddle him with that in case I changed brands so I named him Adolf instead.

"You can't call him that," Coby said. "People will think you're a skinhead."

The one thing you never do is tell me what I can't do, so "Adolf" it was. As my life went on I discovered that he was not only my best friend but one of my only friends. Seeing as how I got home in plenty of time for lunch I barbecue up a couple of plain cheeseburgers. As I take them off the backyard grill and throw them on buns the grease drips down and burns my lower lip. I eat one-and-a-half burgers and give the rest to Adolf, who gobbles it down in one gulp. He knows the routine because we barbecue all the time. The only reason I came home was for our regular cookout.

I nap off my hangover on the couch for a couple of hours with Adolf beside me then get up to go to work. My main transportation is the red, white and blue 700 Interceptor that I ride like a mailman in rain, snow, sleet or gloom of night. I also have a $180 car to take Adolf around in that I bought from the cousin of another friend of mine, Poppa Chulo, who apparently stole it in Texas from his wife's uncle, which doesn't count as stealing according to Poppa Chulo. In any event it's registered and doesn't show up hot when I get pulled over.

It's a mostly silver Chevy Sprint five-speed with a three-cylinder engine and it's small, especially for a big guy like me. Part of it is primer gray and it has no keys, only two toggle switches for an ignition. You hold one down and the other up until it starts. Since no one would ever figure that anyone would be stupid enough to do that it's pretty much theft proof. For music there's a small portable cassette player plugged into the cigarette lighter that plays The Smiths non-stop. The car is a total piece of crap but it has sheepskin seat covers so that makes it cool.

I grab my book bag, hit the toggle switches, push play on the cassette player, and head off to work. I take the usual route down Pacific Crest Highway, past a famous landmark house on stilts made from an old water tower. I always promise myself that someday that house will be mine. A few miles past that I pull up to work at Sea Lion Beach Liquor. It's an old building from the early fifties that has the only local neon sign from that era that still works. I've got work down to a science and I walk in with my book bag so I can study when it's slow. Trike is the manager of the place but he's also a good friend and the guy who hired me.

"What's up, Walter?" he asks.

"Not much," I shrug.

I'm wearing a loose-fitting, green tee-shirt, blue shorts, and untied white basketball high-tops. I settle in and put my book bag on the counter as Trike leaves. I crack open my books, trying to study history as one piece of human trash after another comes into the liquor store. Sea Lion Beach has nothing in it at night but surf and skate punks who have this idea they can talk trash to any clerk behind the counter. But that never works out for them with me.

"Oh, you're the clerk," a drunken scumbag will say. "Serve me and take the verbal abuse I'm giving you."

"No," I always reply. "How about I pick you up by the collar and throw you into the street instead?"

The owners come in now and again and one time caught me tossing a punk into the gutter. But they used to work the late shift themselves so they're always on my side. From 4:00 P.M. to 6:00 P.M. I read about trains, the Russian revolution, and other bullshit that nobody but History majors know or care about. Finally, my homework assignment done, it's time for dinner. Mario, the cook from the Hawaiian restaurant next door, comes in and sets a white bag on the counter containing a well-done prime rib sandwich and fries. In return he grabs a six-pack of Bud out of the cooler and goes out the back door. It's a fair trade just like every night I work.

With dinner done, it's time to crack open a soldier. It's Thursday, the last night of the week for me, so one Coors turns into another and continues to grow exponentially. I stock, mop, count the drawer, and then grab a couple of cases which I get at cost and always mark down on the ledger. I'm finally done with my indentured servitude and would normally head home. But tonight is different. I'm going down to Mexico with Dick and the boys for the weekend to celebrate my friend Grant's birthday.

I'm in a good mood now because I don't have to deal with anymore scumbags tonight. I put the cases of Coors in the hatchback and slam it down with a smile. I slide into the driver's seat, reach behind me, and grab a bottle top through the handle holes of the 12-pack I put in the back seat. I twist the cap off, take a long swig, turn on The Smiths, and flip the toggle switches to start the car. It's a little after 11:00 P.M. and I'll soon be headed to Mexico to whoop it up. *Life is good.*

I maneuver down the alley behind the store and make a left into an older part of town. The houses have been here for over 50 years but they're well-kept with nice yards. When you get a little ways away from the beach it's a nice community. The street is dark and I take another big swig off my soldier. The Smiths are playing and the ocean fog is just starting to roll in.

As I lower my soldier I look down the street and see two shapes in the darkness. At first I think its two guys fighting but then I realize it's a man slapping the shit out of a fat chick. *That's not cool.* I start to slow down the car to get out but then the fat chick breaks free and runs across an unlit crosswalk in front of me in a hurried waddle and rushes into a house. It startles me and I hit the brakes to slow down, nearly spilling my beer. I look down and stabilize it, making sure it's jammed securely between the emergency brake and driver's seat. When I glance up from my beer check a man suddenly appears out of the darkness, rushing in the same direction as the fat chick, forcing me to slam on the brakes.

*Wow*, I think. *I better pay more attention. He came out of nowhere. I could have hit him and something bad could have happened.* I wait for him to cross in front of me but as soon as he gets out of the way he stops in the middle of the street.

"Watch what you're doing, fuck face!" he yells.

I ignore him and slowly let the clutch out, moving the silver Sprint into the quiet darkness. *That guy shouldn't have said that,* I think. But I was in the wrong so I keep going. Then from behind me, I hear a voice calling out again, barely audible over the smooth rhythm of The Smiths. I turn down the volume so I can hear.

"Learn now to drive, dumb ass!" the guy shouts out.

I look in my rearview mirror and see that the guy is still standing in the crosswalk 30 yards behind me. He's five feet, eleven inches tall and maybe 190 pounds dressed all in black with carefully styled hair. He looks like a high school quarterback type who got all the girls and was in everyone's face because the teachers all cut him slack. Both his arms are out in front of him and he's flipping me off with both hands.

"Go to hell!" he yells. "I'll mess you up!"

*Huh? Did he really just say that? He's really begging for it.* I push the clutch in and hit the brakes, watching this guy in my rearview mirror standing in the intersection where our lives have crossed. I slowly move the gearshift into reverse and back up, curious to see if he really wants some. I turn the steering wheel to the right and slowly make a reverse turn until he's in front of me. I grab the driver's window knob to roll it down but the window falls all the way into the door jam, leaving me 10 feet away from this quarterback scumbag dressed all in black. *Just drive off*, I tell myself. *Don't go there.* But this scumbag won't stop yelling at me.

"That car is a piece of shit just like you!" he screams.

"You want something with me, man?" I ask calmly.

"Yeah! I want you to get your fat ass out of that car so I can jack you up!"

*That's it. He has clearly crossed the line. You can only let someone go so far before it becomes a matter of honor.* I open the door and get out. Now it's him and me in the deserted residential intersection with no street lights. My Sprint is parked in the road between two rows of parked cars, Single family dwellings stand behind me and he's in front of a dark, unlit corner church. It's been there forever and is long and narrow, made from big blocks of dark, gray stone.

"Go to hell!" he yells again.

"That's it!" I bark, startling him. "Let's go!"

As I bolt towards him his eyes open wide in shock and he makes a break for the back of an old Volkswagen square-backed sedan parked in front of the church. When I try to chase him down he quickly moves to the front of the car, keeping it safely between us.

"Good luck catching me, fat ass!" he yells from the far side.

I turn towards my Sprint sitting in the middle of the street and walk to the driver's side door. "I knew you were a poser," I yell back. "You talk shit but you're all mouth!"

As I put my hand on the door handle he comes out from behind the Volkswagen and walks towards me, flipping me off again, thinking that I'm going to drive away.

"Fuck you, fat ass!" He yells. "Fat ass! Fat ass! Fat ass!"

I open the door and grab the top of the window frame like I'm going to get in, but then I suddenly spin around and burst into a charge, like a bull elephant going after a jackal. He moved from the safety of the parked car near the church to taunt me and is just 10 feet away. He freezes for just an instant and turns around to run, but I've gotten the jump on him with my surprise charge and all his bullshit is catching up to him. Now it's a foot race and with each stride I'm more pissed. I've been listening to this guy's big mouth for way too long and the bull elephant is getting closer to trampling the jackal with every thunderous echo of its feet in the quiet night air.

The jackal tries to get away from his mistakes but the law of the jungle is overtaking him. I'm mad as hell and as I run I think how much I hate little smartasses with big mouths. We run the length of the old stone church and I draw close enough to grab his shirt. I reach out with my hand and clutch his collar, bringing him to a stop. I can feel his fear in my grasp. His words have caught up to him. The bull elephant has caught the jackal.

As I grab his shoulders and turn him towards me I decide I'm going to shake him around and just scare him a little. I'm not going to hurt him bad because he just yelled at me and ran. Maybe I'll sit on his chest for a minute or two and cut off his air, as opposed to dismembering him with a pair of vice grips a body part at a time, which I sometimes feel mad enough to do but which I've never come close to acting out. *No, I'm going to be nice and just give him a little fright.*

As I hold him by the shoulders facing me, he suddenly shakes one arm free and I think he's going to run. But instead he takes me by surprise and rears back and punches me in the face, sending pain shooting up the side of my head. *Oh, hell. We're going there after all.* I let go of his shirt with my other hand and blast him with a left hook. It's over right there and he falls to his back. Thanks to the glare of a porch light from a nearby apartment I see his glazed-over eyes and know he's done. I lean over him and put my face inches from his.

"That's what happens to smartasses," I say.

With a grunt his eyes pop open and he swings wildly at me, bouncing a left and right off my head before I know what's happening. *Enough with being a nice guy. Now it's time for the jackal to pay full price for his sins.* I pound downward with a straight right and it lands flush. He's on his back on the cement church parking lot with a silly knocked-out look on his face. I'm so mad now that I swear I would crush his head like a grape if I could. I really would. But in the heat of battle I go to what I know best. I straddle his chest, grab his hair, and bash his head onto the cement, trying to bounce this scumbag's head off his body.

Out of the darkness near the church, a long-haired hippie suddenly comes out of the shadows and hovers over me. I haven't seen him before and have no idea who he is. I stop the bashing and look up with surprise.

"Hey, man," the hippie says. "What's going on here? There's no need for this."

I hate hippies so I get off the unconscious loud-mouthed jackal to see if this long-haired freak wants to go. He stands in the shadow of the upstairs apartment light where it hits in the back of the church. He's dressed in a tie-dyed rainbow shirt and dirty white painter pants.

"You want some?" I ask him, panting heavily. The heated breath from my mouth flows into the night air like fog.

"There's no need for this," he shakes his head. "Peace, brother."

"Oh, my god!" a female voice yells out behind me. "What did you do to my boyfriend?"

I turn around and see the fat girl that I saw running across the crosswalk earlier kneeling beside the scumbag and cradling his head.

"Somebody call 9-1-1!" she yells. "Get an ambulance!"

I turn back towards the hippie but he's nowhere to be seen, having disappeared as quickly as he appeared. Lights start coming on from the surrounding apartments and from the houses across the street as the fat chick continues screaming. I hurry to my Sprint in the middle of the street, hit the toggle switches, and take off. I learned a long time ago that it's better to leave before the cops get there, even if you're in the right like I was.

I take the back way home through the naval munitions storage yard with the earthen bunkers lining both sides of the road. I get to my house to meet Dick and the boys a half-hour late and sit in my car. *We were going to go party in Mexico for the weekend,* I think. *Why did that scumbag have to go there?* I grab the soldier that started everything. It's still cold and secure between the seat and emergency brake and tastes great when I power it down. I get out of the Sprint and go to the living room where

Dick and the boys are partying hard. Adolf runs up and I give him a big hug.

"What's up, big boy?" I say through his wild licks to my face. I hold him tightly to calm him down as I look around the room. "I am so ready to party."

"How was your night?" Dick asks.

"The store was fine," I say. "But I had a little trouble after work."

"I can see that," Dick laughs. "You've got blood on your forearms."

"I'll tell you the whole story in Mexico," I say. "Who's all going?"

"Well," he says, counting off on his fingers, "it's going to be Tom, Grant, Mikey, Skip, Phil, me, and you. Jorge has to do something with Shelly this weekend, so he's staying home."

"That's good," I say. "Adolf needs someone to watch him. I've got the beer in the car. Let's load up the coolers and get rolling. It's almost midnight."

As I walk out the door, Adolf knows I'm going somewhere and is pissed. I've slept with him every night since I got him when he was eight weeks old. I hate to leave him but Jorge will hang with him and I need to go on this road trip. I'm already on my next soldier when we all jump into Phil's huge Lincoln Town Car and roar off, heading south.

## Chapter Three
## Impending Doom

We somehow make it to a fleabag hotel in Ensenada, 60 miles south of San Diego on the Pacific side of Baja, smashed on beer. We get a couple of rooms for the seven of us and pass out until 1:00 P.M. Everyone is hung over but after they pound a couple of pots of coffee they're ready to get back into the swing of things. I've never drank coffee and consider it a crutch, compared to vodka which is rich in vitamin B. So I throw down a handful of aspirin and am ready to resume the fun. We grab a cheap lunch at a fish taco stand across the street then head to the hotel bar where we order a margarita pitcher each. By the time we've polished them off and started on another round Grant is cackling like a maniac and everybody is totally wasted.

"So how did you get blood on your forearms last night?" Grant asks.

"I messed up a scumbag who really begged for it."

"Where at?" Grant presses.

"Right by the liquor store," I say regretfully. "It's a small town and I shit in my own backyard. The cops are probably looking for me. Everybody knows me from work."

"Don't worry about it now," Grant answers. "You're in Mexico."

"Right on," I nod. "I'm not going to let it ruin my weekend."

We order margaritas and chips until dusk, and as the sun goes down our volume goes up. *It's time to play.* We're a bunch of drunken hooligans and it's time to find trouble. We leave the hotel and stagger from bar to bar, powering down cheap drinks. The dirty city streets are filled with Mexican *hombres* with macho attitudes that we push out of our way on the crowded sidewalks. We're like a bunch of rowdy kids on spring break, except older and bigger, so no one messes with us.

We get crazier and louder at each bar. There are taco carts cooking cat and dog meat everywhere I look. Each street corner is crowded with beggars, drunks, hookers, and small-time Mexican pimps with cowboy hats trying to lure tourists into local brothels. Being hassled by them is just part of the game and even though they want our money and put up with our bullshit, I can see in their faces they'd just as soon like to kill us. I'm smashed and loud and getting more obnoxious as the night goes on.

"Get out of my way, Paco," I laugh out at nearly everyone I pass.

We turn a corner towards another bar and I stop cold in front of a store selling Mexican women's clothing. "Hold on, guys," I say. "I need a damn dress."

I go into the store and buy a moo-moo style Mexican dress from the astonished female clerk who charges me twice what it's worth. I don't care, though, because it's blue with a white bead necklace that goes perfectly with my hair, or so I tell everyone. Grant gets a yellow nightgown with a pink lace collar and we throw them over our clothes and proceed to walk around Ensenada. I'm fired up now and I'm not going to put up with any more badgering from Mexican street thugs with Napoleon complexes. I have on my new dress and I'm hammered so don't mess with me. *Get out of the way because Big Bertha is coming through.* We walk around for a while wearing the dresses and the locals look at us like we're crazy gringos – which we are. I'm having fun and cursing up a storm.

"Watch your mouth," a little Mexican vendor in black cowboy boots says. It's the end of the night and he's still desperately cooking tacos on a rusty cart; but he looks me straight in the eye.

"You want trouble?" I say.

I move closer until I tower over him. A small woman with two frightened young boys in ragged clothes, who I just notice are huddled behind his cart, scramble up and move back. *Oh, hell.* The man's eyes get wide as I raise my hand but instead of bashing him in the face I slap him on the shoulder good-naturedly.

"Because I just want some tacos," I say.

"Si, senor," he replies, relief written all over his face.

The older kid breaks free of his mom and runs up and hugs his dad's leg. He's a hero to them now. He's stood up to the evil gringo and saved them. I give him a fiver, grab a couple of fifty-cent tacos, and move on, throwing them to some stray dogs when I turn the corner.

We get back to the old, run down, six-story brick hotel and two hookers drive by in a white, pin-striped Datsun B-210 with low-profile rims. It's a Mexican BMW. They pull to the curb in front of the high-rise building across the avenue and get out. They're maybe five feet, three inches tall with dark brown skin and long black hair. They're wearing flowered blouses with tiny white shorts with green platform high heels. The outfits really don't match and I think that Grant and I could give them some hints on how to dress.

They follow us into the hotel and Skip and Phil negotiate with them for a couple of minutes in the lobby, right in front of the bell clerk who couldn't care less. They finally reach an agreement and go up the elevator with us and follow Skip and Phil to one of our two rooms. The rest of us, who have smartly backed off, jam into the other room. *Oh, yeah. You can catch anything in Mexico.* From our balcony we can see Skip and Phil bouncing around on the bed with the two hookers, seeming to do nothing but get in each other's way. We laugh uncontrollably until the hookers leave, with no one apparently happy, then go back into the room. Skip, a little mouse of a guy, gets a ribbing from all the boys for his acrobatics. I climb in bed and pass out immediately in my new dress, leaving it on as an extra shield from the suspect bed sheets.

When I wake up the bead necklace is wrapped around my neck and my head hurts like hell. I think about home and the scumbag I beat up and I can't get away from the thought that I could be in serious trouble. I go into the bathroom with its blue colorful tiles and cheap mustard paint and turn on the water in the sink. As it trickles out, I open my travel bag, grab my razor and cut off my goatee, leaving just a cop mustache. Hopefully that will change my look enough that I can't be picked out of a police line-up.

As I examine my face in the mirror I realize I've got to do something about the double-chin that's been hiding under my beard. By the time I get out of the bathroom the room is empty so I go downstairs and see that everyone is already at the hotel bar where it all started the day before. Everyone is drinking coffee and having a tough time getting revved up again. But I can roll so I forego the java as usual and order a double margarita. At the table next to me are two attractive American women in their early forties, a blond and a brunette, also sipping drinks.

"How's it going?" I ask. "Hair of the dog?"

"You could say that," the blonde laughs. "We're taking a mental health break from selling San Diego timeshares. You?"

"Even worse," I say. "I just cut off my goatee because I have to go back to Orange County where I almost killed somebody last week."

A tense look comes into their eyes and I realize I've probably said too much.

"But it was in self-defense and he deserved it," I say quickly. "He was using his girlfriend as a punching bag."

This seems to make it okay with them and they relax again.

"Well, good," says the brunette. "You'll be fine then. The police are good at sorting those things out."

"Yes. The cops are our friends," I say sarcastically with a wry smile.

I chit-chat with them for a while and am just about ready to get the blonde's phone number when Skip comes over from the bar to grab me. I say a hurried goodbye and go outside with him where the others are already waiting in the car.

"Dude," Skip says as we get in, "she was as old as my mom."

"Yeah, and I'd bang her, too," I say. "So what's the difference?"

The entire car bursts out laughing as Phil pulls onto the main road and heads north. After an hour's drive or so we stop in Rosarito Beach and go into a restaurant we know next to the toll road.

"I'll take a double margarita!" I yell out before we even sit at the bar, "with chips and salsa!"

Everybody follows suit and we get back into our groove, having loud drunken fun and pissing off everybody in the bar who can't hear a soccer game that's on TV. After a couple of hours we've had enough and decide to leave. Mikey offers to pay the entire tab with his credit card and we stumble outside to the dirt parking lot to wait for him. He staggers out a few minutes later with a silly grin on his face.

"Look at my signature," he giggles, waving the bar tab. "I signed it Charles Manson. Just wait till they try to bill him!"

"They'll still charge your credit card, dumbass," I say.

His grin turns upside down and he starts to demand cash from everyone, but we flip him off in turn, grab a case of Coors from a beer shack next door, and head for the border. We make it through the long line at Mexican Customs at the dumpy and rundown Tijuana border crossing in 45 minutes and I pass out in the back seat. The next thing I know we're pulling up in front of my house and Skip is pushing me out the back door. I find my balance and get to my feet as the Lincoln speeds away.

Skip keeps his hand on my shoulder to balance his drunken walk as I go up the walkway, put the key in the door, and open it. Skip immediately heads for his bedroom to crash while I greet Adolf, who is waiting for me as though I never left. I check the phone for any bad news but there are no messages from the cops, the D.A.'s office, or anyone else. I breathe a sigh of relief. It seems that I shaved off my beard for no reason. I must have been paranoid but I'm always worried because Johnny Law wants me bad. Not because I'm wrong for beating people up who deserve it, but because I win. I've beaten up a lot of scumbags and gotten away with it because they all begged for it. They were all wannabe tough guys who picked on the wrong guy.

I beat up that moron who begged for it and now it looks like he turned out to be a stand-up guy. I never would have believed it because he didn't seem to be someone who would man-up from our brief encounter. He must have realized that he drank too much, thought he was tough, started a fight, and lost it fair and square. Every once in a while I'll meet another true warrior who thinks the same way I do and will take what they deserve and then move on. But they're few and far between.

I'm home from Mexico on a Sunday evening and since sleeping on the drive home sobered me up, I grab a soldier from the fridge and do some reading in my history books to get ready for classes. When I walked in Adolf ran to the door, happy to see me; but now that I'm studying he's giving me a you-left-me-so-get-lost attitude. By the time I finish a couple of hours later, though, all is forgiven or forgotten and I turn the TV on and stay up late with him on the couch and drink. He trails me into my bedroom when I'm drunk enough to sleep and dozes off instantly, his cold nose rubbing my ribs while he snorts like a wild boar.

It seems like I had barely closed my eyes when the alarm clock blares into my ear. I hate waking up to the damn alarm and someday hope I won't have to. I only have a couple of late classes on Monday so I take my time getting to campus. It's harder than normal to pay attention to the bullshit lectures today as the professors, wannabe stars of their own lives, talk about trains, the Russian revolution, Cold War politics and other earth-shattering events they seem to think they were personally responsible for. When my classes are finally done, I walk across the Wong Beach State library quadrant towards the parking lot. A guy I know from my high school football team, who's now a muscle-bound steroid user, sees me and comes over.

"Hey, Walter," he says, sticking out his 44-inch chest and sucking in his 32-inch waist. "Looks like you've been losing weight. You're in great shape."

I smile thinly at him and debate dropping him right then and there. This moron knows exactly what he's saying. He's a total idiot who is trying to get over on me. I'm heavier than I've ever been and am worried that my Mexican moo-moo might soon be the only thing I can fit into. I have a sudden vision of me and my Russian professor who looks like the Zig-Zag man, standing next to each other in our dresses. Be that as it may, I still can't believe how this phony steroid-ripped clown, who couldn't hold a candle to me in a fight, has the nerve to come up and play with me. *Does he think he could even last a minute with me in a brawl or a debate?* I guess it proves how dumb he is. I decide to let him live just because I'm as fat as shit and deserve the ridicule. I chat with him for a few minutes before he hurries off to class. *To hell with this! I've got to get back in shape!*

From that day forward, for the next two months, I burn the candle at both ends, tearing it up at night and training every day by lifting weights and going into the wrestling rooms to grapple with whoever's there. I also start boxing to get some formal training on how to punch with power. When I enter Westminster Boxing Gym for the first time Tyrell Biggs, the Olympic gold medal winner, is hitting the punching mitts with his trainer. He looks impressive but he is a boxer and not a real warrior. I know that I would kill him in a street fight. But I want to fight and this is the closest thing I can legally do without the risk of going to jail. I know I'm tough and could beat these boxing stars; I've just got to learn the rules so I can play their game.

The first time I ever sparred hard was a few weeks before I joined the boxing gym, and was what actually got me interesting in doing it. I was visiting a friend in central California and went to his boxing club with him. He told his trainer that I was a bar brawler who liked to fight.

"So you're tough, huh?" the trainer said. "You street fighters never want spar, though."

"I do," I answered without hesitation.

"Okay," he nodded in surprise. "Spar with that guy over there. He's a pro with nine fights. He won't hurt you too bad."

I went out to my car and put on my wrestling shoes that I always have with me. Then they got a mouthpiece and warmed it up with hot water from the cafe next door and melted it around my missing front teeth, which I lost in a car accident.

"Do I really have to go through all this?" I asked the trainer.

"Yep," he replied. "You don't want to get your jaw broken. Your sparring partner is the little brother of Jerry Quarry. His name's Bobby. Keep your mouth closed and try to protect yourself."

I put on the gloves even though I didn't really know what I was doing. I'd never sparred before but I did what I do best and traded with him non-stop, eating three or four jabs to get in one good overhand right. He was out on his feet twice and each time the trainer would have to call me off as I backed him into a corner. I took a bit of a beating too, but it didn't matter. I fought just like I do in the street, with instinct and heart. It made me wonder if maybe I could fight for a living someday. We all need to have our dreams, even if they do seem impossible.

## Chapter Four
## **Boxing and Brawling**

Just five weeks after joining the Westminster Boxing Gym I have my first boxing match against my trainer's advice. I'm not worried about my skills; I'm just here to get down. It's all about scrapping even if there are rules and gloves.

My first official opponent has three years of experience on me and I have no business being in the ring with a guy like that for my first match. But I don't care and it's on. We battle for the first two rounds evenly then in the third I take it to a new level, where skills don't matter, called "gut check time." You have to be from the street to understand it and it's something that a guy who's in it only for sport can't fathom. It's where you throw caution to the winds and don't care how many times you're hit as long as you can deliver punishment and make him pay. I wade in with all guns blazing and knock this boxing wimp down twice and win.

Before I started my new training regimen I'd been going to the wrestling rooms for takedowns during the day and hitting the weights at night. But now I'm boxing, wrestling, and lifting weights during the day and doing real fighting at night in the bars. In just a couple of months I've gained muscle and lost fat. I'm at home after school on my work and training day off, hanging with Adolf, when the phone rings and I pick up.

"It's Monday Night Football," says Ron "Gonzo" Middleton, one of my buddies, who was also the heavyweight on my junior college wrestling team. "The Dead Grunion has free hotdogs and a bunch of drink specials."

"Let's party," I say. "You don't have to ask me twice."

We meet at the club and get down non-stop until the game is over. They clear the tables from the bottom section and the DJ starts playing music and the dance floor comes to life. Long retractable pillows that hang down on chains descend from the ceiling onto the crowded dance floor, like schlongs from heaven, and one comes down right beside me. I'm so drunk that I grab it to help keep my balance and when it starts to retract I hang on. The DJ, who can't stand me because I always bug him to play The Smiths' songs, sees me going up but keeps raising them. I'm hoisted up with the pillow until I'm swinging 10 feet in the air in the rafters. I hang on for as long as I can but I finally get tired and drop to the dance floor, luckily not killing anyone and somehow not breaking my neck. I lay on the dance floor catching my breath as dancers stumble around me to the disco music. *Holy, hell! Now that was a fall!* As I lay on the parquet floor a big black guy looks down at me and steps right on my stomach, almost making all the beer I drank come up.

"What the hell?" I say, scrambling to my feet.

"If you want to be a rug then expect to get stepped on," he says crossly.

I was happy lying on the floor in my drunken state, but now this scumbag with an attitude has to go and ruin my night.

"If you want to be an ass then expect someone to kick it," I shoot back. It sounded better in my head than when I actually said it, but it's hard to be clever when you're hammered.

"If you want some trouble, jumbo," he says, "I'll be waiting for you outside."

He disappears into the crowd and I try to follow, but dancers keep running into me and he's already outside by the time I get to the front. I can see that's he's just outside the double glass door, on the sidewalk that runs between the building and the dark marina water below. By the time I get into the parking lot the idiot is already shadow boxing, warming up like he's Joe Frazier. He sees me coming towards him and puts up his fists.

"It's just fair to tell you," he says, "that I was a Golden Gloves champ and I…"

That's as far as he gets because I take a short run and shoot in on him in a perfect double-leg takedown. I pick him up and put him on my shoulder for just an instant before I slam him down onto the sidewalk, forcing the air out of his lungs with a sharp grunt. As he struggles for air I climb the rope up his body, straddle him, and punch his Golden Glove face a few times. He rolls to his stomach to avoid the blows and struggles to all fours to try to get up. I get off him as he wobbles to his feet then hit him with a right and a left before his hands even come up, putting him on Queer Street with his eyes dancing in their sockets. Before he can crumple to the ground I shoot in again, get him across both shoulders in a fireman's carry, then step across the sidewalk and throw him over the railing into the marina water 10 feet below. I almost go over with him but a hand grabs my shirt from behind and keeps me from toppling over.

I glance behind and see that Gonzo has followed me out and kept me from taking a bath. The golden boy splashes and sputters around for a few seconds before clambering onto some rocks. He looks up and sees us laughing our asses off at him and flips me off now that he's safely out of reach. A small crowd has gathered and are all laughing at this wannabe tough guy floundering in the water like a mackerel. The bouncers come over and start to ask questions and so we get in our cars and head out before the cops arrive.

I go to sleep as soon as I get home and awake the next morning to the hated alarm clock, heading out for another day much like the one that came before it. I'm a creature of habit so I go to school, work out, do my shift at the liquor store, then go out and have fun. I party at a different hotspot every night with different friends, since no one can keep up with me. I had planned to teach school and coach football and wrestling after I graduated but I don't know if things will work out that way for me. I'm pretty sure most schoolteachers don't act the way I do. Regardless, I know that I have to get my college degree out of the way then see if my past catches up to me. I've had a lot of trouble with the law over the years and I know it could cause me problems later. I've been charged with everything from fighting in public to assault with a deadly weapon - me! So far I've skated on all charges because it was all in self-defense, but it still leaves me wondering what I'm going to do with my life when the one thing I have a passion for is bar brawling.

My life is drifting aimlessly and I'm going nowhere from having too much fun. I keep wondering what my life is all about. What am I going to do? Everybody I grew up with has gone through that point in their life and is pursuing a goal. But I'm not your average Joe. My real passion is not to be an accountant, doctor, lawyer or teacher but rather a fighter. I don't want to be what normal people think of as a fighter. No! I want to beat up idiots, morons, scumbags, phonies, and bullies who deserve it. It's even better when they approach me with an attitude and think they can hurt me. I think of all the people they've done that to just because they've always been bigger, stronger, or quicker than everyone else. Now they've gone a step too far and picked on the one person who will exact justice for all their evil deeds.

Every person I've beaten up has begged me for it. Don't get me wrong, I love to fight, but every person I've taken out did something wrong. I just gave them a correction when they disrespected me at some level and proved to me who they really are and what they've really done. There are a bunch of beggars out there who deserve to be punished and when they ask me for it I'm only too happy to oblige.

I'm already done with school and working out when Tim calls. He's one of my best friends who's been stomping with me for a long time and who used to live across the street when we were kids.

"There's a big party at a club on the other side of town," he says.

"So what," I say. "There are a lot of parties on this side of town, too."

"A lot of hot chicks will be there," Tim tempts me. "Okay," I say. "What the hell. Let's go."

Tim comes by a little while later in his truck and we pick up a twelve-pack and drive around killing time, listening to music as we cruise the familiar residential streets of Happening Harbor. There has to be at least a thousand broken beer bottles on the sides of the city streets, most of them ours. Every time we finish a beer we throw it at a street sign and shatter it with a loud splat. We finally end up in the Surfside School parking lot, where we graduated from the fifth grade, to finish off the clip of soldiers.

In our pre-tune travels Tim's friend, Gene, has made it into the truck. Tim has been my friend for a long time and is an average-sized Mexican guy of maybe 150 pounds. I always notice people's weight because I want to know who has my six during a bar fight and if they can handle themselves. Gene is maybe 10 pounds heavier than Tim but is not my friend. But since he's a friend of Tim's he will be tolerated. Gene thinks being goofy is cool so he wears goofy clothes and listens to goofy music. To me he's just weird but to each his own.

We make it to Christian's nightclub and Gene has two quick beers to catch up with me and Tim. Gene has never been able to hold his booze, however, and starts running around the club grabbing a bunch of girls' butts.

"Tim," I say. "What's up with Gene? Is he mental?"

"Probably, Walt," he answers.

"Oh, well," I shrug. "At least he's funny to watch."

The place is packed with a younger crowd in their early twenties and cigarette smoke fills the room. There is loud music with a lot of chicks walking around but for some reason I'm just not feeling the vibe. Maybe it's caused by not enough booze or Gene being so goofy but the vibe just isn't there. It happens sometimes. I hate it when it's so crowded that you can't get a drink and that's the case tonight. Most of these idiots are drunker than me, which is sad. What the hell, though, at least Gene the drunken idiot is supplying plenty of laughs.

After less than an hour there, Gene has predictably managed to get himself kicked out for being a goofball. He came with me and Tim, though, so according to party law we have to leave with everyone we came with, so we get ready to take off. Across the room I see a wannabe tough guy red-haired bouncer talking to idiot Gene, but at least everything is calm. Gene starts winding out of the club escorted by the bouncer with red hair that I recognize from the wrestling rooms around town. He's not very tough but is more than hard enough to be a bouncer here.

Gene is getting a little more agitated now, and is getting physically pushed towards the door. Tim is ahead of me and watching closely but I'm just floating back, actually glad to be out of here. The bouncers are all relatively young and inexperienced but they hustle him out the door without a major scene. Well, Gene needed to be thrown out and I wanted to leave anyway. Still, I could feel the gravity of it building as he got forced out. I continue to move peacefully towards the front door, not emotionally involved and glad they threw that goofball out.

Then out of nowhere and for no good reason, the head bouncer, a big Samoan, slaps me hard on the back from behind. Out of the three of us I was the one he noticed and zeroed in on. I was minding my own business but he saw I was the only threat and had to size me up. I turn my head and see that he's fat, perhaps four hundred pounds, and apparently likes to push people around.

"Move out!" he says sharply when I turn around, pushing me again.

"What the hell?" I snap at him. "I didn't do anything. Keep your hands to yourself and don't touch me. I'm not joking!"

Once again, I'm face-to-face with another stupid moron who thinks he can push his weight around. *Oh, man.* He made my mood turn on a dime. Moments earlier I was happy to be leaving and now this four-hundred pound scumbag is messing with me. *No! No! No!* I walk towards the front door and go out to the entrance area that's like a giant birdcage made of wrought iron. It's a twenty-foot high dome atop a thirty-foot diameter, five-foot tall brick circle with only one opening. He doesn't know it yet, but it's on. When we get outside the iron cage I turn towards him

"Push me now, bitch!" I yell.

He could slap me and talk tough when were in the club, inside his safety zone, but now he looks me over and is hesitant, his face full of uncertainty. He glances behind me, though, and his look changes. He suddenly has new confidence and steps towards me aggressively. I glance behind me and see that his back-up team has arrived, straight from the parking lot. Not bouncers, apparently, but his friends. All of them are in the mid-three- hundred-pound range and are squeezing between the cars towards us.

I slide into a position with my back against the iron cage, where none of them can get behind me. They try to circle me but this is not my first barbeque.

"Bite me, you bunch of fat losers!" I yell. I slide away from the iron cage and then backpedal across the pot-holed parking lot. These dumb idiots think they're going to get me but there is no way. "I'll be back!" I yell out.

"Sure you will," The head bouncer laughs at me, surrounded by his fat friends. "I heard that before."

"Not from me," I answer. I take off running to the truck and get in and we drive off.

I have Tim go around the corner and stop the truck while I dial my wrestling buddy, Gonzo, who lives close by.

"Gonzo," I say, "I need back up. I've got a four-hundred pound Samoan bouncer that wants a beating bad, but he has friends."

"No problem, Walt," Gonzo answers instantly. "I'll be there in a minute."

True to his word he shows up in five minutes with his brother Reilly in tow, who also wrestled in college.

"I need to get this lame duck," I say. "He's another wannabe tough guy bouncer who's messing with me. This is how it's going to go down: you guys keep his back-up away but don't touch the big boy. I'm going to get him good."

We pull into the tire store across the street and get into attack formation. I take off my party shirt so it doesn't get blood on it and cross the street with everybody behind me, acting calmly. I march up to the entrance of the black cage with Gonzo, Reilly, Tim, and Gene trailing behind so as not to seem they're with me. I know they're wondering what's going to happen next. The fat Samoan is in front of me with his back to the wall, thinking his friends will protect him and jump me from behind if I hit him. He is now going to pay for his sins.

"Remember me?" I say. "I'm back and you're never going to forget me."

"You better get out of here," he says toughly, "before I…"

I never do get a chance to hear what this loudmouth is going to do to me because I fire a straight right from a hands-down position into the center of his face. *Damn! It didn't faze him!* This guy is big and I couldn't get my hips into the blow. He starts to bring his hands up slowly, surprised by my first punch, but I follow with a left hook to his jaw which snaps his head back and gets his attention. He drops his head down and bum-rushes in to tackle me. I sprawl but he is so heavy that his weight pushes me back. I don't want him on top of me so I belly up, wrap my hands around his stomach, and get him in a bear hug, my arms hooked under his. He doesn't have anything, but all the worse for him, he thinks he does. I take two steps back to get room to take him down with a spinning throw, but as I do he reaches between my face and his fat chest and slides his thumb into my left eye socket. The bastard has thumb-locked me!

Now I'm getting my eye ripped out and have to do something fast. His feet are close together and he's standing straight up in terrible base, so I squeeze my bear hug with all my might and lean forward, unbalancing him and sending him crashing to his back on the potholed asphalt with me on top. I turn my face away from his thumb it pops out of my eye socket. Now that I'm in control he looks like a fat pig at a Hawaiian luau to me. I can see in his face that he's starting to panic.

"Guess what, Fatso?" I say into his ear. "Thumb-lock on you!"

I push my thumb into his eye and he cuts loose with a high-pitched yell that penetrates my ears. Then I move my other hand to his face.

"Double thumb-lock," I growl. "Payback's a bitch."

He is screaming bloody murder now but I don't let up. I'm seething with anger and feel like a volcano that's about to blow its top.

"Oh, yeah," I say, breathing heavily. "You're going to get it, scumbag. If you poke my eye, I'll poke two of yours. But since you're a bully who can't fight, you don't know how to get away."

This fat bitch is on his back. Why? Because I put him there. Both his eyes have thumbs in them and he's screaming like the stuck pig he is. He starts to claw at my eyes and his index finger falls into my mouth. *Thank you for the nice juicy sausage, Fatso.* I bite down hard and he screams like a woman delivering a baby without drugs. I never scream from someone giving me pain. It's the one rule of the true warrior: never let anyone know they've inflicted pain on you. I push away from this fat piece of shit, rise up into a straddle position, and hit the scumbag with an artistic array of punches, elbows and forearms, smashing his round face into a single dimension and getting in one good shot after another.

I suddenly get pushed off from behind and I'm surprised because my boys were supposed to be watching my six. Somehow somebody snuck by them. I get up quickly and see Gonzo and Reilly grab the offender, throw him to the ground, and pummel him with punches and kicks until he's still. They look around, daring anyone else to try and come through them, but no one does.

My eye is closing fast from the thumb lock and I move towards the fat bouncer who has gotten to his knees. He backs into the patio screaming at the top of his lungs like a parrot.

"Help! Help! Somebody Help!"

He has both hands on his face and blood is pouring down his forearms and dripping off his elbows from the finger food he offered that I chewed to the bone.

"I told you that you'd remember me!" I yell.

He falls back inside the birdcage where the other bouncers are streaming into and I know better than to follow him there. My eye is nearly closed and I've got his blood all over my shirtless upper body. This won't look good when the cops come so I make my move and trot across the street to the tire store. Everybody catches up and we drive to a gas station bathroom where I clean up with paper towels before going to a late night cafe. We sit in a big booth and laugh about the street justice that found the bully bouncer. My eye closes completely as the late night breakfast comes to an end and we go outside.

"Thanks for the back-up," I say to Gonzo and Reilly in the parking lot.

"No problem, Walt," Gonzo says. "That bouncer had it coming."

Tim drops me off at my house and I fall into bed with Adolf.

## Chapter Five
## East Meets West

I wake to the rumbling of my air conditioner. There's no school today so I head out to the weight room. The entire white part of my eye is now blood red and the lid is partially closed. The weight room regulars are all freaked out when they see it. I guess they think it's worse than the usual trophies I come in with after every weekend. Black eyes, cuts, and fat lips are all trophies to me and the regulars have seen them all, but I guess this one is more gruesome. I'm proud of my battle wounds and this one brought me more attention than usual.

I'm doing an upper body workout today so I bench 495 pounds for four sets of four then do 365 pounds for upright rows and go to my neck and other body parts. Then I head upstairs for takedown practice in the open wrestling room. Nobody in the room can wrestle tonight so I slam around some fish and then head out, climbing onto the Interceptor and settling into the duct tape seat for the rocket ride home.

The house is definitely a bachelor pad. It's Jorge, Skip, me and my best friend Adolf. The fridge is well stocked with beer and I'm thirsty. I crack a regular

Coors, turn on the TV, and crack a few more. The phone rings and it's Tim. It's been a few weeks since the fight at Christian's.

"Walt," Tim says. "I'm with Poppa Chulo. We want to come over and pre-tune and then go to the Dead Grunion."

"I'm down for it," I say. "Come over and we'll drink then go."

I down a six pack by the time they show and have a couple more with them. Then it's off to the cry of the wild at the Dead Grunion. Tim's not a big guy and neither is Poppa Chulo and where we're headed there's most likely to be trouble. So I'm going to have to watch my own back. I have on an orange collared shirt, white shorts and black high-tops. Tim drives us to the Dead Grunion and we walk upstairs with the DJ music thumping in my ears and the strobe lights bouncing off my bright clothes.

It's on and crowded with chicks everywhere. The boys in the club are calm and 2:00 A.M. comes quickly The crowd is funneled out the front door and down the marina walkway 50 yards, where they turn at the fountain to get to the parking lot where the fun awaits. It's been the late night arena for many a battle over the years.

Sure enough, some tourists from the East Coast are jacked up and looking for some fun. I know they are not locals from their accents. Paul's Landing, where the Dead Grunion is located in Happening Harbor, is a tourist spot. Being that the Dead Grunion is in the marina it's attractive to the out-of-towners and makes for good hunting.

The four clowns with accents aren't dressed like locals and two of them have on hockey jerseys, not something worn in Happening Beach, California. They start in on me first, throwing out some insults about my clothes. *You guys are out of your league*, I think. *You don't want to go there.*

They keep on, their East Coast accents begging for some. Looks like it'll be me, Poppa Chulo and Tim against these four East Coast goofballs. This could be fun to teach them a West Coast lesson.

"Eat me!" Poppa Chulo finally yells at them, stepping out.

Poppa Chulo is small and not that smart but he's as tough as nails with stainless steel balls. These East Coast tourists are going to get their asses handed to them. It's just about to go down when the bank window, which is on the way to the parking lot, shatters. It diverts everyone's attention and then a moment later a fight breaks out next to it! We leave the East Coast guys and run over to watch the show. It's always a good bet there's going to be a good fight in the Dead Grunion parking lot. There have even been small-scale riots there. I know because I've been in a few.

The Landing hired security cops a while back, badges and all, and they are somewhere in the mix. Scuffles break out in the milling crowd and somehow Tim winds up in handcuffs and me and Poppa Chulo rush to the rescue.

"Hey!" I say. "Let our buddy go. He didn't break the window. Take the cuffs off or you're gonna get messed up."

Tim looks scared. This is the first step towards going to jail and he knows it. I'm getting ready to blast the security guard any second and I'm sure he feels the seriousness of my intent. He acquiesces and lets Tim go, taking off the cuffs. Poppa Chulo and I share a deep sigh of relief as Tim heads for his car before the guard changes his mind. There will be no bullshit tonight.

The late night crowd is undulating in the parking lot like people doing the wave at a baseball game, 40 to 50 people strong, back and forth. Everybody is drunk and screaming. It's like a rowdy rock concert without the band. Then it gets a lot more rowdy as the hockey jerseys re-appear.

"We're still here, you losers!" the biggest one yells.

"Chill, Walt," Poppa Chulo says to me. "I got it."

The East Coast lame duck starts to laugh. "This is going to be fun," he shouts to his friends.

"Get back!" I yell at the crowd.

I'm bigger than anybody there so I walk around telling the crowd to get back and clear out. They form a circle of 40 to 50 drunken people and they are all cheering. Poppa Chulo is a junior college state wrestling champion and even though he is just 140 pounds he's going to mess up this 200-pounder from the East Coast. They move to the middle of the parking lot and get into it.

The east coaster kicks Poppa Chulo in the ribs but it's nothing to write home about. This guy may have kicked a bag in his garage but he is far from a professional and looks like a wannabe striker. I know with Poppa Chulo's wrestling and street fighting abilities that he can handle a half-assed karate kick.

I watch the crowd as much as I watch the fight. Nobody is going to get past me. I'm watching Poppa Chulo's six and am in guard-dog mode. Poppa Chulo takes him down and the crowd grows silent, all of the crowd wondering how the little Mexican took down the east coast hockey jock when they expected him to get trashed. Poppa Chulo climbs the rope from the pelvis to the ribs and works his way past the arms until he's straddled on top of this guy. Now the hockey jersey bigmouth is going to get his just deserts.

The crowd grows restless. They want Poppa Chulo to lose because he's with me and I've been bossing everyone around, telling the crowd what to do. Poppa Chulo has the guy over the speed bump with his knees glued to his shoulders and starts to punch his little fists into Mr. Big-Bad-East-Coaster's face. I'm standing with my arms out to the sides to block the crowd.

"One on one!" I yell out repeatedly. "Stay back!"

I'm doing my best to look all around but the second hockey jersey guy comes out of a blind spot and jumps on Poppa Chulo's back. *How did that guy get past me?* I let Poppa Chulo down. With Tim gone it's just me watching Poppa Chulo's back, with 40 or 50 drunks trying to intervene on behalf of the hockey jersey guy. The bar crowd now has a fight mob mentality like you see in a riot. It's just me and Poppa Chulo against the crazed mob.

Poppa Chulo has two guys in hockey jerseys on him now. Poppa Chula is on the first one's back but the second guy is standing there getting ready to drop jackhammer fists on him. I break rank from controlling the crowd and run full speed at the guy who's about to unload with cheap shots. I've got Poppa Chulo's six. I'm a full sprint when I clothesline this idiot right under his chin and nearly take his damn head off. I can feel my forearm crushing his windpipe as he crumples to the asphalt. Poppa Chulo scrambles up, free of the east coaster that was on top of him. The mob is really pissed now and I know it's time to haul ass.

"Run!" I yell at Poppa Chulo.

From behind me in the crowd I hear, "Kill the ass in the orange shirt!"

*Shit! I'm wearing an orange shirt!* I go into invincible mode and lower my shoulders like Larry Csonka on a goal line rush. Nobody is going to stop me. I'm running hard and can't be taken down but I got this whole mob trying to tackle me. I'm taking arm punches all over more are coming one step after another. Now I've got guys on my back and legs. I slow, teeter from the weight, and then hit the ground.

*You're done for*, an inner voice tells me. *No! Not me!* I yell back inside my head. *I'm not going there!* I try to stand up but I can't. I'm toast. I've got 10 guys on me and I'm taking a bunch of cheap shots. They would never do this face-to-face and one-on-one without being in a mob. As I cover up I actually laugh out loud. These little bitches need a gang and a truckload of booze to be like me. But they'll only do it when it's 100 percent safe for them, never when the outcome is in doubt. I've never played it safe, hence the predicament that I'm in now. You cowards will jump on a guy when you're in a mob – a guy that would put you down like a canary in a gassed-filled coal mine one-on-one – but you wouldn't dare look me in the eye if you passed me on the street alone. All you tough guys on mob steroids are little chicken-shits in real life.

I'm on the ground with these little bitches taking shots at me. I'm taking a beating as blows land to my ribs and the back of my head, over and over. At least I took the heat off of Poppa Chulo. I've been here before and know how to protect myself. It's not my first clambake. I'm being cracked everywhere – legs, ribs, arms, and head – but I can take it; I can weather the storm.

Finally, the wannabe cops from the Landing swarm in and the crowd backs off. It seems that my karma has caught up with me. They must remember that I was threatening to kick their asses just a short while ago. Now it's going to be payback. These geeks are going to mess me up. I'm quickly handcuffed and stretched out on the asphalt but to my surprise they don't rough me up and nobody is taking cheap shots. I'm happy that the little bitches aren't beating on me anymore.

It's over but I know I'm going to jail. The security geeks can't wait for their heroes, the cops, to show up and take me away. I'm handcuffed belly down. Dammit! I wish I could get my hands on one of those little cheese-balls that jumped me. I'll be coming back to find them. At least I'm no worse for the wear. A little bruised, maybe, but I covered up good.

The security guards wander off to disperse the mob and a Dead Grunion bouncer appears in front of me with a chick on his arm.

"Look at this moron," he says. "Not so tough now."

He raises his work-booted foot and smashes it into my face.

"Screw you," I say, my head ringing from the blow.

I get another boot to the face. "Screw you!" I say again.

"Look at this ass," the bouncer says to the chick as he boots me yet again.

"Screw you!" I yell out.

Man! Where are the cops? I never wanted the cops to show up before in my life. *Keep it up, you idiot. I will get you later.*

Red and blue lights start to reflect off the buildings and the bouncer walks off quickly. The cops rush in and grab my handcuffed arms and hoist me to my feet.

"Whoa," says an older, clean-cut cop. "Looks like they got you good."

"Nope," I shake my head, "Just one guy while I was handcuffed."

He puts me in the back of the black-and-white and in the rear view mirror I can see that my faced is all jacked up. I'm ready to keep my mouth shut and go to jail by myself but then the far door opens and they throw Poppa Chulo in with me. His face is as messed up as mine.

"Dammit, Poppa Chulo," I say. "I can't go to jail. The DA has a hard-on for me right now. When the cop comes back act like we're really hurt. Maybe he'll let us go to the hospital instead of jail."

The older cop comes back and gets into the cruiser. We start moaning and groaning like two Mexican hookers looking for a tip.

"Sir," I say, "I think we need to go to the hospital. We're really hurt."

The cop looks back and gives us a skeptical raised-eyebrow look. He's been around a while and isn't impressed.

"Okay, boys," the cop says. "Here's the deal. We can go to the hospital and I'm going to be stuck with a bunch of paperwork and afterwards you'll go to jail for a few days. Or we can go to jail right now and no charges will be filed and you'll be out in three hours and I'll be home for breakfast."

I look at Poppa Chulo in surprise and we both start laughing.

"I don't think I need the hospital after all," I say. "I'm suddenly feeling fine."

"Yeah," Poppa Chulo agrees. "It might look bad but it don't hurt a bit, sir. It really don't."

The cop nods wordlessly and we drive away. We got it handed to us by that mob of morons but no charges will be filed and we'll be out of jail in the morning. So all-in-all it isn't a bad night.

## Chapter Six
## Going Nowhere

I awake the next day in the early afternoon with Adolf licking my face. As I push him away I realize I have a face only a dog would love. I've been dozing on and off in my bedroom since getting out of jail this morning and I can't face the thought of going to work and listening to assholes all night.

I pick up the phone and dial the liquor store. "Hey, Trike. I can't make it in today. I got into it last night and got my face kicked in."

"Yeah, right," Trike says. "Since when?"

"Since I usually don't fight 30 people," I say. He knows that I rarely lose unless I'm really drunk so he doesn't believe me.

"Good try, Walt," Trike laughs. "You've got to come up with something more believable than that."

"The hell with it," I say. "I'll see you at four."

As I hang up the phone I still feel tired from jail but I'll just get drunk at work to dull the pain. My face is bashed up but that's how it goes. You play with fire and you get burned sometimes. I roll out of bed, grab a shower, then get dressed and head over in the Sprint.

"Holy hell," Trike says, walking up to me when I go in the door. "I didn't think you were serious."

"It doesn't really hurt," I say. "I'm just tired from being in jail all night."

"Well, don't worry about stocking and cleaning," Trike says. "Just take it easy and count the drawer. I'll do everything else in the morning."

"Cool," I say. "Thanks."

Trike heads off and after a while a local regular comes in — an older professional guy that I talk to from time to time.

"What in the name of sweet Jesus happened to you?" he says.

"Just a little fun," I say.

"Walter," he shakes his head. "What are you going do with your life? You can't be doing this kind of nonsense anymore. If you want to fight then box professionally. Make a name for yourself. You're not going be a teacher. You messed that up a long time ago with all your arrests."

"No," I say. "I'll be okay on that. I don't think my past will catch up with me. I haven't been to jail for anything big yet. Just overnight stuff."

"Maybe," he says. "But check out your face. It looks like someone took a club to it."

"Yeah, I know. But that's how it goes. You give a beating to someone who begs for it but it goes both ways. I got no problem taking an ass-whipping sometimes."

He shrugs and leaves but I know he's right. I'm not going to be a teacher. What am I going to do? When I think about the future I feel like I'm being choked. I can feel the invisible hands of passing life squeezing my neck and my heart beating in my ears like a clock as time marches on. Is my ultimate fate just to hang out in bars until my vision gets blurry, my thoughts get cloudy, and the final blackness surrounds me? That is the only future I can see right now and I don't like this dead-end feeling. I won't let myself waste the only life I have but what am I going to do with it?

I'm scrambling through my last semester of college. I have enough credits to graduate and I'm getting my social science waiver out of the way so I can teach high school. What a waste, though. I'll be nothing more than a glorified babysitter to a bunch of rude punks. Maybe I'll go to law school. It's a serious option except that I hate all the assistant district attorneys and can't stand how they lie and twist the system just to get convictions to further their careers. Justice is a joke that only the rich can afford. It doesn't matter who's right or wrong, they just want to bring you down to get brownie points.

If some DA geek doesn't like you because you're big and strong they will get their revenge just because they were picked on in high school by somebody just like you. But they can't get me because the most criminal thing I ever do is win. I never start fights but I always finish them. Being a criminal defense attorney doesn't sound all that bad. I've got the discipline and aptitude to pull it off but I can't wear a suit and call some asshole in a robe "Your Honor" with a straight face.

Its closing time at the store and the drawer is counted. I've got on a good buzz and I put a twelver in my jacket, climb on my bike, and ride home. The cold air feels good on my beaten face and all I can do is laugh into the wind. I got my ass stomped last night but it doesn't hurt as bad as it looks. I get home and am still tired so I power down some more beer, watch Letterman with Adolf, then go into my room and pass out. I awake to the ringing telephone the next morning and hear my brother's voice when I pick up.

"Hey, Walter," he says. "My car's in the shop. Can I get a ride to football practice?"

"Okay," I say. "Gimme a couple of minutes."

He's coaching the freshmen team at the local high school. As I hang up I don't think I could ever coach. I tried it and it's not my cup of tea. I pick him up and take him to school. As I pull into the parking lot school is letting out. For the first time in my life all the high-schoolers filtering through the lot look like kids to me. I'm in the Sprint and these punks are carrying their book bags with baggy clothes and smirks on their faces.

"Get the hell out of my way!" I yell out the window as they walk in front of my car. "I'll run your asses over!"

My brother gets out and as I turn around I have to go through the gauntlet of twerps again.

"Get the hell out of the road," I yell out the window to no one in particular.

These punks think nothing of walking in front of a moving car. They think nothing will happen to them. They have no respect for anything and don't worry about the consequences of their actions. I make a left onto the busy street in front of the school and look in the rear view mirror at the mass of clueless kids. *Who are you kidding? You can't deal with that bullshit. That's it*, I decide then and there. *I'm not going to be a teacher.* It seems that college was just a journey to kill time and I will have a degree I'll never use.

As I drive back home I realize that I don't want to grow up. A feeling of panic starts to come over me as my bleak future stares me in the face again. Being an attorney just doesn't seem right. I could kick ass in the courtroom but I don't want to scour books in law school for the next three years and then wear a suit and kiss ass for a living. I could try boxing but the sharks that control the sport are ruthless. I walk in the front door of my house and kick back for a while then glance up at the clock. *Dammit! I lost track of time and I'm going to be late for work!*

I jump into the Sprint, hit the toggle switches, and take my usual route down Warner to PCH past the water tower house. I turn into the residential streets then park behind the old building the liquor store is in. I walk in and my routine starts. I stock the cooler and then Mario comes in with dinner and takes his six-pack. My homework is light so I crack a Coors and thumb through the newest Playboy. As I check out the chicks I pass an ad for something called the No-Holds-Barred Fighting Championship. This has to be a fake pro-wrestling bullshit event even though the ad says it's real. I flip the page and go on to the next chick.

At 11:10 P.M. my work is done, the store is stocked and clean, and I've got a twelve pack under my arm and a good buzz in my head. I get home and wrestle with Adolf and then start my favorite game: drink a twelve pack in an hour by downing a beer every five minutes. After two beers go down I decide that my heart really isn't in it tonight. It's time to take Adolf for a run. I strap on his black nylon harness and pull it over his ripped shoulders and past his big head and neck.

Adolf starts to go crazy. He's been sitting at home waiting for me to get back and now it's time to run. I grab my skateboard and my big down ski jacket with deep pockets, each of them able to hold a tall can of Coors. We start at the end of the cul-de-sac in front of my house and skateboard down the street. I'm pushing three bills now and crunches sound out as the wheels grind the asphalt. I put my left foot on the board and push off with my right. The wheels roar over the uneven knotty asphalt with a distinctive groan that breaks the silence of the cold night. I feel like a Roman gladiator racing around the Coliseum in a war chariot behind a charging warhorse.

My little seventy-pound guy is ripped to shreds and his muscles stand out as he races down the street. We're on our usual track and I pull one of the tall soldiers from my ski jacket, pop the top, and take a swig. As Adolf the stud pulls me onward I look at the stars. At that moment in time life is good. We make a couple quick lefts as the adrenaline from Adolf's quick turns wears off. We make it to a long straightaway of our usual route and Adolf breaks into a gallop as he downshifts from a full charge to high speed cruise.

This street has been freshly paved and it's smooth sailing now. The wheels under the board change from a rough groan to a smooth hum as do the thoughts in my head. What the hell am I going to do with my life? I can't be a teacher; it just won't work. It's a noble profession for morons but it's not for me. Maybe I can get serious about boxing. It's going to take me a while to learn the sweet science but I've got the tools and the discipline and I know I'm tough and definitely have the balls. Most important of all is that I've got the personal integrity to let me sleep at night. If I get into boxing I'm not going to stab anyone in the back. But can I dive into the shark tank and deal with these guys who are trying to get their hands into everyone's pockets? I only have pennies and nickels. I'm an amateur and I just started. How can I make a living while I build up my pro record?

The world comes to a halt and I suddenly find myself flying through the cool night air like Superman. I can see the stars in the cloudless sky. Only a few are not washed out by the city lights. The hum of the skateboard's wheels has gone silent but the click-clack of Adolf's paws is still going strong. Then my left shoulder and head slams into the newly paved road and my tall Coors goes flying away into the darkness like an old girlfriend. Now everything is silent. I know in the back of my buzzed mind what happened: I just hit the ground as hard as hell.

The skateboard wheels must have hit a rock on the newly paved road and sent me skyward. But what goes up must come down and as I skid to a stop in the middle of the road I laugh out loud. Everything was going smoothly then bam! Out of nowhere I got smacked by something beyond my control. I stop laughing and everything is cold and quiet. Nobody was outside this late at night to see my face plant and it's just me and Adolf and my thoughts alone in the universe.

I roll over and lay motionless on my back next to a parked car staring at the dark sky. I'm breathing deeply from the adrenalin burst and the cold air is starting to freeze my face. Wait! That's not cold air but rather Adolf's slobber all over my face from him licking me back to life.

"I love you too, big guy," I say as I get up and dust myself off.

I'm down but not out and I've got backup. I reach into my jacket pocket and pull out the other tall boy. It's dented so I tap the top to settle it down and crack it open.

Foam comes pouring out the top but I pound it anyway. I hit the ground hard and need this beer. I drain it in one continuous gulp then get back on the skateboard. I'm hurt, but not that badly, and feel like I just went through high school football practice. Adolf drags me back to the house, our usual lap over except this time with an abrupt stop in the middle. Shit happens in life and this is just another experience to deal with.

I settle onto the couch just in time for Letterman. The beer drinking game I started earlier resumes. I've tried this many times before but tonight it's different. I know I can do it. A twelve pack in an hour is nothing I can't handle. Not three in ten minutes then a few more, but a steady one beer every five minutes. I've been drinking all night, first at the store then getting down with Adolf on our cruise, and I'm primed. I get through ten with confidence then hit the wall. That's it! I run to the bathroom sink, blow chunks everywhere, then stumble down the hallway and pass out in my bed, Adolf snorting happily beside me.

## Chapter 7
### Rock at Roller's

Beep! Beep! Beep!

I wake to the stench of my own puke on my new cop mustache. I hit the hated snooze button and then nine minutes hit it again. *Why does it feel like an elephant stepped on my head?* Oh, that's right. I tried the twelve pack game last night. That explains the beer puke smell. I also went for the flight of my life with Adolf as the pilot. There's blood on my sheets but what else is new? I've still got my clothes and high-tops on and I can feel the mattress through the holes in the well-worn soles.

The truth is that I would much rather go out and party than spend money on clothes. I live to box, wrestle, lift weights and have fun. I'd rather do that than join the rat race. I get up using every bit of self-discipline I have and go to class. I keep telling myself it will make me a better person but I'm not sure I believe it. After classes are done I hit the boxing gym to work up a good sweat. It's Friday so we're going to Roller's with Rolando and his wrestling buddies from college. They might be little guys but at least they have some of the warrior spirit in them.

69

After hitting the gym I head home and then hit the road to work on my cardio. Say what you will, but running on the street with traffic driving by is the best. I've got my Walkman on with The Cure, NWA, Ice T, and The Smiths blaring in my ears. I go into a hypnotized state and push till it hurts then back off just a little as my lungs burn, heart pounds and sweat pours down my face. I run to the beat of the songs and it hurts so good for all four miles. I know that many of the people driving by would love to run me over. There are a multitude of people in town I've had run-ins with but they don't have the balls to aim their car at me even with my back turned. They know what the consequences would be if they didn't kill me.

I make it back to the house and order a large pepperoni from Kings Pizza before cleaning up. I've been eating there for years because it has a local feeling in the ever-growing corporate suburban sprawl. I get out of the shower, jump on the Interceptor, and make a quick pizza pick-up run. When I get back Skip is there and I tell him about Roller's as I dive into the food. Man, the pizza is good! As I sit at the coffee table and flip through the TV channels Adolf stares at me pitifully, hoping to get scraps. I eat the entire pizza but save the last piece for my best buddy.

As he chomps it down Tim and Poppa Chulo show up and we go out to the garage, where there's a high-dollar foosball table, and pre-tune. The walls are unfinished in typical beach style and a heavy bag hangs from the main crossbeam. The bag is my pride and joy and I come out here by myself a lot at night and do round after round on it. But it's party time tonight so the bag is untouched as we drink beer after beer and go round robin on the foosball table. When we're sufficiently buzzed I put Adolf inside, Tim fires up his red Toyota truck, and we head to Roller's, which is not far away. As we wind through the streets I notice that not many people are out.

"Hell, Tim," I say, "slow down. I'm going to hit this sign coming up. How fast you going?"

"Forty-five," Tim answers, glancing at the dash.

"I'm gonna nail this bastard dead on," I say, leaning out the window and lining up my throw.

Tim knows the drill but instead of keeping it steady he speeds up just to mess with me. I keep my concentration, let the bottle fly, and crack it dead on with a perfect bull's eye.

"Didn't work," I crow to Tim. "I'm too damn good."

"You should be," Tim answers. "You've been practicing for years."

Tim rolls past Naugals Mexican fast food joint and goes down the street to Roller's nightclub by the freeway. The parking lot is full and I know it's going to be a good night. Tim parks and we walk to the front door and go past three bouncer fools. They make a big deal of acting dangerous but I know they've never given or taken a beating in their lives.

"Show me your ID, Bluto," the one on the end says to me.

I don't say a word because I want to get in the door but I think to myself, *Oh, man. Flex your cheap power at someone else. You're gonna get it someday, you dumb bastard.*

We pass through the front door and get hit with pounding music and a heavy bass beat, making it almost impossible to talk. We look around the dance floor and bar area for Rolando and his wrestling buddies before

71

finally spotting them out on the patio. I grab a drink and then walk out.

"What's up, Rolando?" I say.

He hoists his drink at me and I see he's with two baby-faced guys with thick necks and cauliflower ears who are holding cocktails with somewhat lost looks on their faces. Rolando's smoking a cigarette like he owns the joint but his wrestling buddies look like they're out of their element. It's their first time in Southern California from the Midwest and you can tell they're a little cautious. But the boys are all here now and we're going to have some fun.

We're in an outside area that holds about twenty people and most of them are smoking. It's cold and flames flicker from the gas tiki torches by the steel patio gates. The grass lawn is dusted with ice crystals and fog is flowing from everyone's mouths. It might not snow in Southern California but sometimes you get a cold-as-hell breeze blowing off the ocean at night. We drink fast to stay warm and quickly get into the party groove. Everyone is laughing and having fun around a high-top table talking wrestling and other bullshit.

I walk into the club and ask the DJ to play some good music instead of his techno dance bullshit but he is like most hipster fools and shrugs without even looking up and ignores me. *Whatever, idiot.* I just walk away from the little long-haired moron and go back outside to the patio where everyone is getting all juiced up.

"I'm feeling it," I scream at Tim, Poppa Chulo and the wrestling guys. "Let's freaking party!"

As I pound down my beer I feel someone tap me on the shoulder making me spill a little on my shirt. I turn around and see a big six feet, two inch Mexican guy, running maybe 220 pounds but doughboy dumpy, standing there.

"Look, ese," he says. "Shut the hell up. You're making so much noise I can't hear the music."

The whole table stops and everyone looks at him. The moment is frozen in time like the grass on the lawn behind him. A split second turns into a year. I look at him and all I can see is red. This is completely unwarranted and it takes me a few moments to speak.

"I don't know you," I say. "What the hell?"

"You don't want to know me," he says in his best movie tough-guy voice.

Then he turns around and goes back to the table behind us where there are a few other guys. I can hear him boasting about how he tamed the shrew.

I stare holes into his back but he doesn't turn around. *You have a few beers and now you're telling me to shut up? It's your mistake, dumbass.* I sit there and ponder. I can't let this happen to me. Oh man, I'm getting so furious. *Nobody can talk like that to me.*

"What an ass," Rolando says. "Who the hell does he think he is?"

"Get a hold of yourself, Walt," Tim says, seeing the anger build up inside me. "Forget that happened."

"Nope. Can't do it," I say. But everyone knows me here. If I jack up this fool the DA will be all over my ass." I think for a moment and look across the table. "Rolando, you've got to get that guy for me."

A faint smile crosses Rolando's face and he gets up. He has a look in his eyes like he's somewhere else besides a bar; like he's getting ready for a wrestling match. The wheels are turning and the fight computer in his head is running at top speed. "No problem, Walt. I didn't like that dumbass from the beginning."

The two wrestling boys look at each other unsurely, like they don't want to be here.

"Stay close, guys," I say. "It's on."

We swig the last of our drinks. This bastard came up and told me to shut up for no reason. Now it's time for him to get the justice he deserves because of the courage he got from his drink. He's going to get beat down for trying to be a tough guy in front of his friends.

Rolando looks over to the guy, catches his eye, and glares silently at him.

"What the hell do you want?" The Mexican doughboy says finally.

I'm just floating and watching. I want to kill this loser but I don't want to go to jail tonight. Then the big dope makes his biggest mistake and gets up. Oh, yeah. The big, stupid, peanut-brain moron has had way too much to drink.

"Screw you, dumbass," Rolando barks out.

Everybody at our table gets up and starts to laugh. This is going to be funny. I stay way back as Rolando moves forward, ready to pull the trigger. If anything goes wrong. I'll get this big mouth. The dumpy fool squares up with Rolando, dwarfing Rolando's 170 pounds with his 220 pound frame. This guy has no idea he's in big trouble. Rolando looks harmless. He has on long sleeves, dress pants and is wearing his glasses. But if you know what to look for you can tell he has the signs of somebody who's been around.

This big bastard is going to get what he asked for. I don't want to get in trouble in front of all these people who know me and go to jail, but if Rolando doesn't get him then I will. Nobody knows that but me and it brings a smile to my face. Everyone moves off the patio and onto the frozen grass near the back fence. This guy undoubtedly thought Rolando was going to be easy prey, as any fool that matched up with him would wrongly assume. Oh, this is going to be fun to watch.

I don't know much about Rolando's street-fighting skills but I do know that he broke Poppa Chulo's jaw once. So I know he can get down from all his wrestling training. But I've never seen him fight so I'm eager to see what's going to happen.

"Let's go," Rolando says, stepping in range of the big guy.

The guy glances at me, sneers at Rolando, and then shakes his shoulders to loosen them. It's obvious that he thinks Rolando is a little guy trying to stand up for me. The big, dumb goof with the big mouth puts up his hands in a really bad boxing stance and Rolando hits him with a straight right dead center to the face. The big doughboy's eyes roll back in his head and he crumples to the frozen grass, out cold. He told me to shut up and now he just got shut up himself with a one-punch knockout. I laugh as he falls onto the icy green blanket.

Almost before he comes to a stop his friends jump forward and surround him, trying to save him from any more ass-kicking and trying to get him to his feet. They look at us and I think they might make a move since we're outnumbered. They don't realize the bunch of crazies they're up against. They think that beating someone's ass is like winning the Heisman trophy in college football but it isn't. There's no public glory in it. All they're going to get is a serious ass-kicking if they challenge us, with no film at eleven. I can tell they want to go. They have no other option in their minds but to step up. If your buddy gets knocked out then you have to man up and settle the score. But the looks in our eyes keeps them at bay.

I hear a commotion from inside at the bar and see someone from the patio pointing at us and the bartender picking up the phone. A bell goes off in my head. We're seasoned warriors of the bar scene and know it's time to get the hell out before the cops show up. We slowly walk out the front door with almost religious reverence, like we're going to eat a piece of bread and gulp some wine at a Catholic church. Running in a crowd only attracts attention.

"Shalom," I say to the bouncers calmly as we pass them. These steroid dimwits have no idea that some loser is out cold in back.

Once we clear the doors we sprint to Tim's red Toyota truck and pile in. Tim is driving, Poppa Chulo has shotgun and me, Rolando and the wrestling boys are in back. The doughboy's friends have appeared at the front of the club and are pointing us out to the bouncers.

"Let's go!" I yell into the cab, banging on the roof. We speed away out of the parking lot and turn a corner into the night. As we bump along in the back I realize I'm hungry as shit. "Head to AM/PM for late night hotdogs, burritos, and hamburgers," I yell against the rear window.

Tim nods and we make a few turns and pull into the all-night gas station. Poppa Chulo and Rolando go inside to grab the food while Tim fills up. Through the window I can see Poppa Chulo trying to put cheese sauce over some nacho chips, but he is so drunk that he misses and it goes all over the floor. The towel-head attendant yells at him instead of just doing his job and wiping up the floor and I can see him trying to give Poppa Chulo a mop to clean it up. That is a wrong move with these two messed-up guys. Poppa Chulo shoots a double leg on him and Rolando grabs him high. They turn him upside down and try to use his head as a mop to clean up the cheese sauce. After a few halfhearted swipes Rolando and Poppa Chulo throw him down and run out. The towel-head gets up and chases them, infuriated by the liquid cheese smeared all over his headpiece.

"Tim, get the hell outta here," I yell. "These places got a direct line to the cops!"

Tim takes off as Rolando and Poppa Chulo sprint to catch us. The towel-head lunges forward and grabs Rolando from behind. Poppa Chulo turns and kicks him in the balls, stopping him cold and dropping him to the ground screaming. They catch up to us as we turn the corner and I jump out as they jump in.

"Keep going," I yell. "I'm going to stop him from getting Tim's license plate." The towel-head gets off the ground and I wait to see if he runs toward the street but he spots me and goes back inside, cheese dripping onto his face.

This is not my first beach party at this place so I know I'm in for a long trot. I jump the drainage ditch wall next to the road and jog for a half mile, the dust making a cloud behind me as I run from the scene. I jump the fence at the condo complex where Trike lives. Tim knows I'll be there because we've done this before. It's perfect timing because Tim pulls up right away and I jump in the back of the truck where Rolando and his wrestling buddies are still sitting.

"You guys are totally crazy," one of the wrestling boys says.

"Yeah," I nod. "We do this just about every night."

"It's late," Rolando says. "We gotta get back to my girlfriend's house in Irvine. She dropped us off at the bar."

"No way, Rolando," Tim says. "I'm too drunk to drive all the way to south Orange County."

That's ludicrous since Rolando just wasted that doughboy for me and saved the honor of the entire group, so I know it's up to me: "I'll drive."

I jump into the driver's seat while Tim climbs in back and then I pull onto the 405 freeway. I got the Toyota four-banger singing as it hits a hundred miles an hour and I yell for it to go faster. The out-of-state wrestlers are nearly shitting their pants in back as they scream for me to slow down.

"You guys want out?" I yell, not even sure they can hear me. "There's no way out but death!"

"What if the cops pull us over?" one yells back. "We'll get kicked off the wrestling team."

"Bring it! Bring the cops!" I yell drunkenly, out of my mind from a flood of beers. "I don't care. You see crooks run from the cops on TV shows but now you'll see how it's done in real life."

My thoughts fly by just like the blurred road signs. What does "real" actually mean? Anything? I've wrestled my whole life but just because you're a warrior of the wrestling room it doesn't mean you can fight for real. I've been in many wrestling rooms with countless grapplers and most of them think they can fight but it's not true. Most have false courage and if you smack them in the face they will turn away and walk off from the pain. But when I get smacked in the face it's like when I got spanked when I was born. It brings me to life and it's beautiful. It's what started my life and what still makes me tick and drives me forward.

I somehow drop Rolando and the wrestling boys off and make it back to my house and into bed.

## Chapter 8
## Lucky in War

When I wake up the next morning I have no idea how or why I was driving Tim's truck, why it's parked outside, or why Tim is snoring away on my couch. He must've been too drunk to drive and I must've been hammered enough to take over. Just pure luck that I didn't get pulled over. There's no alarm clock today so I slowly come to consciousness. Adolf is getting jumpy and needs to drink some water. I think about passing back out but instead I get up and open my bathroom door. There's a sudden shock as the sun fires into the rods and cones of my eyes from the window. My room is usually dark with constant air conditioning and tin foil over the window to keep the light out.

I go into the shower and hot water beats down on my face. I'm sitting in the corner and the smell of soap is all over me. I'm too hung-over to even hear Tim start up his car but when I come out the snoring has stopped and he's gone. I get dressed but don't really want to do anything. I go out to Jack's and get a supreme cheeseburger and fries and then come back home and read some history about Russians who raped and pillaged in the Caucasian mountains. I have nothing to do so I crack a beer. I have one and then two and pretty soon the fridge is empty.

I jump on my bike and hit the throttle hard down to Sea Lion Beach Liquor. I walk in and have a beer with Trike and we talk about nothing. The sun is out and the crowd is light so I grab a twelve pack, zip it up in my jacket, then head back home. I walk in and Adolf is at least glad to see me. There are no messages on the answering machine and the phone is dead silent. Nobody likes me and nobody cares. I'm bored as hell and know there has to be some fun out there but nobody is calling so the hell with it. Two beers turns into twelve and pretty soon the sun is setting.

I wrestle around with Adolf for a while. He's tough and gives me a good roll but I finally squeeze him so tight that he goes still. I bite his nose nice and softly and then get off of him and sit my ass down on the overstuffed chair. There's nothing on so I flip through the channels until I see what looks like King Kong Bundy getting down.

Oh, that's right. It reminds me that the No-Holds-Barred Fighting Championship wrestling bullshit is on pay-per-view tonight. I saw the ad in Playboy magazine. It was live on Friday but I can still get the rerun. We have a pirate box so we get all the channels and pay-per-view broadcasts. I push the control buttons on the remote but nothing happens. Shit! I hate the damn remote. *This one? No. This one? No. Okay, then this one.* I'm just about to send it sailing out the window when the channel finally changes.

The first thing I see is an animated man beating on a steel cage like it's a drum. Then I see some fools running around in pajama costumes so I know this has to be another fake pro wrestling show. Nobody would wear that stuff if they weren't being paid to do it and they sure as hell wouldn't fight in it. I post up next to Adolf and he kicks me in the ribs to tell me this is his couch. *Whatever, dog.* I stick my thumb in his back leg paw and spread the pads on his foot, not in a hurtful way but in a playful way and he kicks some more. The doorbell rings and I'm glad somebody human remembered me.

"Come on in," I say loudly. "Whoever you are."

My dad walks in, grabs a beer, and drops down on the far end of the couch.

"What's up?" he asks.

"Check this shit out," I say.

Some announcers, including an old pro football star and a former martial arts kickboxer, come on talking about the fights and we watch them.

"Is this for real?" my dad asks.

"I don't know," I say. "It looks like it is but I don't think so. This was on Friday so we're watching the rerun."

A Samoan comes into the pentagon-shaped cage wearing a grass skirt. He runs across the pentagon and gets hit by a pasty-white French guy in karate pants and no shirt. The Samoan falls to his knees and the French guy kicks him in the face. The Samoan's tooth flies across the cage as he falls to the canvas unconscious.

"What the hell?" I say. "This has to be for real!"

"Yeah," my Dad answers. "Sure doesn't look fake."

We watch the rest of the fights and a skinny Mexican guy in pajamas named Garcia wins the eight-man tournament.

"Well, that was pretty cool," I say.

My dad leaves and I stay home with Adolf the rest of the night. I go to bed and when I wake up the next morning Adolf is snorting away. The room is dark and the air conditioner is rumbling, blowing out cold air. I didn't hit the throttle too hard last night so I feel okay. I push my legs straight and flex my quads. They're sore and the lactic acid leaving the muscles feels good. Lactic acid is like an unwanted guest that shows up at your house late at night that you boot out the door in the morning: it's always sweet when they leave.

I don't feel like doing anything today but I get moving, take a shower, put on a tee-shirt, untied high tops and shorts and migrate out to the garage. I turn on the stereo and blast KROQ out of the speakers. Then I slip on my boxing gloves, step in front of my heavy bag and lay into it. The three-minute round buzzer is plugged in and I go into a trance. I start hitting the bag like a programmed robot or an insect whose only purpose is to survive and reproduce.

The bag is the only purpose that I have and I imagine that it's my sole reason for existence. I have to beat on it. I just imagine that the bag did something evil to me. *Screw you, bag*, I say under my hard breathing. I hit it with everything I've got. *I'll kill you, you piece of crap.* The round clock goes off after three minutes and I take a quick sixty second rest. I picture everything that I hate in life and then go off again when the buzzer sounds. I do six rounds then go back into my room just off the garage, where I shower and change into an oversized T-shirt and baggy shorts. Skip and Jorge are home now. They've got their own lives and for the most part are good guys to live with. Live and let live is my mantra and it seems to be theirs, too.

I have nothing to do so I barbeque some food, read some more history book chapters and go to bed early to get ready for my Monday morning classes. I don't know what it is about me but I just like to have starting points to focus on like the first day of the week. Once I have a firm goal in my head then I have no problem working towards it. My big problem now is just deciding what goal I want to pursue.

Monday is pretty typical for me. I get up without bashing my alarm clock then go to school, the boxing gym, the weight room, and out for a jog. Afterwards I hit Monday Night Football at the Dead Grunion then end the day with a stop at Jack's drive-through on the way home. On Tuesday it's school, workout, work, and party. One day turns into a week, a week turns into a month, and pretty soon I've blown through October and into December.

I feel like I'm just spinning my wheels. The harder I put the pedal to the metal the deeper I bury the wheels into the ground. I know I can't be a teacher; it's just not for me no matter how many times I tell myself it's what I want to do. I don't like lawyers so I don't want to play the law school game, either. Not that it's too hard but because I don't want to lose my personal integrity. Kissing ass and screwing people over to get ahead might be fine for someone else but not for me.

So here I am in early December sitting at work at the liquor store and all I can say is to hell with school. All the hoops I jumped through have been for naught. What am I going to do now? The future is rushing towards me like a freight train and doesn't seem that far away. In fact, I can see it like the pink elephant in the room. I'm an ostrich with my head in the sand and nothing will work out unless I pull out my head.

"That'll be five dollars and sixty cents," I say to a customer. "You want a bag?"

"No, bro, I got it," the guy says, taking his twelver and walking out the door.

The last two months have gone by quick and I've been hitting the party circuit hard. I don't do much cardio anymore and I'm eating and drinking like a horse. The realization that I don't know what I'm going to do with my life has put me into a spiraling nose dive. I feel like a World War Two fighter pilot smashing into the German countryside. I guess we won that war, though, so why should I worry? If only real life was as clear as history. I finish with the chores at the liquor store and crack another Coors. The floor is mopped, the cooler stocked and I'm drinking and watching the small black-and-white ten inch TV.

Out of nowhere in walks a smoking hot chick. I take another big swig off of my beer that's in a Coca Cola cup and think to myself that I need to get a piece of this. She walks around the cooler and grabs some wine coolers and comes up to the register.

"Can I get you anything else?" I ask helpfully. *Like a ride to my house?* I think.

"No, that's it," she answers.

"Okay. That's going to be $3.40. I haven't seen you around before. What's your name?"

"Cathy," she says with a giggle, grabbing her bag. "Bye now. Be good."

She turns and parades out like a peacock, her feathers spread across her back like a prized bird you'd see at a world class zoo. When she leaves through the door it's like a vacuum sucking out all the air. I raise the Coca-Cola to my mouth and gulp down my beer in one long swig. I stare out the window into the empty abyss of nothingness. She was like a ton of bricks hitting me between the eyes. It wasn't the ass. There are nice asses everywhere. There was just something in her personality that made me want to have a chance with her.

I get off work thinking about how it's time to take charge of my life. But how? What do I need to do? I pick Tim up and we drive around the Happening Beach back roads, that I call the residential highway, and drink countless beers, looking at the houses in the nice neighborhoods. They look like mansions to me. How did those people get there? I take another swig, crush my empty Coca Cola cup and tell Tim to head home so I can go to sleep.

I get up the next morning still thinking about my life. Screw this. It's time to rebound. I'm over 300 pounds and I'm going to take the bull by the horns. I go down to the beach hoping that my thoughts aren't bigger than my stomach and that I can run at least two miles. Wrong. I can't get more than 200 yards before I'm huffing and puffing like a steam locomotive. Adolf and I turn it into a brisk walk as I suck in the air in huge gasps. This sucks. I've got to get my act together and it won't take long. I'll be back. I force myself to walk two miles, holding Adolf back from a sprint.

It's gray, cloudy and cold when I get back to the car and Adolf grabs shotgun on the sheepskin seat cover. His big head hangs out of the window and his fawn-colored body is pushed tight against the seatback with his black-mask face flopping in the wind. He is thick and in shape and rides like the captain of the ship, looking like he's in control of the world. His cropped ears are up and his head sways in the wind as the Sprint chugs down the street.

"Hey, Adolf!" I yell. "You're the man!"

He turns his head and looks at me as if to say, *You talking to me, fool?*

We get home and I swat the bag in the garage while Adolf hangs out in the driveway. The phone rings and I rush inside to answer.

"Hey, Walt," I hear Tim say. "Let's go get a burger."

"Nope," I answer. "I'm losing weight."

"You gotta be kidding," Tim laughs.

"Nope, "I say. "I'm getting back in shape. I'm going down to one-hundred and ninety pounds."

"Yeah, right," Tim answers.

"You'll see," I say. "Give me a couple of hours to exercise then call me back."

Later that evening Tim calls and we go out with no real plan. We grab a twelve of Coors and spin through the residential highway getting a few beers deep. I tell Tim about the chick in the liquor store that sparked my interest for the first time in years.

"Wow," Tim says. "Wish I could have seen her."

I see a sign coming up and we go through the usual drill with me taking aim out the window and Tim speeding up to throw me off. I nail the sign dead center. Splat!

"Damn, I'm good," I say. "What do you want to do now?"

"I dunno," Tim answers. "Let's go to Lucky's Golden Glove, that old-school boxing bar that pours schooners of Coors."

"Sounds good," I say. As we turn I can't help thinking about Cathy from the store. "That chick was so hot but all I got was the cold shoulder and a giggle. It never used to be that way."

"Well, look at yourself," Tim fires back. "You're a three-hundred pound fat slob, to put it mildly."

I probably should be pissed but he's right and it resonates in my head. "Yeah," I nod. "I've lost track of the important things in my life."

We get to Lucky's and pound a few schooners when Craig and Smitty, two old friends from high school, show up. We're all drinking hard and I have a big smile on my face as I have a rip-roaring good time. I haven't eaten because I've decided to lose weight so the beer goes straight to my head. We all start playing foosball in the old boxing bar.

Lucky, the old midget boxer who owns the joint, is not here but there's a bunch of old boxing pictures and memorabilia to make him think he was good in his day. He might've been tough against other small guys but he's still a midget. If I could kick someone's ass when they were in their prime and I was a freshman in high school then they're not tough and will always be a boy and not a man. It's not their fault, just the genetic lottery and the luck of the draw. Small guys with attitudes are just little dogs with big barks.

The air is smoky and the carpet is dirty but it's still a good place to get a schooner. Not too many people are in tonight and we're getting down at the foosball table. The pool tables are empty and the shuffleboard is silent. There are a few scattered souls around the bar but nobody hard. Most of these guys are the cheapest of drunks. They can't afford good hard alcohol or even decent clothes. Cheap rags are the dress code for the CEOs of this drunken world. I look into a mirror and smile. Life is good right now. I've got a good glow on and I'm laughing my ass off playing round robin foosball with my friends.

There's only one foosball table and I'm sitting next to the boys drinking a beer when these two fools sit down next to me. They're two big goofballs, drunk off their asses, and looking for some fun. That's not a problem because I'm feeling good and looking for some fun myself.

"Hey, what's up?" the bigger of the two says.

"Not much," I say.

"You wanna arm wrestle?" the guy asks me.

"No, man," I say. "I'm just chillin'."

"Really?" the guy asks in a superior tone, like he thinks I'm scared.

"Really," I answer.

Tim, Craig and Smitty step up to the table and Tim raises an eyebrow at me. These two goofs don't have the foggiest idea what they're getting into and keep going on.

"Didn't think you'd be afraid of a little arm wrestling," the big guy says.

The big guy is like a great big Sea of Cortez marlin who's hitting the bait with his big beak. I've played it cool with him and now he's caught hook, line and sinker. It's up to him to be a smart fish: he can either run with the hook in his mouth or he can jump into the boat. *It's up to you, Mr. Marlin. Jump in the boat and make nice and I'll let you go and won't club you, or drag out the drama and try to spool me and get whacked and served for dinner. Make your own destiny. Catch-and-release or club on the head: it's your call.*

The big guy parks next to me at the table and really starts in. "You look pretty strong but I guess those are just show muscles," he says.

"Just chill, man," I say. "I'm here for fun. Don't do something you'll be sorry for later."

"You're the one who'll be sorry, fat boy," he says. "See, we're security guards. We're the Badknock boys. We'll put a bad bump on your ass and a knock on your head."

I'm getting spooled now and Mr. Marlin has made his choice. He is definitely going to get thumped on the head.

"You wanna arm wrestle me or not, fat boy?" he asks again.

"I don't arm wrestle," I say. "But we can do takedowns if you have the guts."

"You shouldn't have gone there, fat boy," he says. "I did some wrestling in junior high and you're in for it now."

So it's on for sure and we all go outside. The trashy barmaid tells me not to go, thinking I'm going to get hurt, but I'm in the zone so we walk over to the strip mall next to the bar. There's a donut shop up front and the light from the donut-shaped sign lights up the parking lot.

Now that I size him up I see that he's at least six feet, four inches tall and around 240 pounds. A small crowd has gathered to watch the fun and the big guy shifts into a boxing stance that will allow me to get an easy takedown. I edge in, getting ready to shoot in on him, but as I get closer he steps to the side and throws a left hook, putting maximum power into the fist at the end of his long arm. As I duck down I hear his fist whiz by my ear and I get jolt of adrenaline into my body. *Damn! This tall sucker almost caught me.* Now it's time to whack the marlin on the head. I know the dangers of fighting on asphalt all too well, but I'm strangely drawn to it like a bug that's attracted to a light that has killed hundreds of others right before it.

I step inside his reach, getting too close for him to strike with any kind of power, put him in a bear hug, and squeeze hard. He struggles to break free but he's not going anywhere. He's obviously had some boxing training but strikers are not dangerous at all on the ground. I put my right leg next to his left thigh and go knee to knee, locking his leg in place. He's tall so I pull him over the top of my bent leg, thinking that he'll slip his leg out allowing me to whizzer him. But he keeps his weight on it and his knee dislocates as I crash him headfirst into the ground, his left leg bent beautifully at a 90 degree angle. He was trying to blast me with a sucker punch but now the big fish is reeled in.

When his head hits the asphalt with me on top I let him go and scramble to my feet. Not because I feel bad for this cheap-shot artist but because it's a good fighting tactic. With my hands free I'm now able to start smacking this dumb fish in the boat. He gets to all fours and starts to wobble up on Queer Street, not really knowing where he is. If he hadn't of tried to cheap-shot me I'd probably let him off the hook. But he made his choice and now he has to live with the consequences. He pauses in that position for just a moment and I kick him in the face, sending blood splattering into the night. He collapses onto the asphalt out cold, convulsing like boxers do after a hard knockout. Mr. Marlin is now in the bait tank.

91

"Don't kill him!" his friend screams, diving on top to shield him.

We take off running to our cars and haul ass out of there. I make it home wondering where the cops are and hoping that whoever saw me beat up that stupid ass knew he started it. He'll think twice before he tries to cheap-shot someone else. I guess the Badknock boys got their bad asses knocked.

# Chapter 9
## Wannabe-Me

Beep! Beep! Beep!

Damn, I hate that alarm clock. It's already January and it's my last semester. I stumble out of bed in the dark and open the bathroom door. The sunlight hurts my eyes and I squint as I jump in the shower to start my day.

After an uneventful day at school I find myself cruising down the freeway on my way to the old-fashioned boxing gym with two rundown rings. All the windows are painted over and duct tape is the only thing holding the punching bags together. As I approach the entrance I can hear the constant melodic ringing of the round clock timer in rhythm with the jump ropes.

As the front door slams shut behind me I leave my everyday life behind and enter another world. Willie, my trainer, who works under my supposed real trainer, Mack, is there. Mack is Japanese and looks like Mister Miyagi from the Karate Kid. Mack is good but he doesn't have time for me. All his attention is on Tyrell Biggs as he hits the punching mitts at machine gun speed.

The boxing gym is a completely different world from the college campus and is a culture that is not easily understood by anyone outside the sport. You have to bite your tongue and take on an outward illusion of stupidity to not let it tarnish your mind. It's hard for me to do but they have knowledge that I want. It's a paradox. I want knowledge from a place that on the surface seems brainless. But I know I can pull some real diamonds out of this crazy place.

Willie comes over to me and we go to the heavy bags. "Okay," he says. "Turn your left foot, screw your big toe into the ground and then..."

I crack the bag and send it rocking back and Willie's eyes get big.

"Not bad," Willie says. "Do it again."

I nail the bag again and Willie smiles and shakes his head. Willy is a really down black dude with a very expressive face. The usual truthful black frankness seems to always come bubbling out of him. He loves boxing and that's what he's all about. Boxing seems simple on the surface but in reality it's very complex.

Mike Tyson is big right now and it cracks me up after every big boxing match to see all these hotshot football and basketball players come into the boxing gym thinking they're going to kill the world. By the end the week more than half of them are gone and by the end of the month only one or two are still around. Then after six weeks go by and it's time to get into the ring and spar, the remaining few do it once and are never seen again.

I finish my workout with a couple of rounds on the speed bag then I head off to pick up Adolf and go run on the beach. I've dropped some weight and I'm able to make it the whole two miles now. Even though I'm slow at least I make it without walking. I go back home and the phone rings as I walk in the front door and I pick up.

"Hey, Walt," Fred, a guy I know from high school says. He owns a garage door company that my roommate Skip works for. "You want to make some extra money?"

"Sure I do," I say.

"Great," Fred answers. "Skip recommended you. Basically what I need is someone to go out and give people a bid when they call in and ask about a garage door. I'll show you how."

"Sounds okay," I say, and we make plans to meet later in the week.

We meet up in a few days and he takes me on a few bids and the week after I'm going on calls by myself. It's easy part-time work. I'm not really into it but at least its real money compared to what I make at the liquor store. I've started my last semester of college and now I also have a new job. I'm taking the four classes I've dreaded but I can't put them off any longer. They are staring me in the face just like the rest of my life. I never know what's around the corner. One day I have the world by the tail and the next I'm fighting for air deep underwater. At least it's good that I'm disciplined and can focus on things when I want to.

A while back I let myself go to pot but now I'm training like a madman. The classes are hard for me but I'll get through them. I just have to stay on top of the class work then it will be easy. Anything can be easy if I want it to be. It all depends on how much effort I put out because that's what I'll get in return.

The next few months are centered on school and workouts and not much else. By the time I get into the middle of April I'm down to 210 pounds, from the three bills I was at the beginning of December. I've lost 90 pounds in that short period of time by hitting it hard. Once I focus on something that's all I can think about. I'm running hard and long, lifting weights, and boxing and wrestling in open rooms wherever I can find them. I'm 210 pounds but I'll slam your ass through the wall.

There's a sneaky little bastard from Santa Ana named Frito James, maybe 190 pounds, going around telling people that he schooled me in takedowns and I hear about it. So I go into a wrestling room one night where I know he'll be. We square up for takedowns and fight for grip. He leans into me and I bang my forehead into his. When I look at his face I can tell he's not digging the takedown session. I drop down a level and lunge forward, double-legging him onto his back.

"Holy hell," Frito gasps, "that hurt."

"We're not done yet," I say. "Let's do some more takedowns."

I circle and bring my right foot to my left heel, to get a deep penetration shot. He doesn't notice, though, because I'm pulling his dyed hair on the back of his head. I suddenly spring into my double-leg penetration and get deep between his legs. My shoulder hits his stomach like a cannonball and his feet come off the mat. I turn the corner and feel a twinge of pain. My left ear is banged up because it's on my shooting side and is tight to his hip. The young 190-pounder is now on my shoulder and I'm on my feet. I throw him over my head for maximum height and he falls five feet down to the mat. I could squash this little punkass bitch like a bug but I let him scramble back to his legs where I get him in a head-and-arm lock.

*You see, dumbass,* I think, *I'm going to squeeze you hard and choke you nice and good.* He starts to whimper like a submissive pup and I hit an arm-spin takedown. You've been running around the wrestling circuit saying you took me down the last time we paired off. Maybe you could do it when I was playing around but not when I'm going hard. I let go and spin to his back. He has tears in his eyes and cries out in pain.

"I'm not wrestling with you anymore," he says. "You're trying to hurt me."

"Nope," I answer. "That's just how you wrestle hard."

He runs out the door.

"Bye-bye, Frito," I say, laughing out loud. "What a pussy."

An idiot that I've known for a long time sees Frito scamper away and comes up to me. "What are you doing, Walt?" he says. "That wasn't called for."

"Shut up, you dumb little moron," I say, "before I knock you back to the stone age. You're already as stupid as a caveman so you might as well look like one."

The guy stares at the floor silently, eyes cast downward, afraid to say a word. Some dumb guys have to be put in their place because they don't know that they're idiots. I grab my weight belt, walk out to my bike and cruise home. It's evening and time to go out. I've been training hard and losing weight for months and I plan on boxing in a match at the end of April under 200 pounds. I've been skipping meals, running four-to-twelve miles a day and boxing, lifting and slapping around punks in wrestling rooms. Now it's time to party.

The Smiths are blaring on the stereo and I've got Adolf on his hind legs with his front paws in my hands and we're boogying down, dancing our asses off in the living room. There's a big tube TV along the wall and an old sectional couch and a paisley pullout sofa sitting diagonally in the corner. There's an entrance from the kitchen and another on the hallway by the front door. There's an 8 x 4 foot finished oak panel that closes it off, making it secluded. There are a few empty beer cans with notebook paper shoved out of the tops, spread out like Japanese origami flowers. A while back Jorge, Coby and I ate some mushrooms and Jorge decided to make flowers with notebook paper and beer cans.

"They're beautiful," he said. "I'm going to sell them at the swap meet."

The funny thing was that they *were* beautiful and we kept a couple sitting around to remind us of that night. Dusk turns into darkness and I've slammed more than a few soldiers. Steve, an old friend, shows up and I shut down the house. We go over to Tom's house, a friend from high school and have a few more beers. Then we head out to this hole-in-the-wall bar, 2095, that's hidden in the corner of a shopping center and plays crazy punk rock music from a few years ago. I walk to the front and am greeted by a big Samoan guy named Bimbo. He's seen me flatten many a beggar in the parking lot and always gives me a lot of respect.

"Hello, Mr. Foxx," Bimbo says. "Let me get you a table."

Bimbo has on a denim vest that he always wears and flexes his steroid-pumped arms as he leads us inside. He's jumpy and a bit on the excited side which are standard steroid side effects.

The usual drinking begins and we start getting into the music. Wannabe punks are everywhere. Screechy Ron, a happy old guy with an unmistakable high-pitched raspy voice, is behind the bar pouring drinks. There's a bunch of chicks here: fresh fish to spear. There's also a bunch of drunks in punk rock costumes. That look lost its shine years ago. Jeans, tattered shirt and a ragged haircut doesn't get you anything now but a laugh.

Back in the day you put on a punk rock uniform to get into fights but nobody cares anymore. So what's the point? Kind of like white kids from the suburbs dressing up like boys in the hood and pretending to be rappers. It's something to laugh at not to get in a fight over. It's a different crowd that wears the punk costume now. They don't want to pay the price of fighting or run the risk of getting hurt. They want to pretend to be rebels without actually being against anything or suffering any consequences.

We get down for a while, sitting in a booth in this rundown bar with its ripped upholstery. All around us in this dark room are a bunch of fools dressed up like its Halloween. A few of them bump into me but I give them a sharp glace and they shy away. The problem with them is the lack of warrior attitude that goes with their costumes. But guess what? I am the consequence. This bunch of fools thinks that nothing is going to happen to them regardless of how they act. If they behave then nothing will.

The bar is not the same as it used to be and nothing fun is happening so Tom, Steve and I decide to leave. We walk by the bouncers and make it out the door. A crowd is gathered outside around the front door and everybody is drunk and disorderly.

"This bar has gone downhill if they let you in, Foxx," a voice says behind me.

I turn and it's this little itty-bitty guy named Joe with a smartass look on his face. He's as little as it gets in every respect. He's small in stature, small in his life, and most of all small in personal integrity. It has to be the fact that he was born in a woman-sized body and never got over it. Some small guys can be as tough as hell but this idiot isn't one of them. For him, being little makes everything he does little. He's been a wannabe punker his whole life but he isn't punk rock. He can't hurt anyone so he tries to be intellectual but he doesn't have the brainpower. He falls short because he's just a suck-ass midget with nothing inside to back it up. He's a jealous wannabe who tries to get over on people to make himself feel adequate.

"Joe," I say, "It's time you considered getting a sex change. You would be a good-looking girl. You could talk strategies on how to suck-off real fighters except you don't know any."

His punk rock wannabe friends laugh despite themselves and he turns a shade of red and flips me off.

I've always had a strong dislike for Joe's view of life. He has nothing I respect but I am strong and he is weak and he has crossed the line. So I cup my right hand and smack him on his left ear with a satisfying pop that seems to come from inside his head. A real man would either take a swing at me or shake it off knowing that he had it coming; but not Joe, the ultimate midget of the world. The little weasel holds his ear with one hand and waves his other hand at Bimbo.

"Call the cops! You're a witness that Foxx assaulted me!"

"I didn't see anything," Bimbo says. "As a matter of fact I think they need me inside." He laughs and walks away into the building.

We turn away and walk to Tom's black Toyota Maxima and get in. As I shut the front door from the shotgun position I hear Joe screaming at the top of his lungs.

"Get everyone from inside!"

Two guys run in and seconds later 20 or so other wannabe twerps run out the door. Small-Time Joe is trying to rally the small-time wannabe fighters.

"There they are!" Joe points at us in the Maxima.

Tom backs out of the angled parking spot and his headlights illuminate the bunch of posers who think they're going to save Small-Time's honor. As 20 wannabe punks come running Tom puts the car into reverse then shifts into drive and takes off. These purple-haired idiots, swinging the chains that normally hold their empty wallets on their baggy corduroy pants, run after the car like they're going to catch it.

"Stop the car," I say to Tom. "I'm going to kill these fools."

This sad group in Doc Marten boots and wife-beater tank tops are what Joe thinks passes for tough. They think being a warrior is stealing change out of car ashtrays in parking garages.

"Stop," I say again. "I am going to kill these posers."

"No!" Tom says, continuing to drive. "We're leaving."

Tom is a good partier but he isn't up for a brawl. He drops us off at his apartment and Steve and I transfer to the Sprint and head to the Jack's Burgers on PCH and Warner, across from Mr. B's Liquor. The Sprint's windows rattle as we make our way there and pull into the drive-through lane. It's amazingly slow and its several minutes before the car in front of us pulls away from the order board and we're able get in front of the microphone.

"Hello?" I say.

Thirty seconds pass without a word from the speaker, giving me time to pull a few dollars from my wallet and scrounge for loose change on the floorboard.

"Hello?" I say again. "Did you hear me? Anyone there?"

Another couple of minutes go by. I just want four plain cheeseburgers and it's taking a year to order. Someone in an old van directly behind me lays on their horn, honking at me repeatedly.

"Order your food, you stupid ass," the driver yells out of his window.

"No way," I say to Steve. "He is not talking to me. I'll jump out of this car and rip his head off."

The guy honks again. "Move it, you moron," he screams.

"Okay, that's it," I tell Steve. "I am going to kill this idiot." As I reach for the door handle the microphone light on the order board suddenly comes on.

"Can I take your order?" a voice says.

I calm down and release the door handle. "Steve, you want anything?" He shakes his head so I order my cheeseburgers.

"Please pull forward to the next window to pay," the voice says.

I pull up and start looking for another 46 cents on the floorboard, spotting a quarter under the floor mat and some nickels and pennies under the seat. The drive-through moment from earlier is over. I just want to get my food and get out of there. Suddenly from behind me I hear a horn go off again.

"About time you moved," the van driver yells. "You took your sweet time!"

I can see the guy now in the light from the ordering board. He's a long-haired hippie in an old-time VW Jesus van; the usual late night drunk. My temper is short tonight after Small Time and his wannabe punk rockers. Now a dumb hippie at the Jack's Burgers drive-through is fanning the flames. I must pay him back for his big mouth and overuse of the horn. I'm not taking his drunken bullshit anymore. He's going to get it and get it good. I take a deep breath to calm myself and try to let good reason overcome my anger. I try to force myself to ignore this long-haired hippie in the van but his horn sounds again. He just won't stop.

"Where'd you get your driver's license, asshole?" he yells, his words echoing in my window. "K-Mart?"

That's it. I open the Sprint's door quickly, causing the loose glass to rattle in the frame. Now it's on. The VW van is gold with red stripes on front and as I walk back its headlights blind me almost as much as my rage. The driver jumps out, keeping his door open and pushed tight against the order board, cursing at me through the V-shaped opening between the door and hood. He's in his late thirties with long, dirty blond hair and a Fu-Manchu moustache. I've been putting up with this idiot's bullshit too long. This is going to be fun.

I clear the back of my Sprint and break into a full charge, my arms extended straight in front of me. In a split-second I smash through the barrier of his open door. To my surprise it's quite easy to get past. I thought I would have to squash him into the front seat of the van to get the door shut. But I don't want him in the van. No. I want to get my hands on his big mouth. He was hungry enough to go to a late night drive-through, so the least I can do is put my fist in his mouth to chew on.

I slide past the edge of the door, moving towards him, and get smacked hard in the head. A flash of light goes across the inside of my closed eyelids as I fight to stay conscious. *This hippie hits damn hard,* I think. I get inside his reach and wrap him up in a tight bear hug and feel him squirm. I'm like a python and I squeeze tighter and tighter. The lights go off again as he cracks me in the head a second time. This guy punches like Mike Tyson. I'm trapped between his van and the order board with my arms around him and I take yet another hard shot to the head.

Burning pain ripples around my skull like vibrations from a tuning fork. He has hit me three or four times and I can feel the pain moving from the top of my head down to my chin in waves. One thing for sure, this hippie can crack. He must be a boxer or something because he sure packs a wallop in his shots. It won't do him any good, though. He can't get any clear shots on me because I'm squeezing him nice and tight like the rat he is. I lift him off the ground and walk with him in a bear hug, squeezing hard and looking for an open place to slam him to the ground.

"Can I take your order?" a voice says from the order board speaker.

I stagger and see stars again as the hippie lands another hard blow to my head. You've got to be kidding me. Another shot? I can't wait to slam this prick. I finally get him past the back of the van, arch my back to get more elevation, and pull him over my left hip with explosive acceleration. The hippie is going to get flying lessons at the Jack's Burgers airport. The landing strip is the drive-through asphalt, though, and he's not coming down smoothly. He crashes onto the ground, the exhaust pumping out of the van's tail pipe and into his face. It's like a smoky dark scene from a horror movie. Too bad for the hippie with the heavy hands this is not a movie. This is real life and the cavalry won't be coming to his rescue.

His body goes temporarily limp from the impact and in that split second I jump on his chest and sit on his sternum with my knees across his shoulders. Now we're going to see who hits hard. I go full throttle and give this idiot a right, smashing his nose flat. Then I hit him with a left to the eye.

In a fight you go down like a Japanese aircraft carrier captain at the battle of Leyte Gulf. You never give up despite the odds and scream defiance at your opponent even as the last breath leaves your body. At this stage of the fight, though, the fury has left the hippie's eyes but has grown exponentially in mine. I fire a left and two more heavy rights. This thirty-something hippie loudmouth has left the realm of the conscious world. I blast him with another right. I'm not speed-bagging this guy's face, I'm heavy-bagging it. His head turns into an overripe melon; a cantaloupe that's been left in the sun too long, squishy with texture but no substance. Something you could dig your thumb into and puncture the skin so the juice flows out.

I hit him a few more times and the veil of red fury starts to lift from in front of my eyes. I look over my shoulder and see Steve beating on the hippie's legs with a short wooden cop nightstick.

"What the hell are you doing, Steve?" I shout. "That's not cool!"

Steve stops and looks at me in one of those cone-of-silence moments, where you feel that nobody else in the world can hear you speak.

"Hell, Walt," Steve says. "He's been hitting you over the head with this club the whole time."

"He has?"

"Yeah. He's been trying to bash your skull in."

"Then kill him!" I yell, the red rage returning.

I continue pounding his face while Steve goes back to hitting the loser's legs with his own club.

I land two last signature punches on this waste of a human life and we run back to the Sprint, the hippie's club in hand. I think for a second about pulling up to the drive-through window and grabbing my cheeseburgers but I know the cops are on their way so I buzz out of the driveway, the Sprint rumbling and chugging down Warner Ave. We turn at the first stop light, make a left two streets later then cruise home along the residential highway. I can get across town taking city housing-tract roads faster than taking the main streets. Best of all there's no cops. We're safe even though my head hurts and throbs like crazy.

"Shit," Steve says, "that guy was beating on you with a club."

I reach up and feel my head. I have two huge lumps on top of my skull. I have a sudden vision of the hippie's beaten body lying at the back of his van with exhaust fumes blowing over his bloody face. I laugh at how trivial a couple of bumps on my head are compared to that. It was all worth it.

Before Steve takes off I pass the cul-de-sac my house is on to make sure no cops are there. They're not, so I pull up and Steve takes off. Adolf is waiting for me but there's no TV tonight. We go straight to bed and I can only lay on the right side of my head because of the lumps that have grown to the size of eggs on my left.

That dumb hippie learned to keep his mouth shut. He will probably eventually forget the lesson, but for a while, at least, he'll lay off the horn when he goes to a drive-through.

# Chapter 10
## Road to Ruin

Beep! Beep! Beep!

"Damn!" I slam the alarm clock and get up to go to school early. I've got to give a speech in my History Seminar class and since I was the last person to pick a topic the professor picked me first to give a presentation. But instead of spending the night before preparing my thesis on Vietnam, which is supposed to last for ten minutes, I went out and partied it up with the boys and had fun at Jack's Burgers.

With just an hour to go before class, I go to the library and try to pull shit out of my ass. I read the prefaces of a few Vietnam history books but I know I'm screwed. I have a deer-in-the-headlight moment and think maybe I shouldn't show up. But I have a residue buzz and the fool's bravery that goes with it. I finish scanning the books and rush out on the road to ruin.

"So, Mr. Foxx," the professor says after everyone in class has taken a seat, "you're first. Could you address the class with your project?"

I go to the front of the class and stare out at these scholarly students. I want to say, *If I could only tell you about last night, I would enlighten you children about real life and how we create our future history in the present, but instead I'm here to tell you about Vietnam.*

Instead I start off with as much of the bullshit I can remember from the books I read just an hour ago. I ramble on and on about everything *but* history. It doesn't make any sense but what does in my life? Only the things like what happened last night have any logic to me.

I finish lamely by saying, "So that's going to be my paper." I finish rambling and look at the professor.

"Mr. Foxx," my professor says. "What kind of a presentation was that?"

"Not a very good one, I guess," I say.

The professor nods his head. "Not only was it not very good, it was a waste of class time."

I sit down and three others in the class give their presentations. As class gets ready to adjourn the professor looks in my direction. "Mr. Foxx," he says. "Will you please stay after class? I'd like to have a word with you."

The professor is a small Middle Eastern guy who calls himself a Palestinian and wears a red dishtowel on his head that makes him look a little like Yasser Arafat. My buzz residue is still strong so I'll take the browbeating like a man. The classroom empties and I sit at the end of the long conference table, packing my bag and getting ready to head out.

"Mr. Foxx," the professor says gently. "Don't take what I said in front of the class personally. I was sharp with you because I know you can do a much better job. I had to let the class know that was not acceptable."

"I'm sorry, sir," I say. "I had a rough night."

"Yes," he says. "I could tell. Just do what you're capable of and you'll be fine."

"Thank you," I say. "I will."

I go to the rest of my classes in a daze as the residue buzz fades away to nothing. After school I go to the gym where I'm working with a new trainer named Jesse. My boxing match is Saturday and I'm not eating anything because I've got to be under 200 pounds in five days. The lumps on my head are throbbing so I just do a light workout then hit an easy six-mile jog. Afterwards I grab a shower and watch TV with Adolf before sleeping early to make-up for the hours I missed the night before. I spend the next few days gearing up for Saturday. I grind through school, do light workouts, and get lots of sleep. By Friday night I'm less than 200 pounds and ready to get down.

I spring out of bed the next morning well-rested and ready to go. I jump into the Sprint and drive to the boxing gym which is already set-up for the show. A local gym rat is checking everyone's weight. He was a punching bag for Meldric Taylor in a tune-up match once so he thinks he's tough.

"Hey, Walt," he says before I step on the scale. "Super heavyweight, right?"

"Nope," I answer. "I'm fighting in the under two-hundred class."

"Really?" he says. "You look bigger."

I get onto the balance beam scale and he starts fiddling with the little weights. I wonder how it feels to be a former opponent of Meldric Taylor now doing weigh-ins at an amateur boxing show telling yourself you're still tough. When I first went to the gym this little rat popped off, asking me what a wrestler was doing in a boxing match. I just bit my tongue and smiled like I do now as I step off the scale.

"You're right," he says. "Two-hundred pounds. You've been training hard."

"Yup," I say. "Put me down for heavyweight."

After the sign-ups are completed there's a total of 15 heavyweights, so there shouldn't be any problem getting a match. The amateur officials circle around and begin to match the boxers up, all trying to get their favorite fighters the easiest opponents. As the scumbag politics unfold I walk across the street to MacDonald's, I haven't been under 200 pounds in a long time and I've been starving myself since the beginning of December. Now that I've weighed-in it's time for a big breakfast of pancakes, syrup, sausage, hash browns and milk. It feels so good to eat after making weight. I finish and go back across the street to see who the officials matched me against. The old street is in bad need of repaving and there are potholes everywhere. I walk into the old warehouse that's been converted into a boxing gym and go over to Jesse.

"So who am I boxing?" I ask.

He shakes his head. "You don't have a match, Walt."

"What? There are fifteen guys in my weight class."

"Yeah," he says. "But everybody has seen you in the gym. Nobody at two hundred will fight you."

"You've got to be kidding," I say. "I weighed-in below two hundred."

"That's why nobody wants to face you," Jesse shrugs. "They know you're a cut-down superheavyweight who can crack."

"Well, I want to box," I say. "Tell them that I'll fight at super heavy. I'll fight anyone. I don't care."

He walks away for five minutes and I see him talking to three or four different guys before he finally returns. "They've got someone," he says. "He needs a match but he's six-feet-four and two-forty-eight."

"Tell him it's on," I say.

Five matches are ahead of mine but they finish quickly and soon it's time to go. I'm 199 pounds fighting a huge black guy who looks like he's chiseled out of a single piece of obsidian. He's a hot prospect and a lot of people have come to watch him fight. He has on red-white-and-blue headgear and an official-looking boxing team tank-top and shorts. He looks to be backed up by some big-time sponsors. I have on my wrestling shoes, hot pink shorts, and a white wife-beater.

I get into the ring where he's already standing. I can't wait. *Let's go, you big bastard.* The bell goes off and from the start I turn up the heat. I smack the hell out of him from the inside, not giving him room to punch me from distance. I'm lighter than him but I steamroll his ass for the entire first round until the bell rings. The second round is more of the same with me inside teeing off and him covering up and backpedaling. This was obviously not supposed to go this way and my opponent's cornermen look concerned and are unusually quiet.

Round three starts and the crowd of casual onlookers is going crazy while the hardcore boxing regulars and officials looked stunned. Their boxing phenom is getting his ass waxed by a crazy-looking white guy in a wife-beater who was not supposed to go the distance with him, much less win. My ears are laid back and I've got the fight in the bag. I could stall out the final round and win easily by decision but I want to knock him the hell out. *Bring it on!* I'm taking it to him again but with thirty seconds left I get careless and get hit with a nice overhand right. It's a good shot but I'm far from hurt and am surprised when the referee starts an eight count.

"What the hell?" I say through my mouthpiece. "You kidding me?"

The referee finishes the count and restarts the fight. I circle to the right and fire a couple of shots then take another overhand right in return. With less than ten seconds left in the match the referee steps in and calls the fight, lifting the big guy's arm for a TKO win. He looks over and nods at the big guy's cornermen.

"It's over?" I say to Jesse, who steps into the ring. "But I wasn't hurt and I had the decision in the bag. This is bullshit!"

"Yep," Jesse says, guiding me out of the ring. "Welcome to the politics of boxing."

As I leave the gym I know that regardless of the official outcome this guy knows he just got his ass handed to him by a 199-pounder. Because the referee knew the trainer, though, they cheated me. That is so typical of the scumbag boxing world and why I'm so hesitant to go into it professionally.

I take the tape of the fight that my dad filmed and go home and pound beers and watch it. I can't believe how badly they jobbed me. I kicked his ass the whole bout but the boxing officials wanted him to win and fairness had nothing to do with it. It's all scumbag politics. I watch the entire match several times and it's clear to me the fix was in. This is actually what I expected from the scumbag boxing judges, referees and promoters so I'm actually not all that outraged. I know who won and that's all that matters.

I stay in with Adolf and drink all night, thinking about how I just got screwed over in my boxing match. That's the way it is but that isn't the way it should be. Screw this boxing bullshit with all its scumbags. Boxing needs truth. How can I turn pro and deal with all this shit? The sport is tough to a certain level and the average Joe is captivated by the perceived violence. But it's hard to get really hurt or to hurt someone. It's all a smoke screen but the public seems to buy it.

Most boxers have a little warrior spirit in them but they're not hardcore. If you went to a boxing gym and told everyone inside that a bunch of wrestlers were in the parking lot and wanted to fight, the boxers would call the cops. But if you went to a wrestling room and told everyone that a bunch of boxers were outside and wanted to fight, the wresters would be crawling all over each other to get out the door: *Let's get down!. Let's kill those pieces of shit!*

My mind is rambling. I just got my eyes opened to the fact that I can't go into boxing as a career option. Another door in my life has closed. The sport is crooked, but now what? I'm in my last semester of college and before today boxing was always a viable alternative. Now I'm back to crashing my fighter plane into the German countryside. My life is so messed up. *What am I going to do?* I've got to find something that has meaning. Soon I won't have school and now I don't have boxing. *Dammit!* I don't have a life to look forward to. All I can do is try to muddle through the present. My best option now is to be an ostrich and stick my head in the sand until I find a reason to pull it out.

I put the boxing match behind me and dive back into my normal routine for the next few weeks, hoping that everything will somehow fall into place. Life is a blur of schoolwork and working out. When it comes to going out I'm mellow as well, chilling at home and drinking with Adolf. I go on several more garage door bids for Fred and it's easy. I've just about had my fill of the assholes that come into the liquor store but I hang onto the job for security, using Fred and his garage door company just for extra spending money.

I'm keeping both jobs because I've known Fred for many years and he's not to be trusted. He's a fat guy with black curly hair and a giant beer gut sitting in the middle of his Buddha-like body. When you shake hands with him you'd better check your fingers to make sure they're all still there. I have to remind myself constantly of who he is. He tries to dress nice but it feels fake; like a college kid who has to go to an opera for his freshman music class and borrows his dad's clothes. No one at the opera says anything but they all know he's a poser. I'm doing the bids in my mom's car and it's going well and I'm making good money relative to the liquor store. But I'm not planning on making a career out of being a garage door salesman; that's for high school dropouts and losers like Fred.

As the days continue to tick by school is more of the usual boredom and the boxing gym is flat. I let the boxing loss go and just keep training. It's just politics and I can't do anything about that. He didn't and couldn't kick my ass. One day after working out I pack my gear into my boxing bag, climb on my Interceptor and head out of the barrio where the gym's at. I feel comfortable out on the main drag and hit the throttle hard. I look up from the speedometer just in time to see a cop going the opposite way.

I look in my rear view mirror and see his reds and blues come on. As he pulls a U-turn to come after me I tighten the strap on my helmet, downshift, and take off. The red needle on the tachometer moves from left to right as I go through the gears and pick up speed. The scenery turns blurry and as I go across the freeway overpass I can see him in my mirror tracking me. The light just turned green and the cars in all lanes are four deep. I split them in seconds and get way in front of everyone. I turn right into the first housing tract and get on the residential highway.

Now that I'm in the tract homes I'm gone. Nobody can catch me. I cross over a few major streets that separate the housing tracts and make it home, parking the Interceptor on the side of the house just in case the cop gets lucky and drives down my street. But the cop can't catch me. I'm too good. I walk through the side door into my room and fall on my bed. I've got a couple of hours until I go to work at the liquor store and I'm just chilling. Adolf sticks his head in the bedroom, discovers that I'm there, and jumps on the bed in happy surprise. I hang with him for ten minutes then get up and make a sandwich, share it with Adolf, then try to read some history. The ever-present weight around my neck is getting heavier and heavier by the day but I know I'll somehow work it out. I always do.

The phone rings and I pick it up and say hello.

"Walter," I hear my dad say. "The police are here looking for you. There are two cops at the door and a squad car at each end of the street."

An icy, cold spear goes through my heart. "What? What the hell are you talking about? There's no way! I'll call my lawyer and figure out what this is about. The cops can't be looking for me. I haven't been in a fight for months."

"Well," my dad says grimly, hanging up, "they're after you."

Suddenly the weight on my shoulders about my future career is gone. Now I have a bigger thing to worry about than what I'm going to do after college. I'm instantly tense and nervous. *What the hell is this about?* I've been low key the last couple of months just trying to figure out what I'm going to do with my life. Why are the cops looking for me?

I pick up the phone and call Barry Repel, my attorney. I've used him so much in the past that he's now more like a friend. "Hey, Barry," I say when he picks up, "it's Walt. The cops are looking for me and I don't know why."

Barry is quiet for a moment as he thinks over what I've said. "Okay, just lay low. I'll go in with you to talk to them. Meet me at the courthouse tomorrow at two o' clock."

I tell him okay and then hang up the phone and go to the liquor store and start my shift. I turn my head every second to see if the cops are coming in. A cold and misty fog blankets the old beach town. It's slow and every time the front door chimes my head pops up from the book I'm reading. In my head I picture SWAT cops storming in to hook my ass up. I don't get it. I haven't done anything. This is the first time that I'm happy to see the scumbags come in. They can ask for pack of Red Dogs and I won't care. I've eaten my prime rib sandwich and I can't read more than two sentences without wondering what the cops want me for. I haven't a clue.

*The hell with this!* I grab a beer, slam it down in one gulp, smash the can into a flat piece of aluminum, and repeat the process several times. I'm too distracted to watch the 10 inch black-and-white so I play The Smiths and serve a few stragglers as I mop the floor, moving the handle to the rhythm of Morrissey's vocals, mouthing the words silently: *Girlfriend in a coma I know...I KNOW.* The store is stocked and cleaned so I grab an empty box and put out all the loose trash and numerous flattened beer-cans I've made. It's finally closing time so I hit the alarm and go out to the Sprint with a fresh twelver. The sheepskin seat covers are cold tonight and frost has glazed over the windows. I can't see to save my life so I hit the toggle switches and start the car. The defroster is one of the few things that actually work.

I sit and listen to The Smiths while I drink a beer and wait for the windshield to clear. When I can finally see I take off down the alley and turn onto the dark street that goes past the church and eventually runs through the Navel Weapons Yard. This long stretch has no streetlights and is extra foggy because of the huge field of ammunition bunkers with grass tops and cement fronts. I feel like I'm on a road that has no end and leads nowhere. The Sprint is humming along, the Smiths are playing, and I'm lost in my buzz. But the big question is still looming over my head like a guillotine ready to drop: *What the hell do the cops want?*

# Chapter 11
## Liar, Liar

I awake in the morning in less of a bad mood than I had imagined. I'm not happy by any means but facing a problem is a lot better than thinking about facing it. I get through my morning classes and head to the courthouse after lunch to meet my attorney, Barry.

The building isn't that impressive from the outside but it's definitely intimidating from the inside. It's a two-story gray cement structure with just a few windows and Spartan landscaping. I go in the first set of glass doors, past the Division 1 section and make a right at the first hallway. It's long and I can see my reflection in the freshly polished marble floors that almost look like water to me. I go by Divisions 2, 3, 4, and 5, finally passing the Traffic section. Every time I come to the courthouse somebody knows me, and sure enough I see a man holding a file folder in the hallway.

"Hey Walt," a fifty-something guy with a stained tie says. "What are you doing here?"

I think about telling him to piss off and mind his own damn business but I can't remember what his name is or what he does. He could end up being the judge who presides over my case so I just smile, shrug and keep marching down to the Public Offensives section. I go through the open hallway door and Barry is waiting for me at the furthest window, dressed in a suit. The office workers are clustered around desks on the other side of the glass that separates them from the public. Like all typical government employees they are walking around like zombies with nothing to do.

At one of the other windows a young attorney is being helped indifferently and at yet another window a female lawyer has a pissed-off look on her face. The government workers are utilizing the only cheap power they have: making people wait.

I sit down on a hard wooden bench at the bottom of the wheelchair ramp that is uncomfortable on purpose; like anyone would want to stay here longer than needed. I'm edgy and nervous and I can feel my heart pounding in my throat. *What is this about?*

Barry grabs a folder from the window clerk and walks toward me. He has a talent for making serious legal issues turn into nothing and has done it for me many times before. He's wearing a gray, pinstriped Armani suit with a red silk tie that really pops. His salt-and-pepper hair is slicked backed with gel and his face is tanned from living at the beach.

"Hey, Walt," Barry says. "What's up?"

"I truly don't know," I reply. "I've been good for the most part since I saw you last." *In reality that just means I've had clean getaways.*

"Okay," he nods, "let me look at this folder and see what it says."

The other two attorneys are still waiting for paperwork at their windows and I can see they're steamed because Barry got his so fast. An office girl passes and Barry smiles at her, turning on the charm.

"Hi, Barry," she stops. "It's good to see you. Do you need anything?"

"No, thanks, Shirley," he says. "I just picked up what I needed. But if I knew you were coming I would have waited."

"Oh, Barry," she laughs. She gives him a playful nudge and walks on.

Barry starts reading the indictment inside the dark brown folder and I watch him as though lottery balls are falling out of a spinning cage on TV. It takes him five minutes or so to finish.

"Did you get into a fight at Sea Lion Beach six months ago?" Barry finally asks, looking up.

"I can't remember what I did six days ago. Tell me what it says."

Barry clears his throat. "It says that you and a long-haired associate were urinating on the side of a church and the victim came up with his girlfriend and asked you to stop. The victim said, 'That's not cool,' and you replied 'I'll show you cool,' and then proceeded to assault him. He says that you couldn't catch him and so your long-haired friend tackled him and held him down while you banged his head on the ground and then took off in your car. His girlfriend corroborates the story."

For a moment I'm speechless, not believing what I just heard. "Barry," I say finally, "That never happened. This is all bullshit and lies."

Barry nods. "It looks like he changed his story three times because he couldn't remember what happened."

"That's because he wanted to fight and got beat up," I say. "I was driving home from work when I saw him slapping his girlfriend around. When I stopped to see what was going on he started swearing at me and flipping me off. It was at the intersection across from the church, I wasn't taking a leak and no one was with me."

"His name is Jerome La Mentiroso," says Barry. "Did you ever meet him before that night?"

I shake my head. "Never."

"It looks like his dad is a detective for the Sea Lion Beach police department," Barry continues. "It seems he's been pushing this with the DA ever since it happened, trying to build a case against you."

As I hear his words I explode, my temper raging. "Dammit, Barry! The DA and the dad are liars too, then! You can be a cop or a DA or whatever and that's fine; but when you lie you become a total piece of shit. You know what, Barry? If they want to lie then I'll play the same game. If you start a fight and get beaten up then take it like a man. Don't try to get even through the courts by lying. I'll lie too and say I was never there. If the DA is a scumbag then I'll lie, too. I'll be just like them!"

I'm nearly screaming and the other attorneys in the area are listening to our conversation carefully, as well as the office workers behind the glass partition.

"Come on, Walter," Barry says abruptly, getting up. "We need to go outside."

We walk out the door on the brightly polished floor and turn down a hallway that leads to an alley behind the courthouse. The hallway is empty this afternoon and Barry's Ferragamo shoes click on the marble hall as he leads me outside through a steel door. A loud hum is coming from the traffic on Beach Blvd. and Barry turns around and gets close to me so I can hear him. We're face to face; our eyes six inches apart.

"Walt," Barry says, "I can't represent you now."

"What?" I'm speechless once again so I look at the bush next to us where a butterfly is flying around the top of some purple flowers.

"I've been working here a long time," Barry says. "Everyone knows me. I can't let a client tell me they're going to lie in front of witnesses then represent them. If I do that I could get disbarred. I like you, Walter, and I know you don't lie; but in the future if you decide to lie then tell me after the fact. If you're going to tell stories then I don't need to know."

"I won't say it again, Barry," I plead.

"It's too late. The other attorneys heard you and so did the court clerks," Barry interrupts. "There's nothing I can do. I'll call you later with the names of some other attorneys you can contact."

Barry walks back into the courthouse, leaving me alone on the street. I look back at the bush and the butterfly floats to the ground without flapping its wings. I walk out to my bike, climb on top, and shoot back to the house. As I go over the freeway overpass I look in my rearview mirror to make sure no cops are around. I lay low for a couple of days until Barry finally calls me in the afternoon at home and gives me the names and numbers of some lawyer friends.

"These guys are good," Barry says. "They'll take care of you. If they ask why I'm not taking the case say I have problems with the story."

It seems that I'm sliding down a slippery slope just as I started to make some progress. I'm getting ready to graduate from school, I'm back in shape, and I've got a job where I'm making a bit of money; but now my past is coming back to haunt me. Not only do I not know what I'm going to do in life, now I've got to deal with this bullshit first.

The next day I call Barry's friends. Since I haven't dealt with them before they're a lot more expensive than what I can afford. I'm a frequent flier on Barry's legal airline so he cuts me a deal; but not these guys. I get a weird feeling from them also. They try to use my potential loss of freedom as a hammer to squeeze every dollar they can from me. I've been with Barry for the past eight years and we have a good rapport. I don't have the same vibe with Barry's friends!

After checking around I decide to use a different attorney that my friends have been using the last couple of years. All the guys in this circle rant and rave about how John has gotten them out of trouble. Although I think they're stupid, and I have a gut feeling I shouldn't, I decide to use him. I make an appointment to meet him at his office in Santa Ana and fire up the Interceptor when the date rolls around.

As I head east from Happening Harbor the scenery gradually changes. I'm in the middle of downtown Santa Ana and border brothers are everywhere, wearing cowboy hats, pushing food carts, and selling ice cream and churros. Cholos in low riders with metallic paint jobs and chain steering wheels are at every stoplight. A taco truck cuts in front of me at a clearly marked no left turn lane and I have to swerve to not get splattered.

"Get the hell out of my way, Paco!" I yell.

If I didn't know better I would swear I was in the trashy border town of Tijuana. I make it through the barrio, cross over a freeway bridge, make another right into an office building parking lot, and park my bike near the main entrance.

Driving through that bullshit has put me in a bad mood. I'm not pissed at anyone in particular except myself. *How did I get here?* It was a long ride, it's hot, and I have to deal with illegals that don't understand street signs and almost run me over. All because of a lie from little bitch Jerome who got his ass kicked when he begged for it. Now that I think about it I should have just killed him. That way his lies wouldn't have put me here. This whole process is his form of chicken-shit payback. I make it up the elevator and into the office lobby.

"I'm here to see John Wittless," I tell the heavy middle-aged and definitely un-hot receptionist.

"He will see you shortly," she says in a reedy nasal voice that grates on my nerves.

I sit down and pick up a Sports Illustrated with Mike Tyson on the cover. They are pushing him like a God and saying he's the baddest man on the planet. That's only because they aren't talking about the planet I live on. *Come to my world and I'll show you bad. If you want you can wear your boxing gloves and I'll still kick your face into one dimension.*

"Mr. Foxx?" The receptionist says, jerking me back to reality. "Mr. Wittless will see you now."

I toss the Sports Illustrated onto the table and go down two hallways to his small office. He must rent from the firm whose name is on the front door. His back window takes up the entire rear wall and I have a nice view of the freeway I just crossed to get here.

Wittless is a small guy, maybe five feet, eight inches tall and is wearing a tan suit and black glasses that go well with his blonde hair. He has a worm-like look to his clean-shaven face and sits behind a small wooden desk framed by two bookcases filled with legal books.

"So, Mr. Foxx," he says. "What can I help you with?"

"Please call me Walt," I say. "Well, in short, this guy started a fight with me by flipping me off and cursing at me. He ran off when I chased him down but then turned and hit me when I was about to let him go. So I protected myself and beat him down pretty good."

He laces his fingers together and nods. "My secretary told me that you have a regular attorney. Why isn't he taking the case?"\

"He has problems with the story," I answer,

"Okay," Wittless nods, "fair enough. What do you want me to do?"

"I want this shit to go away," I say. "This guy is lying his ass off. He and his dumb cop dad want payback because he got the beating he begged for."

"If I settle this without going to trial it will be twenty-five hundred dollars," Wittless explains. "If we go to trial it will be twenty-five hundred more."

"Let's do it, John," I say, getting up to shake his hand. "Work your magic. How do we handle the warrant they have out on me?"

"Bring the first check to the courthouse tomorrow at 1:00 P.M.," he says. "I'll take care of it then."

I walk out of the building, get on my bike, and cruise through downtown Santa Ana again. It's ridiculously hot and in no time these idiots from Mexico get me pissed off again. *Move it, you freaking idiots.* I make it home, make a sandwich, and drink a diet coke. I only have 10 minutes to get to work so I hop back on my bike and cruise down PCH past the water tower house.

I have a sick feeling in the pit of my stomach. I knew my job in this town would lead to something bad. I just want to puke all over this place. I want to watch all the little worms burn in the hot bile that erupts from my mouth. I know it's time to make my move. It's like when you're playing chess and staring at the board and it's your opponent's move and you notice he could put you in checkmate. He doesn't see it, though, and moves a pawn one insignificant space forward and you say to yourself, *Shit, that was close.*

I get to the liquor store, call the owners and tell them it's been three great years but college is almost over and I'm giving them two weeks' notice so I can go to work fulltime for the garage door company. They are very nice about it and thank me for the time I've spent there and wish me the best. I eat my usual prime rib sandwich dinner and try to read but I can't focus on the words with all this bullshit hanging over my head. *To hell with it*! I crack a beer then another and another and watch the small black-and-white TV. A woman comes in and buys a pack of Marlboro Light 100s.

"That'll be two dollars and ten cents," I say, reaching out to accept the change she hands me. She's dressed in a white pants suit and stares at me intensely. "Anything else?" I ask.

"No," she answers. "Oh, can I have some matches?"

I give her some and she takes a couple of steps towards the door before turning around and looking at me with a shocked expression. She stares at me for two or three seconds before spinning away and walking out. *That was weird. Oh, well. This is Sea Lion Beach.*

I crack another beer and flip the black-and-white TV over to Jeopardy. I watch a couple of episodes, answering most of the questions before the contestants, and 11:00 P.M. comes quickly. I finish all the store work and only grab a tall traveler and his twin since I know the fridge at home has a fresh case. When I get home I take Adolf for his cruise, watch Letterman, and then fall into a restless sleep. I awake without the alarm clock and look out the window. It's dark outside and I look at the clock and see that it's 4:00 A.M. This legal bullshit is eating away at me from the inside out like an ulcer. I manage to fall asleep again and wake up to the usual beeping of the alarm clock.

I put on my white jeans and a nice Hawaiian floral-print spooner. I go to school but I'm a shell with nothing inside. When I finish my classes I ride to the courthouse and make my way to the Public Offenses bulletin board where I see that I'm in Division 13. I go down the hall and walk into the courtroom and look at the bench. *Great. I have a woman judge.* She looks familiar to me but then so do all the judges. John Witless walks in shortly after.

Something feels wrong to me. John doesn't have the same presence that Barry does and people don't give him the same respect. Plus, the seats are full of scumbags. The judge calls my name and John stands up and says he's representing me.

"The infamous Mr. Foxx is in court again," the judge says. The deputy district attorney in charge of the case, Abe Contrary, is late and the judge looks at John. "It seems the DA is afraid of you, Mr. Wittless."

Almost on cue Abe Contrary walks in and the double wooden doors slam shut behind him. He's a young geek wearing a cheap blue suit and black framed glasses with a soft mushy body and a pudgy face. *Everything is going bad for me. There's no Barry, I have a woman judge who has heard about me, Abe Contrary is a geek, and John Witless is my attorney.*

"Since Mr. Foxx is here," says Wittless, "there's no need for bail because he turned himself in today."

The judge nods. "We'll set pretrial at four weeks from today."

Wittless goes over and pow-wows with Contrary, the geek DA, and then comes back. "He tells me that the victim's father is a detective and that you're a convicted felon and crystal meth dealer in Happening Beach."

"That's ridiculous," I say.

"They're offering you 180 days," Wittless says.

"What? His detective Dad must be as stupid as his son that got spanked," I say. "This is all bullshit. No way."

Okay," Wittless says. "I've got another case. I'll be back in 10 minutes."

Wittless walks over to the other side of the courtroom where a scumbag named Mark, who I know from high school, is sitting. He stole things out of my car and got his ass kicked more than once by me and my friends. I heard that he got popped for sexual assault and it seems he hired Wittless to represent him. The two talk and I see Mark gesturing towards me. After talking to Mark, Wittless comes back

"You didn't tell me you were a famous bar brawler," Wittless says.

"I told you I beat him up," I say. "He begged for it, John. This is not a bullshit story."

"Okay, Walt," Wittless says. "We've got pretrial in four weeks so we've got to come up with something by then."

"We need to get set for trial," I say. "I'm not doing time for these bullshit lies."

"Okay," Wittless nods. "Bring the other twenty-five hundred dollars to pretrial. The warrant is gone and you're free and clear until then."

I leave Wittless and walk down the hallway past all the scumbag trash sitting on the benches outside the various courtrooms. In my mind, the light panels that cover the fluorescent lights transform themselves into fast lane road markers on a one-way street. As I stare at the highway on the ceiling I don't like where it seems to be taking me.

I slam open the swinging doors that lead outside and go down the concrete stairs to terra firma and out to the parking lot. I climb on my Interceptor, hit the starter button, kick it down to first gear and let the clutch out hard while twisting the throttle. I've got to get away from these scumbags as fast as possible. I make it home, strap on Adolf's harness, and he pulls me over to Mom's and Dad's house.

"Can you believe these assholes?" I say to my mom. "I hope the damn cops do show up today. I'll tell those bastards where to go."

"Just calm down, Walter," my mom says.

"But they're liars!"

"Don't worry, Walter," she says. "The truth will always come out."

## Chapter 12
## **Fight Night**

Adolf pulls me back home. The phone is ringing and everybody wants to go out but I just want to be alone. In the midst of all of this bullshit I just got a new truck through Jorge, whose dad owns a used car lot. It's not brand new but it's new to me and I want to take it for a cruise. It's a white midsize GMC truck that I can use for my garage door estimates. It's plain and non- descript but is pure luxury compared to the Sprint.

I mix up a siren in a red plastic cup, fill it with Stoli and a splash of cranberry, and walk outside to take the truck for a spin. It's Friday and I don't want to hang out with anyone. Adolf doesn't count, though, being that he isn't human, so I open the front door and call him outside where he jumps in the cab. We cruise around the residential highway until 10:00 P.M. and I go back home and mix a freshy. It's my fourth or fifth and now that my buzz is on I'm looking for some people to have fun with.

I go to Rollers but there are no cars there I know, so I go to Trike's condo and he isn't home either. I then drive to where the Happening Harbor Cafe and Dead Grunion are and pull into the Grunion end of the parking lot. A bunch of people are pre-tuning, including three chicks with short skirts and fishnet stockings and two guys a couple of parking spots down drinking beer. I don't recognize any of the cars so I take a big pop off my siren and drive to the café end. I see a guy from high school named Chris in his VW Bug. He's younger than me and was a freshman when I was a senior. We're both older now so we don't seem that far apart anymore.

"Hey, Walt," he says with a friendly look. "What's up?"

"Just cruising," I say. "Let me park."

I pull next to him and we sit on the tailgate of my new truck. His three friends also get out of his car and we start drinking and talking. After a while we see some pretty boy with his shirt off and some other jack-off wearing a flannel lumberjack shirt yelling at each other at the other end of the parking lot. They must have gotten into an argument inside the Dead Grunion and came outside to settle it. We're the only audience and go over to watch the show. You can always tell the guys who aren't going to fight each other and are just talkers, like these two. They just stand there yelling no matter what kind of encouragement we give them,

"Kick his ass!" I yell to the pretty boy. Then I scream to the punk kid in the lumberjack shirt. "You gonna let this no-shirt loser talk shit to you?" But they just keep pushing each other and don't throw down. They're just looking for an excuse to get out of what they've gotten themselves into.

Finally, the pretty boy says to the lumberjack, "I don't want to fight you. Let's trash these loudmouth asses who are yelling at us."

The lumberjack nods and they break into a full charge towards us. Chris and his boys wrestle the lumberjack down but the pretty boy keeps coming at me. It's like a lion running at a hunter, not knowing he's going to be shot between the eyes. I just stand there and wait and as soon as he gets close I pull the trigger. I shoot a double leg, wrap and lock my arms around his legs, and then stand up. His sternum is on top of my head and I have my arms wrapped around his thighs. I snap him down on his back like an old Greek Mediterranean fisherman slapping his daily catch of octopus on the volcanic rocks to tenderize it.

Both his hands are clawing at my face with his fingers fully extended. He tries to fishhook me and sticks his finger in mouth but I bite down reflexively. He feels the pain and pulls his arms back with a yelp. I don't have time to open my mouth and my dental bridge flies out and lands on the asphalt.

The wannabe-cop security guards finally show up and break everything up. The pretty boy and his new lumberjack buddy stand to one side of the security guards with me and Chris and his friends on the other side. I bend over and pick up my bridge from the asphalt. *Screw it. I am so out of here.* I turn and jump into my new truck, put it in reverse, and leave without anyone paying attention to me. I drive out of the parking lot, make a left, and go behind the café to make a freshy. With drink in hand I cruise up and down the green belt, the long park that runs through the small community of Moonrise Beach. My new siren is blaring and I stop in a handicapped parking spot and put my bridge in the ashtray.

*What the hell?* The hollowed-out part of the bridge holding the cemented mouth post has broken off, leaving a jagged cylinder in my bridge plate. I swish my tongue around my mouth to take inventory and all my molars are present, but the post on the left side is missing. It must have snapped off when the pretty boy pulled his fingers out of my mouth. From that second on my plan is set in stone: I've got to get this guy and really jack him up. I have to go to the dentist now because of this pretty boy and he's going to pay.

I've got a nearly full siren and I go for a short cruise through the neighborhood before going back to the parking lot. I'm swigging my siren, my truck is in first gear, and my head is on a swivel as I scan the parking lot for a pretty boy with a bloody finger. I look all over but he's nowhere in sight. I park my truck at the café' end of the lot, away from the Dead Grunion, so I only have a short jog to get away. It'll make for an easy escape. I take the last swig from the siren and leave my wallet, keys, and pager underneath the floor mat. I leave the door unlocked with Adolf in the passenger seat to guard the truck. I sit on the tailgate and tie my high-tops tightly then march across the parking lot to the front door.

"Hey, Walt," the bouncer says. "What's up?"

I shrug nonchalantly and go inside where Chris sees me and comes up.

"What's going on, dude?" he says.

"I'm going to get that pretty boy," I answer.

"Let me help you," Chris offers.

"No," I say. "Don't do anything unless someone cheap-shots me. Stay away unless the shit hits the fan."

I go upstairs and the music is loud, vibrating off the floor and through my body. The lights reflecting from the mirrored disco ball bounce off every corner of the darkened bar. I start my search at the bathroom but there's no one inside except a bunch of idiots doing coke.

I walk back down the hallway, past the pay phones, and veer towards the DJ booth, where a tragically hip long-haired music goof is playing another lame song: *You've dropped a bomb on me, baby, you dropped a bomb.*

The pretty boy isn't by the DJ or the area where the pillows come down from the ceiling so I survey the dance floor. I almost decide that he's not there anymore when I spot him with six guys at the far end of the main bar. I circle around to get the right approach angle for the circle formation they're in. I come in at about 6:00 and he's standing at 10:30.

"What's up, dipshit?" I say. "I'm back."

His friends have puzzled looks on their faces, wondering who the hell I am.

"Piss off," the pretty boy says, squaring up and raising his fists.

He throws a right but I beat him to the punch and blast him with a straight left then a right cross. His knees buckle and he's instantly on Queer Street. His friends are shocked for a moment but then attack, one getting me in a chokehold from behind. Like sand through an hourglass, so are the seconds of my consciousness unless I get this snake off my neck. I'm taking shots and the room in growing dim and I have to break the chokehold or it's all over. I launch myself backwards, hit the ground, and then twist into the guy, breaking the choke. I get back to all fours then hit a stand up. Two other guys start to come at me but Chris and his friends suddenly appear and start scuffling with them, pushing them into the wall.

The bouncers rush through the crowd and break it up, separating everyone. Out of the corner of my eye I see the pretty boy sitting on a bar stool with red splattered all over his face from blood pouring out of a cut over his eye. His hand is wrapped up in a cloth napkin from where I bit him. As the bouncers try to sort things out I back through the crowd, catch his eye, and smile and wave. I walk calmly out the front door then hit an escape trot as soon as I'm in the parking lot. *Run, you bastard, run.* I move fast enough to cover distance quickly but slow enough so as to not alarm onlookers and draw attention so they can remember me.

I make it back to the truck where Adolf is laying on the cloth bench seat and we make it home. It's cool not having to worry about getting pulled over because I'm not in the Sprint, which everyone knows I drive. I like being in an incognito and nondescript truck, something that people won't notice or remember.

The next day I go down to the boxing gym. I'm physically and mentally tired but I make it to the dungeon-like warehouse. The speed bags are rattling like the wheels of a locomotive and the weekend warriors are swatting the heavy bags. Some of the old timers are sparring with each other like they were young kids. I sit down next to the ring with my bag and pull out my tightly-rolled hand wraps. I grab one at the end and toss it onto the floor to unravel it. All the beginners try to hold the rolled-up wrap and drape it across their hands and wrists, which takes forever.

Jesse sees me and comes over. "What's up, Walt?"

"Gonna get a bag workout in then go for a run."

"They jobbed you in your last fight," Jesse says.

"I don't care. It doesn't bother me because I know I beat him."

Jesse ties on my gloves and I get to a heavy bag just as the round clock goes off. I crack it hard enough to kill someone, wishing that it was that lying La Mentiroso ass. The bag quivers at the end of the chain as if complaining about my harsh treatment. I think about La Mentiroso flopping like a fish behind the church as I bang through my ten rounds. When I finish I walk out between the posers and wannabes, training so they can give themselves something to brag about to other posers. They respectfully get out of my way. I don't come in here so I can tell people I'm bad; I come in here because I know I am. There's a big difference.

I get on the Interceptor and ride to my old high school that everyone calls "The Prison." It has drab gray walls with a drainage ditch around it that looks like a moat. I pull over the bridge and out to the athletic field where I played my freshman and sophomore football games. I dig my Walkman out of my workout bag and put on some music. The sun has burned off the marine layer and it's hot.

I start my two-mile run down the backstretch of the red clay track with NWA blaring in my ears. Some goofs are playing flag football on the grass with no idea that the guy running around the track could rip all their heads off. The further I go into my run, the harder I want to push. It's the end of the week and I'm beaten down mentally and physically. The heat has me in a trance and I start to daydream about ripping this La Mentiroso liar apart with my bare hands.

The channel switches abruptly in my mind. *What am I going to do with my life?* I feel like I'm 100 yards in front of a tidal wave and I'm running my ass off so I don't get swallowed up. It's impossible to figure out career choices when I've got this jail bullshit to worry about. Well, I've been doing this legal circus my whole life so the hell with it. I won't get into any serious trouble.

I finish my run and I'm a sweaty pig. I walk back to the Interceptor and climb on and take off. The cool air blasting my face is like heaven on earth. I make it home and kill a cold, orange Gatorade straight from the fridge. I go into my room with Adolf, jump in and out of the shower, then brush my teeth and smile in the mirror, admiring my Leon Spinks grin. *I've got to go to the dentist this week, but first things first.*

"C'mon, Adolf," I say, getting dressed. "Let's go make a drink."

# Chapter 13
## Ready, Aim, Fire

I spend Saturday morning mainly chilling and hit another light workout. My mouth is feeling marginally better as evening rolls around and just as I sit down on the sofa and turn on the stereo the phone rings and I pick-up and hear Tim's voice.

"What did you do last night?" Tim asks.

"Nothing much," I say. "Went to the Dead Grunion and got into a little scrap. Come by and we'll pre-tune then head out."

Tim shows up a little later and is greeted at the door by Adolf.

"What do you wanna do?" Tim says, wrestling playfully with Adolf and taking a seat.

"Let's cruise the residential highway," I say. "I'm sure fun will find us."

We get well into a twelver as we drive around and it's shaping up to be a quiet night. Tim has been my buddy for many years and is at the top of the best friend list. I tell him about the bullshit that I'm going through with La Mentiroso and he wants to kill the loser for me.

"This predicament is a thorn in my side," I say. "We're getting older. What are we going to do with our lives?"

"I'm going to chiropractor school," Tim says. "It's like being a doctor except you don't have to know anything. You can do pretty well. What about you?"

"I'm doing garage door estimates for Fred," I say. "I can do two estimates a week and make more than working a week at the liquor store."

"That's cool," Tim says. "But you're better than selling garage doors."

"I know," I say. "It's just a Band-Aid to buy time."

I see a school crossing sign coming up and instinct takes over. "Slow down. I'm going to nail this sucker."

He hits the accelerator just as I let the bottle fly and it sails past the sign and crashes on the sidewalk, sending glass everywhere.

"You missed," Tim laughs. "I thought you were good."

"Screw you," I say, as I crack another beer.

We go down the street and I recognize the set of headlights coming towards us and the rumble of oversized tires. It's Gonzo, another guy who's pretty high up on my best friend list. I flag him down and he follows us back to the house where we play a few rounds of foosball, with Tim kicking everyone's ass. We're getting down when I notice something seriously wrong.

"Guys," I say. "We're out of beer. Let's go to Trike's uncle's liquor store and grab a fresh twelver."

We jump into Gonzo's old, light green Blazer. It doesn't have a top, just a roll bar and a loud stereo. I grab shotgun and brace myself by grabbing the roll bar as Gonzo speeds off. Trike's uncle's store is just around the corner, just up from the beach where the tourists play on the sand until 2:00 A.M. with bonfires and booze. I can't remember the clerk's name but he knows me and gives us a free pack of Beer Nuts to go with the twelver.

"What's going on tonight?" the clerk says.

"Nothing much," I reply, "just trying to be good."

Those are always famous last words, and as fate would have it, as we walk out, a designer roidhead in mall-bought new clothes comes stomping in, not giving us any room and shoving Tim aside. When he gets to me I dip my shoulder and plow into him even though my teeth aren't in my mouth.

Why are 90 percent of the morons who mess with me pretty-boy roidheads? I've never done steroids but from dealing with these guys I know it messes with their heads and makes them think they can fly. Well, try to fly with me and you're going to get your wings clipped.

"Get the hell out of my way, bozo," I say as I shoulder past.

I stop at the door and turn around and I can almost see the steroids flowing through his veins; they are going to get him hurt bad. He glares at me in his white Miami Vice suit with the sleeves pushed up and his blonde hair feathered back. He's the definition of a total idiot.

"Screw you," he says.

"How about you screw with me instead?" I ask.

I start to step forward but then I hear the voice of the Little Man of Reason sitting on my shoulder: *Don't do it, Walter. You're in enough trouble already and this place has security cameras.* I actually listen to him this time and walk to the Blazer, get in, and crack a beer. Tim climbs over the big off-road tire in the back and gets into the rear seat.

"What the hell was that about?" Gonzo asks.

"That idiot was messing with you, Walt," Tim says. "Forget it."

*Forget it?* All day I've been thinking about the lying ass who filed charges on me and how I can't do anything about it. That shit is simmering inside me like a diesel-filled drum soaking in a storage tank of napalm. *I can't let someone talk to me that way and get away with it.* The Miami Vice roidhead comes out of the liquor store and gets into a brand new thirty-foot Winnebago with dealer plates and a friend in the driver's seat. As they back out beside us the roidhead and his friend both flip me off. *That's it. It's on.*

I jump out of the Blazer with my full beer bottle and rifle it at their front windshield. It's an expensive wraparound that goes all the way back to the rear of the front seats. The bottle shatters and foam explodes across the glass. The two morons inside are shocked and their mouths literally hang open. I turn away but Tim is there handing me another soldier as he winds up with his. He lets the bottle fly and I'm a split second behind him. They both hit nearly simultaneously and shattered glass flies everywhere. We must have cracked the windshield but I can't tell because of the beer foam.

Gonzo rushes to our side with the rest of the twelver for ammunition. I fire another, hoping the Miami Vice moron will come out and back up his words. But he stays inside and starts to drive away as the beer bottles start hitting the now-exposed side windows. They crack under the barrage and one of them breaks out entirely. The motor home's diesel motor groans like a semi-trailer truck as it accelerates away. I throw the last bottle and it arcs through the air and shatters on the rear window.

We pile into the Blazer and do a full-throttle run down the back alley. Our own laughter is the only thing I can hear and it reaches a point where tears are rolling down my face. We slow down when we're a few streets away.

"Dammit," I say, still chuckling, "we're out of beer again. We need a twelver…and another motor home."

The laughter starts up again and we go to a 7-11, get a fresh short case, and then drive to the moon. It's a huge open field at the end of the Happening Harbor residential development by the boat launch, with dirt and sand hills in the middle and boats parked on the perimeter. Craters pockmark the ground where it has been excavated for building material. Gonzo's four-wheeler eats up the landscape with no problem. Off to the left are the navy munitions bunkers and we keep far away from the surrounding fence.

We're in the middle of nowhere with encroaching suburbia all around us. Out here there are no police, no people, no nothing. Gonzo turns up the stereo as we relive our urban beer-bottle assault. After a while, though the conversation turns serious.

"Walt," Tim says. "What are you going to do about that loser who's lying his ass off?"

I don't immediately answer but instead tilt my head back and stare at the stars. I've looked at them before and every time I do a million thoughts race through my head in a split second. *To hell with it. What happens, happens.* You can't go through life hiding from who you are. I'm not going to be like those guys I know who are quiet midgets, coaching wrestling teams and teaching high school and saying size doesn't matter and proper technique will make you tough. What a joke. When you're the runt of the litter that's all you *can* say. *Get to the back of the food line, little dog, your small body matches your small brain. Watch out, runt, my girlfriend might spank your sorry ass if you get out of line.*

When I was a kid I never wished I was bigger than I was. I never wanted to be a midget tough guy who only fought guys their own size. I've always been the guy who would kick anybody's ass ever since I was 14, no matter what technique they knew. I never hid behind a weight or size difference. *I weigh 190 pounds and you're over 300. So what? Let's go.* I never cared how much bigger someone was than me. So this lying moron and his idiot cop dad trying to bring the full force of the law against me can kiss my ass. Karma will always win in the end. *Bring it.*

I snap out of my reverie and lob a glass grenade over the Naval Weapon Station's chain link fence. The bottle breaks on a boulder and we all start laughing again. We showered that roid-head's motor home with beer just like that. He was being a bully, bumping into Tim and mad-dogging us. He should have stepped up but he was just another poser. Screw him.

"Let's freaking party!" I yell.

We polish off the rest of the clip and Gonzo fires up the Blazer and hits the gas. The tires rip into the dirt moonscape as we make it to the paved road. I go home without a care in the world. There's a dark cloud looming in the future, but not tonight. I get dropped off in my driveway and stumble to bed and fall instantly asleep.

In the morning I awake to the groaning air conditioner and the snores of my best friend, Adolf, who's under my arm. It's already Sunday afternoon and there's no alarm clock to worry about because this is my day off. I squeeze Adolf's ribs and he grunts as if to say, *Leave me alone.* I roll out of bed, stumble down the hall, and grab a Diet Pepsi out of the fridge. Adolf runs to the doggie door to take care of business and sunbathe.

Sunday is my fun day when I take a break from training and eat whatever I want. I order a large pepperoni thin crust from Kings and its delivered 15 minutes later. Adolf hears the doorbell and runs in and starts begging for food but I ignore him. I start out telling myself that I'm only going to eat one piece and leave the rest for Jorge and Skip, but then I eat the whole thing and give the last piece to Adolf.

Afterwards I take a shower and start powering beers. After a few it's time to crank things up so I pour a rooster, put Adolf in the truck, and head out to navigate the residential highway on my usual loop. Unlike my old Sprint, the radio works in my plain white truck so I let it blast. As I drive towards the harbor I can see that no one looks at me like they did in the Sprint. For some reason a huge guy in a mid-sized truck seems normal while a huge guy in a tiny car attracts attention.

We make it to the harbor islands and as I cross over the bridge and look down the channel I can see rows of yachts moored behind all the luxury homes. I can't fathom how they got here. Maybe someday I'll figure it out. Dick comes driving up the other way and we roll down our windows and stop in the road. We both raise up our cups with booze in them and laugh.

"Meet me at the Golden Glove," Dick says.

"Okay," I say. "See ya in fifteen."

I take Adolf back home and drive over and park. I walk into the darkened room and see Dick in back at a table with a schooner in front of him and one across the table for me. Jimi Hendrix is playing on the jukebox and we sip our drinks to the strains of *Purple Haze*. Dick kicks my ass in a little shuffleboard and then we sit back down and I tell him about the bullshit that is going down with the little bitch from Sea Lion Beach and his dumbass detective dad.

At first he doesn't know what I'm talking about but then I remind him that it happened right before we went to Mexico and his memory finally clicks.

"No shit?" Dick says. "They're trying to get you after all this time?"

"Yeah," I say. "They want me so bad that they're all lying and they've got the DA on their side."

"What are you gonna do?" Dick asks.

"They want me to take a plea and do 180 days but I'm taking it to trial," I say.

Dick nods. "Why don't you have Grant, Mikey and me testify?

"Dick, I don't want to make up stories."

"You don't have to," he insists. "We'll just testify that we were following you and saw what really happened. You told us the story already so we know it's the truth. There won't be any lies, just what happened."

I think for a moment and it sounds pretty good. "I've got this trial beat if you guys show up," I say.

"Not a problem," Dick says. "Consider it done."

I feel like a ton of bricks has been lifted off my chest and I'm suddenly relaxed. I gulp down half my beer and look around the room and freeze. *Holy hell.* A pretty boy who I hate, who has been talking shit about me for a long time and has caused me a lot of needless trouble, is playing pool. He's on my list and I've been chasing him for years. He's a typical poser with color-coordinated surfer clothes and an ever-present smirk on his face. I have a quick internal conversation with myself.

Devil: "Do it, you dumbass. He's got it coming!"

Angel: "Leave him alone, Walter. You've got too much going on right now to risk it."

Devil: "He's been begging for a beating for years, you pussy. You're not going to let him off the hook, are you?"

*Screw it*, I decide. *It's on.* He doesn't see me so I creep up on him like a lion stalking a zebra through the grass. Just as I'm ready to pounce he catches sight of me and runs to the far side of the pool table, opposite me. I move to the right and he darts to the left. Around and around the table we go. The whole dirty beer joint is watching and the white-trash barmaid comes from the back and sees us. She's in her thirties but her years of working in smoke-filled bars have made her look sixty.

"What's going on?" she pops off. "Leave him alone."

All the dirtbags are sitting back watching silently, but the barmaid's whiskey-worn voice is shouting louder: "Leave him alone, you asshole!"

*The pretty boy must be popping her*, I think. Jimi Hendrix's *Cross Town Traffic* is playing on the jukebox and he's at the long end of the table, tantalizing eight-feet away. He has fear in his eyes and he knows he's done for, but screw it. There are too many people around and I'm sick of hearing the barmaid's raspy voice. There will be another day. Any of these dirtbags would sing to the cops for a free schooner from this white trash tramp.

"I'll get you someday," I say.

The tension in the air lessens and all the dirtbags let out a sigh of relief. The fear leaves the pretty-boy's eyes but then I make a quick quarter-turn to the right and the tension rises and fear creeps back into his eyes.

I lean onto the felt that covers the pool table. "Go to hell, you worthless moron."

The pretty boy and the dirtbags don't realize that I grabbed a pool ball when I leaned forward. I step back quickly, like a major league pitcher making a pick-off move, and fire a fastball straight down the pipe. It glances off his shoulder and as he turns his back and hunches over and I nail him with another and then another.

A wail from the barmaid echoes through the bar: "Stop it! I'm calling the cops!"

She said the magic word so I exit stage left and Dick follows after me, leaving in his car while I leave in my truck. I make it home where Adolf is waiting for me at the door. Sunday is supposed to be a day of rest and I actually feel pretty relaxed after getting payback on that pretty boy and hearing Dick's plan. Maybe I'll be able to sleep tonight. I grab Adolf's face and kiss his wet nose. "Let's go to bed, buddy."

# Chapter 14
## Railroad Job

I awake to the beeping of my worst enemy: the alarm clock. Over the past four weeks I've finished my final semester, sewn up all my classes, and have been peddling garage doors and making a little money. The only bad thing I've had to worry about is today's court date. The time went by like a blur. I became an official college graduate and kept going to the gym and working out. Through it all, though, I felt like a rat on a wheel in a cage, running faster and faster but going nowhere.

Although I'm wide eyed and bushy tailed that's mainly from nervousness as I really didn't sleep at all. When I get out of the shower my face is vibrant, my eyes are clear, and my heart is pumping like it does when I'm about to fight. I jump into my white truck, head north on Beach Blvd., take a right on 13th Street, park my car, and march across the crosswalk to the courthouse.

"Hey, Walt," a voice behind me says. "What did you do now?"

I ignore whoever it is that's talking and go to the board and see that I'm in Division 9 today. I make my way up the steps to the second floor where my attorney, John Witless, is waiting for me.

"Here's the deal, Walt," he says. "I talked to Abe Contrary, the deputy DA, into giving you only ninety-nine days. They have a strong case and it's a good offer."

"What?" I say. "Forget that. You've got to be kidding me. I'm not doing time for these lies. Tell that geek DA to shove it up his ass."

Wittless shrugs, goes into the courtroom, and comes back five minutes later after telling Contrary to get set for trial. He also asks me if I've got a problem with Judge Paris in Division 1.

"Would it matter if I did?" I say.

"Nope," he says. "Especially since I already told Contrary we're not going to challenge it. Nothing would change other than putting us on her bad side."

I'm not sure I follow his logic but it's obviously too late to do anything about it. With a sigh, I follow John downstairs to the courtroom where I catch a detailed look of the woman who will preside over my fate with a sinking feeling in my gut. *Holy shit.* The judge is an old blueblood; tall and skinny with grayish brown hair. I can tell she's an intellectual with no concept of the street rules of behavior or of personal combat. Why did John agree to go into her courtroom without a fight? He should've known that a blueblood judge wouldn't be sympathetic to me. She's the type of person who's read a thousand books but never lived a page.

As I sit in her courtroom I know I'm in deep shit. The room is full of fools with the defendants in orange jail coveralls and the young district attorneys in goofy, ill-fitting suits. All the geek DAs get off on the cheap power they get from their jobs. Just like your typical cop, they've been put down their entire lives at every level and now they're getting their revenge on the world by jerking around small-time criminals with room temperature IQs. Not a hard thing to do. They act like big shots but are putting a good portion of their checks into paying off student loans. I look at them sitting at the prosecutors' desk and am not impressed by their bullshit. *Guess what, you geeks. I've met many of you smart guys before and you've never got over on me. I always get the last laugh.*

Wittless looks as stupid as his name today. His short stature is accentuated by his blond feathered hair that is combed up to try to make him look taller and he's wearing a suit right out of Saturday Night Fever. He looks up into my eyes and at the same time looks down at my life. If Barry was trying my case I wouldn't have a worry in the world.

"You sure you don't want to plea out?" he asks.

"Forget it, John," I say. "Let's go to trial."

"Well, it's going to be more money," Wittless answers.

"I don't care," I say. "Let's do this."

"Are you sure you don't want the 99 days?" he tries once more.

"No," I say firmly.

He nods and starts shuffling through a stack of papers in his briefcase. The courtroom is sterile with no personality, just the hum of the fluorescent lights to break the blandness. My gray matter is rattling and I feel like my neck is in a guillotine. The odds of me getting out with my head attached aren't good. I morbidly imagine the blade coming down and the blood spurting from my neck into the basket. With my last second of life I'll mouth to the executioner, *Screw you. I'll put your face in my ghostly memory and come back and haunt your ass, you bastard.*

The sound of the judge's voice in the courtroom snaps me back to reality. "What's going on with the Foxx matter?" the judge is saying.

"I'm John Witless," my attorney says. "I'd like to enter a plea of not guilty on behalf of Mr. Foxx and ask the court for a trial date."

The judge looks over a calendar on her podium. "How about two weeks from today?"

"Fine with us, Your Honor," Wittless answers.

The prosecution agrees and the trial date is set. I smile and stare into the DA's eyes and he smirks back and then looks away, not able to gaze into my eyes for long. *It's on.* Despite my outward defiance, as I walk out of the courtroom I have a feeling this whole thing is spinning out of control. Wittless better get his ducks in a row because I'm going to battle and he's throwing down next to me. Even as I think that, I know inside that he isn't a good back-up and won't have my six. But I'm a fighter and we don't back down from a challenge even when things look bad.

The cold air slaps my face as I leave the building and walk to my truck and get in. I realize I'm mentally spent. There's nothing I can do until trial starts except try to put it out of my mind. I turn the key and in seconds I'm out of the court parking lot and heading towards home. I stop off at MacDonald's and get a Big Breakfast to go. I walk into my house and as I eat at the coffee table Adolf comes in and stares at me. *They want to put me in jail for 99 days, Adolf.* His only concern, though, is trying to get a piece of my bacon. He is slobbering all over his black mask and snorts in heavenly delight when I throw him a piece. I look out the back window with a blank stare. *Do they have me?* I'm lost in a haze. My eyes fall on the cinder block fence in the backyard that's meant to keep people out. I can't help but think that a fence can also keep people in. Thankfully, my thoughts are broken by a cold nose on my leg and I rip another piece of my breakfast apart and throw it to Adolf.

With breakfast done I grab the black cardboard file that I carry my garage door pamphlets and Thomas Guide in and map out my route for today's bids. Then I get back into my truck and start driving. No more dealing with liquor store losers for me. I just cruise to people's houses who already want a door. I get to my first stop and ring the doorbell. The door is opened by a well-dressed woman with short, gray hair. I show her the different options for her door, measure her opening, and we fill out her order and she signs the contract.

"I like you," she says as I'm packing up.

"Thanks," I say.

'No, really," she continues. "There's something different about you. I don't see you doing this. You just have those gunslinger eyes. I'm not a psychic but you're meant to do something else in your life. You need to know that you're better than this."

"Uh, okay," I stammer. *I'm at a little bit of a loss for words. For someone who says they aren't psychic she pretty much read my mind.*

I go and start my truck and head to Albertsons where the automatic door opens smoothly in front of me. I march down the food-packed shelves and with practiced efficiency grab a stack of red plastic cups, a bottle of cranberry, a fifth of Stoli, and a bag of ice. I've got the rooster run down to a science and could do it in the dark with the fewest steps possible. I know because I've actually counted them before.

I walk back to the truck, close the door, make a traveler, and then wind over to the house to pick up Adolf for a ride. I buzz up Edwards Street just as the sun is setting. Adolf has his head out the window and I stare out over the ocean at the distant horizon. I grit my teeth and suck the nectar over my tongue. As the sun goes down and my buzz gets higher my court problems gradually fade away. It's time to find some fun. I go home and let Adolf out and he runs to the house where Jorge lets him in. I stay in the truck and head to the store where I pick up a twelver. I drive around but nothing is going on so I end up at home watching TV with Adolf and go to bed early.

I awake to Adolf fidgeting in bed, get up and shower, and then head to the boxing club with him in tow. The hypnotic sound of speed bags resonates from inside as I open the gym door. I've got my bag of smelly gear in one hand and Adolf's leash in the other. I tie him up to the ring post then wrap my hands and pick a heavy bag. Today my imaginary opponent isn't Mike Tyson or someone on my list but rather a geek lawyer in a suit named Abe Contrary.

The chain that holds up the bag nearly snaps from my first punch as I lay into the bag with everything I have, killing the lying geek DA several times over. *What did you say you lying piece of shit? It's on!* The bag vibrates up through the chain and into the rafters as sweat pours down my face. After 10 rounds and 20 dead DAs my workout is done and Adolf is bored. I cool off and stop at Sizzler on the way home for lunch. I'm being good so I order a chicken breast with a plain baked potato. As I eat I stare out the window at Adolf in my truck cab. After I take him home it's off to the weight room and then back to the house for a long run.

I put my headphones on outside the front door and stuff my Walkman into my rubber waist belt before starting. It's actually made for losing fat around the midsection but it doesn't work for shit so I just use it to hold my Walkman. As the cars race by I run on the white line that divides the bike path from the car lanes. The bike path is wider than normal on this street so the cars are at least 10 feet away. Every now and then someone honks at me to get out of the way and I always hope that someday someone will stop. That way I can beat the crap out of them for all the idiots who have honked at me over the years.

I repeat this pattern daily, with an occasional party thrown in, and manage to stay out of any serious trouble. Before I know it two weeks have passed and it's time for my day in court. I get up in the morning and put on my best clothes: a nice dress shirt and black slacks. *I'm not overselling this*, I tell myself. *This is how I dress up when I go out.* I get to the courthouse in plenty of time and walk to Division 1. Wittless is waiting for me inside, in front of the judge's podium. At that second I realize that the moment I've been dreading is finally here. I tuck my chin down and lay my ears back. I'm going to war.

"The DA is still offering you 99 days," John says as I greet him. "He thinks this case is a slam dunk."

"Tell him to go screw himself," I say. "He's a worthless geek."

"Okay, "Wittless replies. "It's your call."

As we start the process of picking a jury I stare at Abe Contrary. He's a complete tool from head to toe.

"Contrary said he saw you a couple of weeks back at the junior college," Wittless says. "He was with his wife and kids and you were walking out of the weight room towards them. He said he turned around real quick and walked off fast."

I tilt my head back and stare at the ceiling, rewinding my memory tape in my head.

"Oh, yeah," I say. "I was snapping my weight belt on the ground and this idiot with slicked-back hair walked by wearing clip-on sunglasses, a skin-tight pink tee-shirt, red-and-white striped dolphin shorts like Richard Simmons wears, and white K-Mart tennis shoes. I know most everyone in the weight room but I couldn't tell who he was because of the goofy sunglasses. He bolted like a rabbit as soon as I looked at him. Wish I woulda known."

The judge walks in and the geek DA is at the table closest to me. John is going through his papers and getting organized. The courtroom has a sanitary feel, like a grade school classroom in the morning when the teacher first opens the door. My dad walks through the double doors and shortly after the 30 person jury pool filters in. They sit in rows of wooden chairs and look like churchgoers getting ready for Sunday service. The judge asks if anyone can't serve and an older guy stands up and explains he has his own business and needs to be there to run it. The judge dismisses him and the rest of the jury pool waits expectantly.

Abe Contrary starts his *voir doir* and evaluates the jurors. He stumbles over his questions, is very nervous, and seems like a novice at best. Things are looking good for me. Wittless gets up and is much more plausible and credible than Contrary. He has the polish and confidence of someone who has been here before as he questions potential jurors: *Have you ever been in a fight? Do you understand that fights happen? Do you understand the concept of self-defense?*

After three hours of going back and forth, Wittless and Contrary have selected a jury. There's an old hard-ass construction-looking guy with a red face from drinking too much, sitting next to a hatchet-faced surfer dude with long, thin, slicked-back hair wearing a flowered Hawaiian shirt. There are six middle-aged to older women, two white collar guys in suits and three college girls in their early twenties. I'm not feeling or seeing any love in any of their faces. Judge Paris then adjourns us for lunch and drops her hammer, quickly emptying the court. My dad is three rows back with a blank stare on his face.

Wittless pulls out the prosecution's witness list and I look it over. "Who's this Jesus Martinez?" I ask. "There was no Mexican guy there."

"He's the long-haired guy that got your license plate," Wittless says. "That's how they knew it was you."

"Perfect," I say. "Call him as a witness. He can verify there was no second person there who held down La Mentiroso while I beat him."

"Got it," John said, scribbling on a notepad. "Anything else?"

"I thought the DA's story was that I was walking in the neighborhood with a friend and La Mentiroso and his girlfriend saw me pissing on the church," I say. "How could this guy get my license plate if I was walking?"

Wittless nods and clears his throat. "Good point. I should have caught that, too."

"Who's this Amy Lightfoot?"

"Jerome's girlfriend."

"Oh. The fat bitch I stopped to help. Nothing light about her. Why is Bo Bradley on the list?"

"He's a witness who heard the altercation from his upstairs apartment window behind the church," Wittless explains.

"Okay, John," I say. "My witnesses are ready to go. I'm going to lunch."

I immediately go to a pay phone and call Mikey. "Did you know that Bo is on the prosecution witness list? Tell him he better not show up if he knows what's good for him."

"It's done, Walt," Mikey says. "Everyone is ready to go."

I hang up the phone, get my dad and head down to Hoff's, a bakery down the street within easy driving distance. It feels good to leave the courthouse and all the dirtbags behind. We sit down in a booth and order lunch.

"What do you think, Dad?" I ask.

He shakes his head. "I don't know. It's too early to tell."

Not much conversation goes down after that and we settle the bill and leave. On the short drive back thoughts shoot through my head like in the traffic in downtown Santa Ana when I met Wittless. They're racing all over the place with no apparent rhyme or reason. Unlike the taco trucks in Santa Ana, though, my thoughts all lead to the same destination: jail.

We pull into the courthouse parking lot in my dad's van and walk in. Now that the morning crowd for traffic violations is gone the battleground is sparse with not many people around. We return to the main floor of the legal arena, the courtroom, and I get focused for battle. I pass through the hip-high wooden gate to the chosen ring for this type of combat and take my place at the defendant's table next to Wittless. Across from us, Contrary is shuffling through his papers like a Vegas blackjack dealer and Wittless is tilted back in his chair with a blank yellow legal pad in front of him.

I look at the eight or so courtroom observers and only recognize my dad. The bailiff orders everyone to rise for the Honorable Judge Paris and the old blueblood walks in and glances at me with a distasteful expression on her face. She stands tall and gangly at the top of the podium, takes her gavel, hits the wooden pad on her desk loudly, and sits down.

Contrary stands up. "The State would like to call Jose Ganuze as a witness for the prosecution."

## Chapter 15
### Trial of Error

A middle-aged, clean-cut Latin man in his mid-forties walks in and sits down. He's 170 pounds and five feet, eleven inches tall and wearing black dress pants and a long-sleeved, yellow, button-down shirt. I can't figure out who this guy is. I've never seen him before in my life.

"What exactly did you see on the night in question, Mr. Ganuze?" the DA asks.

"I received a call from dispatch and when I showed up the victim was in serious shape. It looked like the medics were trying to save his life or even worse. The defendant here was running down the street away from me."

*What? Who is this liar?* Then a light bulb goes off. This is a stooge for the detective dad of the little lying bitch. But cops don't lie, everyone knows that. *Yeah, right.* There it is, happening on the stand right in front of me, orchestrated by none other than DA Abe Contrary himself.

The DA finishes with his case and John Wittless gets up and struts to the witness stand like the little man he is, all form and no substance in his ice cream suit and pompadour blond hair. But I can't blame anyone but myself for having chosen this goofball.

"What do you do for a living, Mr. Ganuze?" Wittless asks.

"Uh, I'm a patrol officer for the Sea Lion Beach police department," he says uncomfortably.

Ah, I knew it. He can't even look at me while he speaks. He's telling lies for his detective buddy whose spoiled son, obviously protected by his cop dad his entire life, met his destiny at my hands for being a big mouth, smartass, wannabe bully who likes to slap women around.

Wittless sticks to slick questions that do no good. I'm trying to whisper to him to ask the cop how he knew it was me if I was running away from him but he gives me a look that says, *Shut up. I'm in charge.* I don't give up, though, and he finally nods to me in agreement.

"Could you tell if he fell on his head or if someone bashed it?" says Wittless, finally asking a question that I fed him.

"Oh, it was bashed in," says Ganuze, looking past me to someone in the courtroom audience. "It was pretty clear, you know. I could tell right away."

*How did he know it was me?* He'll have to say that someone saw my license plate and that will contradict La Mentiroso's testimony that I was on foot. That one question will clear me but Wittless never asks it and the little snake cop slithers off the stand, still refusing to look me in the eye.

I watch him walk towards the courtroom door, exchanging glances with an older man and woman sitting on the other side of the courtroom. Now I recognize the woman. She was the one that bought cigarettes from me at the liquor store and then turned around and stared at me liked she wanted to kill me. It's his mother, I realize, and the man next to her must be the idiot's detective dad, the one who claimed I was a meth dealer in Happening Harbor. He never figured out it was another Walter Foxx; or he probably did and just kept it to himself.

The whole conspiracy of how I'm getting totally screwed is becoming perfectly clear to me. The detective, with his ability to lie and intimidate others, is about the same level of scumbag as his son. But Wittless won't challenge the obvious holes in their testimonies. It's now becoming obvious that if I'm telling Wittless what to do then he isn't any better than Contrary, the rookie DA. Adolf could do a better job than Wittless – at least he would bite somebody. My head feels like it's going to explode. My life is on the line and Wittless is not doing anything.

Contrary next calls a friend of La Mentiroso's girlfriend to the witness stand: "Can you tell me what happened on the night in question?"

"We all went out to dinner and had a few beers afterwards," she says.

"Was anyone drinking a lot?" Contrary asks.

"Oh, no," she answers. "Jerome was especially sober. He only had one beer."

The State is finished with this witness," say Contrary. "No further questions."

Wittless gets up and approaches the witness stand. "You expect us to believe it was Friday night but yet you weren't drinking?

"That's right," she says.

"Was Jerome drunk?" Wittless asks.

"Not even a little," she replies.

"No further questions," Wittless say.

He walks back to table, sits in his wooden chair and crosses his right foot on top of his left knee, leaning back with his fingers interlaced behind his head.

"She's a tough nut, Walt," he says, looking over at me. "I couldn't get anything out of her."

I look him in the eye. "What the hell? You barely asked her anything."

He unfolds his hands and huddles up close. "We'd never get anything from this witness. It's his girlfriend's friend."

"Don't you think we should try?" I say. "Jerome was drunk off his ass. We can find out where they were drinking, go talk to the bartender, and catch her in a lie."

Wittless glances at his watch. "She'll never crack."

*I can't believe this.* I put my head into my hands and bend over.

The judge bangs her gavel and announces a fifteen minute recess.

"About time," Wittless says. "I could do with a latte and a croissant."

Before he can leave, my dad comes up to the table. The bailiff and other courtroom staff are milling around, talking among themselves.

"Don't look like it's going too well," my dad says with a sheepish expression on his face.

"Don't worry," says Wittless. "There's still our side to present. I'll get them in my closing arguments. I'm known for that." He packs his briefcase and walks out of the courtroom.

"Oh, man," I say to my dad. "Let's go outside. I need some fresh air."

We walk out of the building and down the cement steps to the middle of the courthouse lawn. I lay down with my back flat on the grass and my eyes wide open. I stare at the blue sky and start to laugh.

"Come on, Walter," my dad says after a while. "Let's go back inside."

I brush myself off and make the trek back to the courtroom. Everyone is standing around and talking but they suddenly become quiet when Judge Paris enters the room with a regal air and ascends to her throne. The court comes to attention and I sit down with Wittless as the legal machine starts pumping for the State. This whole thing is a bad dream that I can't wake up from.

Contrary now calls La Mentiroso's fat girlfriend to the stand and she waddles down the aisle. She's graceless and big, with the shoulders of an NFL linebacker, and is balanced precariously on her high heels. As she walks past me I can see the rolls of fat move on her back. She has a look of self-righteous indignation, as if she can do no wrong and is better than everyone else, but especially me.

"Will you tell the court what you saw that night?" Contrary asks her.

"Jerome and I were walking home from dinner to our house and we came across that guy," she says, pointing at me, "and a long-haired man pissing on the church. Jerome told him that wasn't cool and the big jerk swore and started to chase him. Jerome was too fast for him but the long-haired guy tackled him and I ran home to call the police. When I came back the big guy was smashing Jerome's head into the pavement. I yelled at him to stop but he wouldn't listen to me."

She dabs at her face with a tissue and the courtroom is so quiet I can hear the jury breathing. Suddenly she bursts into tears. I sit there in total disbelief at the lies she's spouting. If I could kill with a look she would have been dead last week. I look at the jury and can see they're buying her bullshit. Two of the older women glance at me and glare. Jerome's girlfriend manages to stop blubbering.

"Then the big guy got off Jerome," she continues, "and high-fived his long-haired friend and they both walked-off laughing."

"John, this is total bullshit," I whisper in complete shock. "All of it."

Contrary finishes his questions and Wittless stands up. "Let's go back to the beginning," Wittless says as her crying turns into sniveling. "How many beers did you have at dinner?"

"One or two," she says. "I'm a marathon runner and I don't drink very much."

I have to stop myself from laughing. A runner? The only place this bitch ever ran to was the all-you-can-eat buffet.

"What about Jerome?" Wittless asks.

"He runs with me," she says. "We have a beer now and then but we never get drunk."

"Were you and Jerome fighting that night?" Wittless asks.

"Why no," she says. "We have a wonderful relationship."

Wittless asks several more inane questions that do nothing to get her to contradict herself and she gives bland answers that support her story.

"Did you actually see Mr. Foxx smash Jerome's head into the ground?" Wittless asks.

"No, they were behind a car, but I heard it," she says. "It was horrible. It sounded like a bowling ball smashing into a pin." Tears start rolling off her face again.

Wittless finishes and walks back to the table. I ask him why he didn't suggest that the long-haired guy could have been the one to smash Jerome's head, since she said she didn't see me do it, just to give the jury reasonable doubt. But Wittless just shrugs and doesn't answer. Even though I suspected it, for the first time I know for sure that Wittless doesn't believe my story and has no interest in getting me off. I begin to suspect that I am royally and truly screwed.

Contrary stands up again. "The State would like to call Jerome La Mentiroso to the stand."

I sit back in the wooden chair and it squeaks as I recline. The sound makes me feel like a rat sleeping in a boa constrictor's cage at the pet store. As Jerome takes the stand I feel like the snake is awakening and all I can do as the trapped rat is to sit quietly and not move.

This daddy's boy punkass loser has a smile on his face and looks all prim and proper. But his expression goes hard when he looks at me, like he's certain he's now going to pay me back. The usual soft, leading questions come out of Contrary's mouth as Jerome rehashes the fake story that all the witnesses have testified to. When he gets to where I beat him up he starts to cry.

"It was so awful," Jerome blubbers, tears streaming down his face. "I thought I was going to die. I could have defended myself against one of them but I didn't have a chance against both."

Contrary hands La Mentiroso a box of Kleenex. I can't believe what I'm hearing. I grab the arms of the chair and squeeze them harder with every lie that comes out of his mouth, wishing they were Jerome's neck. *You're officially on the list, pal. You just got another date with me at a future time and place of my choosing.*

Wittless gets up and asks several patty-cake questions but all he can get is more tears out of this lying loser. He comes back to the table and looks at me: "Wow. He's really traumatized." Wittless doesn't know how close he is to getting on the list himself.

"Your Honor," Contrary says, "the State would like to rest its case."

Judge Paris, the queen of the courtroom, nods her approval. "It's too late to continue so we'll start tomorrow at 8:00 A.M. sharp. I'll see everyone then."

John rushes off with a few brief words about how we'll get them tomorrow and the courtroom empties quickly, leaving just myself, my dad, and the courtroom clerks.

"Holy hell, Dad," I say as I walk up to him. "We are screwed."

I walk down the rows of pew-like wooden benches towards the door. It's only six rows away but I feel like I smoked a joint because it seems to take an hour to get there. My dad and I exit the courthouse and stop by our cars in the parking lot.

"Make sure you have everything ready for tomorrow," my dad says, obviously not trusting Wittless now.

"My witnesses are good to go," I say. "Everyone knows what's up."

We separate and I get into my truck, turn on The Smiths, and drive down Beach Blvd. I'm right in the middle of all the nine-to-fiver drones going home to their hives after being told what to do and think by their corporate masters. I get pulled along by the heavy traffic all the way home and Adolf is waiting for me when I get there. He's happy to see me and jumps around like a jackrabbit, thinking I'm going to take him for a run.

"Sorry, buddy," I tell him, scratching behind his ears. "I'm busy."

I get on the phone and make sure the boys are lined up for tomorrow. I think about going out and maybe getting dinner and a drink but I have no energy. I lay down in bed for a quick nap and the next thing I know the alarm clock is beeping and it's time to get up. I jump out of bed like an earthquake is shaking the house and hop into the shower and get dressed. I have a manic energy, like I'm going on the mat for the finals of a wrestling tournament. I get in my truck and am carried along in traffic by the worker drones again, not noticing anything on the drive. My mind is racing. I'm going to kick the DA's ass and expose his bullshit story. I talked to all the boys last night and I'm ready to go.

I enter the courtroom five minutes early and the jury is already there with Queen Paris sitting on her thrown. I sit next to Wittless, who has his briefcase open.

"Is the defense ready to call their first witness?" Judge Paris asks.

"Yes, Your Honor," Wittless says. "We'd like to call Marty Manley."

Marty is the guy that I trained to replace me at the liquor store before I left, and he heard me tell the fight story at least a hundred times before I ever knew there was going to be a trial. He wasn't there but he knows the truth and tells it under questioning by Wittless.

Marty is big and bald and wearing a sport jacket that looks like he bought it at Goodwill the day before. Before he spoke everyone expected him to have a deep thunderous voice, but it is meek and soft just like him and he moves like a sloth. I'm nervous that he's going to screw up as the DA gets up to cross-examine him. Contrary asks him the same questions several different ways, hoping to catch an inconsistency, but the rookie DA can't break him and Marty does well and his testimony holds up.

*Finally my story is being told, but who will the jury believe?* They are all stoned-face and a couple of them have their arms crossed. Marty finishes and walks out of the courtroom while Wittless call Mikey to the stand.

Mikey looks much more confident than Marty and walks to the witness stand with almost a swagger. He has on dress slacks and a long-sleeved, button-down shirt and projects an aura of competency. Wittless starts with his usual questions and Mikey answers them all with ease. Wittless and Mikey play off each other well. Wittless is finally starting to get into the groove and is sounding like a well-oiled machine. Contrary gets up and Mikey fends off his questions without breaking a sweat.

I take a deep breath and sigh with relief. Things are finally going my way. Yesterday I was down and out now it seems I'm making a comeback. Mikey finishes and now it's Dick's turn to get on the stand.

Dick tells the story as it really happened, including how La Mentiroso instigated the entire fight and threw the first punch and how I was driving, not walking, and how there was no long-haired hippy with me. Wittless finishes and the DA gets up and goes after Dick, who answers all the questions flawlessly, down to the minor details, leaving the DA befuddled. Dick leaves the stand and walks confidently out the door, several jurors nodding at him as he leaves.

The judge's voice fills the vacuum that Dick's exit created as the old blue blood asks Wittless how much longer he needs before we break for lunch. Wittless tells Her Royal Highness that this will be the last witness and then calls Grant to the stand.

Grant walks in wearing a spooner and jeans. It isn't exactly court attire but he still looks clean cut and presentable. He has a red face, though, that gives him a nervous look, which makes me nervous. Wittless asks a few questions and Grant loosens up and does well. Despite being wishy-washy on a few minor points everything goes smoothly as he validates the story that Marty, Mikey and Dick told.

Wittless finishes and the geek DA approaches Grant when his usual bullshit confidence, like he's the smartest guy in the world. Grant's face turns an even brighter red and my heart starts pounding. *Don't screw up, Grant.* Obviously pissed off by the DA's bullshit, though, Grant gets more confident under questioning and answers quickly and firmly without missing a beat. I take a deep breath as the DA announces he has no further questions.

As I sit back in the old, creaking wooden chair the DA turns in my direction and we look into each other's eyes. He has a pissed off look on his face and I shrug at him nonchalantly, hoping he feels my disdainful vibe. The court recesses for lunch and the jury files out, the DA following them with his head down. *That's right, scumbag, the truth will prevail!*

## Chapter 16
## **Truth Will Prevail**

*Shove it up your ass, you lying DA geek*, I think, as my dad walks up to Wittless and me. The room is empty for lunch but the ever-present hum of the fluorescent lights remains.

"How do you think it's going, John?" I ask.

"Good," says Wittless. "Hopefully we can wrap this up in the early afternoon and beat rush-hour traffic."

My dad and I go to Hoff's again. I have a lot of anxiety and my dad has his poker face on. He's says it looks better than yesterday but that doesn't tell me anything because yesterday was a total disaster. We finish and go back to the courthouse but our room is locked. I walk down the aisle towards the DA's office and am passed by her royal highness, Judge Paris, walking fast.

The old blue blood won't look me in the eye. The only way she acknowledges me is by not acknowledging me. It must be nice to be so much better than everyone else in the world. I follow her back to the courtroom, which is open now, and slide next to Wittless, who's reading a newspaper at the table.

"Are we ready, John?" I ask.

"Oh, yeah," he says, not even bothering to look up. "I'm dialed in,"

I watch the courtroom audience file in and see the Marlboro 100 woman from the liquor store. *Oh, mommy, do you know that your son is a lying scumbag?* She would never let herself believe it. If he told her the earth was flat, she'd take it as the truth. *Okay, John,* I think, *let's kick their ass. We got them down, now let's take them out. Yesterday everybody in the court thought I was toast, but I told you I have the truth on my side and it will come out.*

I turn and stare at Contrary, the DA. I know the little worm can feel my eyes on him. He's getting his ass kicked now just like his lying so-called victim did. Right now, if I could get away with it, I'd rip his geek ass out of the chair by his tie, pull him over my hip, and straighten my left leg to make his feet leave the ground. His cheap jacket would be spread open by the rush of wind from his rapid lift-off. His arms would extend as he flew over my elevated hips and as soon as he crested I would collapse, folding my body into a hard cannonball and driving him downwards. As his body hit the ground it would make a sound like thunder and air would blow out of his mouth and his eyes would go blank from the concussion. Underneath me would be the lying DA geek, totally under my control. He wouldn't be able to suck in any air from the impact and the end result would be like someone squeezing his throat. I would then swisher my hips, put my knee on his Adam's apple, ball up my fist, draw a bead on his geeky face, and...

The judge's gavel hits her desk with a sharp noise and it jerks me out of my pleasant dream. I'm back to reality in the courtroom and out of my trance.

"The defense would like to call Dick Johnson to the stand," Wittless is saying.

I turn my eyes away from the locked stare I had on the DA. He gives me a strange look, like a minnow looking at a shark. If he only knew what I'd love to do to him his look would be a lot stranger. Dick is on the witness stand and looking very professional. He has on slacks, dress shirt, sport coat and is clean cut and well dressed. Wittless asks Dick all the easy questions and he recounts the night's events. When Wittless finishes, Contrary tries to make him stumble but to no avail. Dick is a flawless witness. If the DA wants to find any inconsistencies in Dick's testimony he might as well give up now. The truth has been told.

Dick is the final witness and the closing arguments start. The DA's closing is as lame as he is, just going over what the lying witnesses said. John gets up when Contrary finishes. My elbows are resting on the tabletop with my fingers laced together. I look at Wittless like I have full confidence in what he's saying, but I'm only doing it for the jury, Inside my head I'm shitting a brick. I know his closing argument is coming up and I also know that he is a complete idiot.

"My client, Mr. Foxx, was simply defending himself," says Wittless. "Mr. Foxx is a college student who got involved in an altercation that was instigated by Jerome La Mantiroso. Mr. Foxx was verbally abused, challenged to a fight, was struck first, responded in self-defense, and left afterwards. If you need any evidence that the alleged victim was really the instigator then simply look at the

173

chipped tooth in my mouth. This is what happens when you say the wrong thing to the wrong person. I found out on the street that you take your medicine like a man. The State has done nothing to prove their case. You must find my client, Mr. Foxx, not guilty."

I have to force myself to not laugh out loud. I'd put money on him having chipped it falling down in the bathroom. He wouldn't know the street from a hole in his head – which is what I feel like giving him. This was his killer closing argument?

Witless sits down and her royal highness, the blue blood judge, reads the instructions to the jury and for the first time in the trial I feel I can unbutton the top button of my jeans. *What a relief.* When I'm super fat, like I am now, I just want to rub my gut. The jury heads to the deliberation room. Finally it's almost over. The truth will prevail. I get up from the table and walk out to the hallway. The floors have lost their shine and don't look like water anymore. I walk down the hallway to take a break from everything and sit on one of the uncomfortable benches, with my dad beside me with arms crossed.

"What do you think, Dad?" I ask.

"You're alright," he says.

As we sit there I watch the parade of court goers passing by. For the most part they're dirty and unshaven with shirts un-tucked, torn-up flip-flops, greasy jeans, and a vacant look like there's nothing behind their eyes. I imagine they're all fresh from a shady motel. One hour of the parade quickly turns into two. The bench is uncomfortable and made so you won't sit there for very long. But, in fact, the State is in the business of making people wait.

It's taking too long and I'm afraid that means I'm going to lose. I walk out to the grass where I laid down before and stare at the sky, watching the clouds float pass me. *Come on. I want a verdict.* The grass is making my back itch so I get up and go inside the courthouse where I see Wittless.

"It's okay," he says to me. "The longer the jury is out the better."

"Yesterday, when you stayed with the DA and judge during lunch what went down?" I ask.

"Nothing," Wittless answers. "Just some paperwork."

"Is there going to be a verdict today?" I ask.

"Definitely. They don't want to come back tomorrow."

As if proving Wittless a prophet the clerk comes out and tells us the jury is back. I take a deep breath and look at my dad with big eyes. *Let's do it.* We walk down the hall to the courtroom. As I sit down the doors crash closed behind me. I sit hunched at the table with my right hand balled into a fist and my left hand cupped around it. My back is straight as though I'm ready to take a flogging. I turn my head and wait for the jury. One minute runs into the next and it takes an hour before they finally file in.

I study them and look at their posture and little movements. The most important fact is that they won't look at me. *Oh, hell.* I catch a side glance of the old red-faced guy. He has a new self-righteous look. He's too dumb to realize that he's too much of an idiot to judge anyone; but then he showed up for jury duty which tells you something. They sit down and stare at the judge's throne.

Her Highness, Judge Paris, walks in with a steely look, like a hard-nosed professor believing their own bullshit. Thinking that she's better than everyone else is the only thing that gives her life meaning. But everything she does will be forgotten in just a few years if not months. If someone was writing a book her name wouldn't even be a footnote to a footnote. But here she is thinking that she rules the world.

The courtroom is full of electricity as the jury foreman, the red-faced self-righteous fool, stands and announces they have reached a verdict. As he raises the paper to read I know the guillotine blade is falling. I feel every sensation in my body: my itchy back from lying in the grass, my cramped muscles from the uncomfortable seat, and my fat stomach pressing against my too-tight jeans. *Just let this be over with.*

"On the sole count of assault with a deadly weapon," the old man reads, "we, the jury, find the defendant not guilty."

*Yes!* I sit there stone-faced but I'm about to scream *FUCK YOU* to the DA. The truth has come out.

"On the lesser included count of simple assault," the old bastard suddenly continues, "we find the defendant guilty as charged."

*WHAT?* The guillotine blade just cut off my head. The DA put my head through the wooden block and the jury pulled the cord. The blade has fallen down from the menacing frame and cut through my neck. Off goes my skull into the basket and I have one second to look at my body. I turn and focus my attention on Wittless.

"John," I say. "What's this bullshit about an included lesser charge? I was never told anything about that. It was supposed to be all or nothing."

John looks uncomfortable and keeps his eyes on his briefcase. "They asked me about it at lunch yesterday and I told them it was okay. I didn't think it would matter."

I don't say a thing but just stare at him, letting my silence speak volumes. *You screwed me, John. You did it just so you could win points with the DA and the judge.*

Wittless starts to fidget and acts like he is not paying attention to me and instead focuses on the court proceedings. I feel the knife of betrayal tearing a hole in my back.

"Would you like to put off sentencing for two weeks or do it now," the judge asks Wittless, an edge in her voice.

"If I could have 15 minutes to confer with my client we should be able to do it today," Wittless says.

The court is quiet and I feel like I'm the only person in the room. I hear nothing but the pounding of my own heart as I get up and walk down the aisle with John behind me, crashing through the courtroom door. The sound of the world comes back to me as the door slams shut. John is obviously kissing the judge's flabby ass because he doesn't want to have to come back in two weeks and do more work. We stop at a bench and sit down.

"Now what?" I ask.

"Well," he says, "You have to understand that waiting two weeks for sentencing will only make the judge mad and make it worse."

*And you have to understand that I'm thinking about killing you, John*, I think. I had thought Wittless was a more polished version of Abe Contrary, the geek DA, but now I understand that they're the same animal, using peoples' lives to advance their own careers and bank accounts. The judge and both lawyers were in it together from the beginning and were going to get me no matter what the truth was. I just got totally and royally reamed.

My itchy back from lying on the grass doesn't seem so bad, now that my attention is on other matters. I have to go back and listen using my head that fell into the guillotine basket a few minutes ago. I realize that Wittless was just sucking money out of me but I was the one that bought into it. I'm steamed, but ultimately who can I blame but myself?

We get up and walk back. Wittless is quiet all the way back to the courtroom but stops outside the double doors.

"Look, Walter," he says. "You have to be cool in there. No screaming or yelling. I'm going to ask the judge to give you a sentence that fits what you were convicted of: simple assault. That should land you a small fine and a community service sentence."

I shake my head back and forth several times trying to clear it. I imagine I can feel the gray matter of my head hit the inside of my skull. I've gone from being acquitted of all charges to being sentenced to jail in a matter of 15 minutes.

"Okay," I say. "Let's get this done."

We walk back in the door and through the swinging wooden gate to the circus arena that is the defendant's desk. The geek DA gets up and tells the judge more untruths about me. As he speaks I imagine my head in the basket below the guillotine, looking at my headless body with blood pumping out.

The DA finishes and Judge Paris starts flipping through the legal file that I've amassed over the years. She reads the first page and looks up and glances at me. Her reading glasses are down to the tip of her nose as she reads page after page. She looks up and surveys the court, flips through a few more pages then appears to quit before getting to the end. She closes the folder and leans back, causing the springs in her big leather chair to squeak. She reaches up, takes off her reading glasses and pushes the sleeves of her robe up to expose an expensive, diamond-studded wristwatch with a leather band. Screwing people over apparently pays well; but I don't need a watch to tell me that my time is almost up.

John stands up and speaks, "This was an act that both men engaged in consensually. My client's only crime was being the one who won the fight. He should pay a fine and then be forced to do community service at most, preferably teaching youth about the dangers of violence."

At least I've got another chance now and a bit of hope. As the DA stands there in his cheap suit with high-water pants I know for sure it was him at the gym a couple of weeks back. Now I clearly remember the geek in Dolphin shorts with his wife and kids at the college gym. I had just finished lifting and was walking out to my bike and was cracking my lifting belt on the blacktop. He looked at me then turned his family around and briskly walked the other way. The truth was looking him right in the face and he couldn't handle it. Now he's calling me a menace to society and trying to take away my freedom. If I would have known that the geek DA was in front of me at the weight room he might not be here right now.

The judge appears to make a decision. She looks over the courtroom and puts her elbows on the desk and speaks over the hum of the fluorescent lights. "I've read your file," she says, looking at me. "You, sir, are a maniac. Your file is quite extensive and it's a wonder you've slipped through the cracks of the justice system as long as you have. You are going to be stopped right here, right now, in this courtroom, by me, Mr. Foxx. It's lucky that you've never been interested in guns; otherwise I believe you would have killed someone by now. This could easily be a murder trial."

If I wanted Jerome dead that night he wouldn't be here now – and neither would I. Was it mercy that stayed my hand or stupidity? He's lucky to still have a heartbeat. With every word she speaks I can't believe what I'm hearing. Everything she says is a lie. Everyone I've beat-up was a phony who begged for it and had it coming. They act tough and pretend to be warriors but when they lose they don't know how to take a beating. They have no clue about the warrior's code of conduct. If you bite off more than you can chew and then choke on it, don't lie and use the legal system that you profess to disdain to get back at the person who whipped your ass. It's bad karma and it will come back to haunt you.

"Mr. Foxx," the judge continues, "in view of your past record I have no alternative but to give you the maximum sentence. Unfortunately, the law only allows me to give you six months. I wish I could give you more but my hands are tied." She pounds her gavel on her desk. "Court is adjourned."

*Oh. man.* I need to get out of this place to someplace familiar. I need to hear the sound of a bar with the glasses clanking, the pool cues clicking, and laughter echoing through the air. *Let the laughter roar.* I need to be light years away from here. The courtroom has come alive with conversation and all of La Mantiroso's relatives are smiling at each other. *Isn't it great? We got the big bad bully right between the eyes.* I make eye contact with my dad and he just shakes his head.

I look at the lying fool who got me here. He's talking to a group of people and smiling and nodding. My stare is burning a hole into his soul and he can feel it. He looks up and our eyes lock. It's like I'm chasing him around the car again and he's at the trunk and I'm at the hood and he's yelling at me, *Fuck you, fat ass.* But now he looks at me with a raised eyebrow as if to say, *I knew this was coming. I knew my dad would get you.*

I make a small motion towards him with my index finger. I'm pointing at him and only he knows it. *Here's a flash, liar. There will be another foot race one day and I'll be chasing you again. You won't know the time or the place but I will. You're on the list and I never forget.* He looks down and breaks eye contact. *That's right, you poser. Look away. You can't look into the eyes of the gorgon for long without turning to stone.*

"Am I going to jail today?" I ask Wittless.

"No," he says quietly. "What do you need? Two months?"

I nod. I'm deflated inside but I keep my expression blank: *never let them know that you're hurt.* I walk back to the defense table, my head held high. The electricity left the room an hour ago and it's business as usual now.

"When does your client wish to start his sentence?" the judge asks.

"In eight weeks," Wittless says.

What has happened to me is really starting to set in. This is my private kangaroo court. It's time to go to jail and it's crystal clear that I've been screwed since day one. *Oh, the lessons I've learned.* At least it's late afternoon and the worst day of my life is almost over.

181

"I'll give him five weeks to prepare," the ruler of the world says.

"Thank you, Judge," the fawning Wittless says.

"Sentencing is completed," says her Highness.

I get up without a word and head out. *To hell with this.* I'm not talking to anyone. I want to be free and I'm pissed I won't. Outside the courthouse the cold air is still. *Fuck it. Be a man. It's only six months, not my entire life. I still have my pride.* I don't see Wittless anywhere. I will contact him later. I look back at the DA talking with Jerome's family in the lobby. They are gathered around each other as if they pulled off the same beating I gave him.

I smile when I think of Jerome the loudmouth on the ground bleeding; it's not even close. It took all their pygmy lies to slay the giant. I walk towards the parking lot and pass a thirty-something stranger with a buzz cut and sleeve tats.

"Hey, Walter," he says. "Who'd you beat-up this time?"

I ignore him, get to my truck, pull out of the parking lot and make a left onto Beach Blvd. In front of me is an old, gold-colored Toyota Maxima with a little American flag sticker, faded and tattered, on the trunk. For some reason it catches my eye. I glance inside and see Jerome behind the wheel, driving to his freedom while I'm giving up mine. As his car accelerates away I keep my eye on the weathered flag, maybe because I'm feeling a little weathered myself. It strangely makes me feel a little better. I just made it through the rocket's red glare, too, and I'm still here as well.

## Chapter 17
### Mud, Guts and Beer

Adolf has been in the house all day and Skip and Jorge have also been out so he's happy to see me when I walk in.

"Hey, buddy," I say, grabbing his ears playfully. "My day has been like yours except I got sentenced to six months." He tippy-toes up to me, curls up his spine and wags his tail, trying to get a back scratch. His tail starts to beat faster as I pet him for a minute. *I need to calm my nerves. It's time for a drink.* I call Fred and tell him I need another day off.

"How did it go?" Fred asks.

"Not good," I reply. "They strung me out for six months. They screwed me good."

"Take as much time as you want, Walt," Fred says. "Just call me when you want to work again."

"Yeah, thanks," I say. "I'll ring you in a day or two."

I open the fridge door, grab a soldier, go into the living room and fall onto the couch. I listen to the sprinklers spewing water on the front lawn and their constant tick hypnotizes me. Adolf's cold nose pulls me out of the nightmare of my impending doom. *Fuck it.* I push my upcoming situation to the back of my mind. *It's light years away so have fun now.*

I grab the phone and call Gonzo. "Let's go out, man."

"Hell, yes," he answers. "I'm ready. How was court?"

"Pretty bad," I say.

"Aw, hell. I'll pick you up in a little bit."

I kick back with Adolf with the chrome ceiling fan blowing cold air down on me. I start slamming and get up to eight beers before Gonzo's Blazer pulls into the driveway. His headlights shine in the living room windows so I get up and meet him at the door.

"Damn, bro," he says. "They railroaded you."

"Yep," I nod. I really don't want to talk about it so I change the subject. "Let head to Trike's Liquor."

We pick up a clip and it's gone almost immediately so we stop at a 7-11, grab another twelver, and continue to cruise around town looking for fun. We decide to go to Sugar's, a seedy bar where the barmaids wear high heels and thongs with fishnet stockings. We belly-up and order a couple of beers. *Hot Blooded* from Foreigner is playing on the jukebox and I'm pounding soldiers hard. Half of my cylinder is gone within seconds and I check out the bar to make sure my surroundings are safe.

A guy named Big Cal is at one of the smoky pool tables, swinging his cue stick around like he's the conductor of an orchestra for dirtbag bar idiots. He steps back to take a shot and his ass is high in the air. He has on dirty jeans, biker boots with a studded belt, and a black cut-off tee-shirt with *Harley-Davidson* across the back. He has a confident swagger as he changes position to take his next shot. I've known Big Cal for years and he hasn't seen us yet.

"Hey, big daddy!" I scream across the bar.

He looks up from where he's bent over the table and sees me. Stretching his six feet, two inch frame up into the cloud of cigarette smoke he comes over and sits on a bar stool next to us.

"Hey, Walt," he says, "long time. What the hell is up?

"I just got sentenced to six months for something I didn't do," I say glumly. "I go in five weeks from today so I'm just partying down." I gesture next to me. "You know Gonzo. I wrestled with him on my junior college team."

"Yo, yo," Big Cal says, reaching out to shake hands. "What's up, Gonzo?"

"Let's play some pool," I say to them.

Cal is killing the old guy he's playing with. He's on his last legs and his weathered face tells me he's been hanging out in cheap, smoky dives for far too long. He's wearing a torn-up tee-shirt and dirty jeans that have an aura of prison.

"Hey," the dirtbag says to Cal, as we all walk up to the table with him. "I was playing pool with you."

"I know," Cal says. "But I'm going to play with my friend for a while. Maybe we'll play later." Cal knocks in the last ball and it's over.

The old dirtbag is drunk and he raises himself up to his full five feet, six inch height. "Tell your friends to piss off. I'm not leaving."

My temper starts to rise. "You need to blow out of here. I've had a very bad day and you don't want to mess with me right now."

"Cut the old-timer some slack, Walt," Cal says.

"No," I say. "He just told me to piss off. You want some, old drunk?"

185

The dirtbag knows I'm not playing around. He can see it in my eyes. After the day I've had I will stomp anyone who disrespects me flatter than a pancake. He can feel my vibe so he grabs his beer and heads to the other side of the bar. As he leaves he looks over his shoulder and walks faster.

"That sucks about your six months," Big Cal says racking up the balls.

"All because of some lying scumbag from Sea Lion Beach," I say. "Typical story: the guy acted like a badass and started a fight with me. Then when he got his ass handed to him he changed his story to get even. His dad's a detective and pushed it with the DA. It's all bullshit."

Big Cal breaks with a loud crack, scattering the balls to all corners. Big Cal runs the table without even giving me a shot. Cal racks again and he and Gonzo go at it while I order another beer from a barmaid in a thong. They're down to the last ball and Big Cal sinks it. He's on a roll and so is my buzz. I'm hitting the throttle hard and Gonzo is also feeling no pain. We leave the pool table and move to a high-top and start shooting the shit out of life.

After a while Big Cal and Gonzo start talking about scrapping. I remind Big Cal that Gonzo was an All-American wrestler and highly accomplished. I've known Big Cal for many years and know he never wrestled in college, but he's always ready to step in and bang in an open wrestling room. Gonzo tells Big Cal how you can't really wrestle well unless you've been on a team. Pretty soon one beer leads to another and they start to get heated.

"Hey, chill out," I finally say with a laugh. "We're all eagles but we can flock together now and then. We don't need to fight each other."

The mood is light and they just want to establish a pecking order. If shit hit the fan we'd all stick together but they want to test each other.

"Gonzo's a top NCAA guy," I tell Big Cal. "I don't think it would go good for you if you wrestled."

"You never know," Big Cal says. "Let's do takedowns and see."

Gonzo agrees and we pour out the back door, going through the fan that blows air to keep the insects out. We go to the middle of the back lot with its one small light on a distant pole. Gonzo takes off his jacket and stretches a little. There's a foggy gloom in the dark night and the air is damp. The lot's surface is loose gravel and mud with stones the size of golf balls. The mud makes it feel like we're walking in refried beans. The old clunker cars belonging to the dirtbag drunks are parked around us, making it seem like a gladiatorial arena. It's a perfect stage.

"Just takedowns, guys," I say. "I love you both. Stay friendly."

"Right on," Big Cal says. "Let's have some fun."

Gonzo is over 300 pounds while Big Cal is around 250. I stand between them as the referee and give them the signal to go. They rush at each other with their ears back and there's a thud as chests collide. As they drunkenly slam into each other, they lock up and start to circle. Gonzo snaps Big Cal down to the gravel and rocks and mud fly. Big Cal manages to bounce up and immediately shoots a single leg. Gonzo sprawls back to counter Big Cal's leg grip but it's tight and he can't break it. It isn't a very technical shot but it is effective. They slop around in the mud and rocks fly everywhere as they bang hard.

Gonzo finally kicks out and shoots a double leg. Cal moves quickly to the side and whizzers Gonzo, slamming him into the gravel as mud flies into my face from the impact. It's hard to believe that Gonzo got taken down. He really must have had too much to drink.

"You just got taken down by a high school wrestler," I laugh at Gonzo.

"I know, Walter," Gonzo says unhappily, getting up and brushing himself off. "Good job, Cal. Let's go again."

"Are you ready?" I ask as Gonzo and Big Cal square up again.

Both Gonzo and Big Cal snort fire as they nod. I drop my hand and again they charge, their chests meeting again with a jarring thud and throwing them back from each other from the impact. Gonzo shoots in on Big Cal's legs, going for the early kill, but he sprawls to defend. Gonzo drives forward like a bulldozer as he churns through the gravel and mud. Air is rumbling out of his mouth from his exertion and he sounds like a big-rig diesel going uphill.

Big Cal is floating away and keeping his legs clear while Gonzo's legs slow down. They were pumping like diesel pistons 10 seconds earlier, but now black smoke is pouring out of their exhaust pipes and their motors are getting louder from the effort. Gonzo has got his pedal to the metal but can't sustain his drive and falls down onto the muddy gravel. Big Cal spins to Gonzo's back easily for the takedown.

Both of the bigs are huffin' and puffin' now and Cal is covered in muddy gravel from head to toe and taking deep breaths. Gonzo is bent over with both hands on his knees, a technique used in wrestling when you need to get air.

Gonzo shakes his head and gravel and blood from a small scratch fall from his face: "I don't know, Walt. I guess I'm too drunk."

"It's okay, Gonzo," I say. "Put on your concentration cap and wrestle like I know you can. It's best out of five and you're down two. You need three in a row to win."

"Okay, Walt," Gonzo says. "I'm drunk but I'll get him."

They line up and charge once again but it's the same result as before as Big Cal spins behind Gonzo and takes him down quickly.

"Sorry, Walter," Gonzo says. "I'm just too drunk."

"Don't be sorry," I say. "Big Cal is tough. Besides it's a muddy field not a wrestling mat so who cares? We're just having a little fun. You guys take a break, okay?"

I go back into the bar for a freshy. I have a full-throttle buzz going and am speaking Drunkenese, trying to get the bartender to understand me. I finally manage to order a beer. I would have made a bet that Gonzo would have done better but I know how it goes when you drink too much. Guys who couldn't hold a candle to you normally can get lucky sometimes. Oh, well. I've got other things on my mind to be too concerned. As much as I try not to think about it, the days' events keep coming into my head. I've got five weeks before I go in, though, so I might as well make the most of it. It won't do me any good to think about things I can't change, that's for sure.

I power down the new soldier and go out the back door. The roar of the insect fan goes off but now the sound is different to me. Now it's like the roar of the crowd as I enter an arena to fight. The cars are still parked to make a stadium and the gravel and mud have settled to form a stage with a perfect takedown surface.

"Gonzo's too drunk to play," I tell Big Cal. "I'll take over for him."

"Okay, cool," says Big Cal. "I want to go some more."

I bend over to tie my shoes tight and almost do a face-plant into the mud. I'm drunk; but if you play with fire you'll get burned now and then. If you never get burned then you haven't played enough. If you drink and fight in bars and you haven't got your ass kicked a few times then you haven't been in very many fights.

"Okay, Big Cal," I say with a laugh, "let's get it on. I need to save the honor of wrestling."

We tie up and grab hands and he starts curling his arm inward. His cut-off sleeves reveal his muddy and blood-pumped arms and his hands are callused and rough from pumping iron. We lock into each other like we've done this a hundred times before; and, in fact, we have. Big Cal and I have been on the opposite sides of drunken wrestling matches many times; all in good fun and for a few laughs. What are a few cuts and bruises between good friends? I squeeze the hand that is pulling me close and his biker rings pinch my fingers. But I will never let him know that he hurt me. We bang foreheads together. "Come on, big daddy," I say. "Let's do it.

We both start to laugh. We're having a great time mixing it up; not in a safe and controlled wrestling room but on the street where pain lives. Most wrestlers won't street wrestle. It's a great concept but there is a high risk of injury and pain. Ideas are always easy and safe but real life is about danger and pain. That's why it isn't easy. Concepts and words are safe compared to action.

The action is right here, right now, as we push each other around. Big Cal is sloshing around in the mud and I hear the mud bubbling out from the air pockets in the straps and buckles of his biker boots. I suddenly spring forward with the quickness of a bear trap and get deep around his hips. He tries to sprawl but I can hold my booze better than Gonzo and I pick up Big Cal and slam him into the mix of gravel and mud: 1-0 for me.

I'm bleeding on my forehead, just above the brow of my right eye, and I suck the blood into my mouth and start to laugh. I've tasted it many times before and it's heaven sent. We're getting down in the foggy arena with the mud and gravel stage and it's the perfect end to my bullshit day. We circle for round two and Big Cal starts to chuckle nervously. The fog is getting thicker and the blood, rocks mud and booze give me a feeling of hard reality. Why don't they have something like this in my civilization? I go to jail for six months for doing nothing wrong besides acting like a warrior and answering a challenge.

I swat Big Cal with a claw across his ear and he shakes his head from the blow. Seeing he's distracted, which was the point of the slap, I shoot in. He sprawls on top of me and we scramble. He loses his base and I pick him up on my shoulder and pile-drive him headfirst into the rocks. Big Cal groans as his head hits the ground, making me laugh out loud. We're both standing ankle-deep in the mud with the blood flowing out of our heads onto our faces.

"That's two," I say.

Yeah, I know," Big Cal says, rubbing his head. "That's it for me, bro. I'm done for tonight."

We shake hands with an arm-wrestling grip. Big Cal looks like a German soldier that just threw a potato-masher from a trench in World War I like in one of my history books. On my end, I can feel my eye closing. This is too much fun to end now. "Let's go one more," I say.

Big Cal is a warrior and he nods and we square up one more time. I shoot in for a single leg and table-top my back. I peek out from under my right elbow, get to the side, and then pivot behind him for the quickest takedown yet. Now that we've torn it up we can rest. Gonzo is as beaten and bloody as me and Big Cal. We climb into Gonzo's Blazer, turn on the radio, and drink beer and laugh for the rest of the night.

I have no idea what time I got home but when I wake in the morning it's to the familiar groan of the air conditioner and Adolf trying to hog the bed from me. As I make my way to the bathroom I know it's going to be good. I hit the light switch and am surprised to see that it isn't bad at all; just a little road rash from the middle of my forehead four inches down my face and two inches wide. It's just a nice scrape with a slightly swollen eye.

I get dressed for the gym and cruise down on my bike for a nice heavy-bag workout. I get a good lift in afterwards and head down to the liquor store where Brian, a local, is working.

"Did you hear about the bullshit at court?" I ask.

"Yeah, I heard," Brian says. "He'll get his someday. What the hell happened to your head?"

"Just a little fun last night with some friends," I say.

"Oh, I thought maybe you went out and got Jerome or something," Brian says.

"No way can I do that," I say. "There's too much heat on me. Okay if I grab a clip?"

"Of course," Brian says. "How's the garage door job?"

"It's good but I haven't been working much because of the trial," I say.

"Hang in there, Walt," Brian says. "Let me know if you need anything."

I nod, head outside, get on the bike, and push the button to start the Interceptor. I cruise down the streets of the sleepy beach town with my head on a swivel, looking in bar and restaurant windows, hoping to catch sight of anyone on my list who needs a serious dose of payback - with Jerome at the top. I know it's only a fantasy, but I start to seriously consider it. I twist the throttle and my bike carries me away from temptation and danger. I'm knee deep in shit and six months is long enough. I'm not in the mood to go out when I get home so I crack a soldier and get on the phone.

"Hey, Fred," I say when he picks up. "Any bids? I've got to get off my ass and make some money before I start my sentence in five weeks.

"No problem," says Fred. "I got three bids tomorrow starting at 10:00 A.M."

"Cool," I answer. "I'll be there."

I sit and try not to think and drink four beers in the process. The phone rings just as I'm considering number five and it's Trike from the liquor store. He hired me in the beginning but quit a while back, so I haven't seen him in a while but everyone I run with knows what has been going on.

Trike tells me that he's leaving for Germany in just over a month and wants to cruise by. He shows up a few minutes later with a twelver and we burn through it, climb into my truck, and go for a cruise. Trike is maybe 160 pounds and we've run together for a long time. When it comes to beating people that are begging for it we're alike. One cylinder quickly turns into a bunch and I get to the point where some of my best thoughts appear.

"So what should we do with this fool," Trike asks as we cruise around the harbor in my truck.

"I'll find out where he works," I say.

"I already know," Trike answers. He's a waiter at Hidden Shores and I got a plan. I'll wait for him to get off work then I'll trash him. He needs to pay for lying. You're doing six months because of that loser. I'll bust his ass from head to toe starting at the shins and working my way up. I'll give him a six month sentence in the hospital."

Trike definitely thinks like me.

"I started checking on him before the trial started," Trike says. "This is how it needs to go down. He gets off work around 10:30 P.M. and walks through the parking lot. I'll park next to him and I'll back in so I can get away quickly. When he goes to get in his car I'll blast him."

"Don't be stupid, Trike," I say. "You know better than that."

He pauses. "What do you mean?"

"Don't use your fists, use a club," I say. "Make sure it's light weight so it won't kill him. Use a closet coat-hanger pole. Blast him like I would and he'll curl up into a ball because he's a pussy. Hit him on the head so his scalp splits and blood goes everywhere. Then lay into his arms and legs so he hurts bad. Hit him 180 times: one shot for each day that his lies put me behind bars. Then tell him, 'I wish I could hit you more but that's all that the law of the street will allow.'"

"I'll do it," Trike says. "I'll wait till you're in jail then I'll get him right before I leave for Germany. Consider it done."

"He screwed me good," I say. "If I did what he said then okay, I'd deserve the time. But he started the fight, threw the first punch, and then lied about everything afterwards just because he lost. He needs to pay."

"I'll take care of it," Trike says. "Put it out of your mind."

Trike is not dumb and he won't get caught. I feel good that La Mentiroso is going to get what he deserves for messing up my life. I know Trike will do it because that's what I would do for him. Trike and I have run together for a long time. He'll make sure that justice finds the people who need it.

## Chapter 18
## **Delaying Destiny**

Beep! Beep! Beep!

*Dammit!* That sound hasn't bothered me for a while but I'm still in bed with a hangover and I've got bids to do in an hour. I shower and spruce up with my white jeans and a spooner before heading off to Fred's office. Once I get the addresses I head to Fullerton, ten miles away, and go to three appointments and by noon have sold one for $200. Not bad money for just three hours' time and a pretty good sales average.

I hit the boxing gym after lunch and settle for a bag workout as there's no one there to spar with. Then it's on to the wrestling room where I can only find a couple of soft heavyweights to play with. I'm down to 190 pounds but these guys are easy for me so I pick one and we go for takedowns.

I shoot a nice single from the outside and my head crashes into his short ribs like a hard punch. He gasps in pain as I grind my head into the bones. I hit a chain pull, making his gasp turn into a moan, as he falls on his ass. I look at him like a great white shark eying a seal: *It's time for dinner but this is just lunch so I won't eat you now, you fat fish.* I sit against the wall and the sweat on my drenched shirt makes my back slip on the thick padding. As I watch the roomful of guys I can't believe that I'm going to jail for six months in a few weeks. I go for a few more takedowns before I get my fill.

I grab my workout bag, climb onto my bike and head home. The cool rush of air is pleasant on my sweat-soaked shirt. I go the speed limit because I'm tired of being hassled by Johnny Law. I'm being screwed everywhere I go. No matter what I do, the fact that I'm doing six months is always in the back of my mind. Oh, well. I've got a little bit of time before the shit hits the fan. I pull up and go inside and the patter of paws on the tile floor makes me smile.

"Hey, Adolf," I say, rubbing his head. "Good boy."

I head straight to the fridge, grab a beer, then get a Milk-Bone from the box on top of the fridge and lay it on Adolf's nose. He sits motionless, his eyes staring at me though the treat.

"Get it!" I finally say.

He flips the Milk-Bone into the air and snaps it up with his tartar-encrusted canines. His face shows pure contentment and I grab the loose skin on the back of his neck and pull him towards me. He knows this means playtime and his face turns to instant aggression as he looks for a hand or arm to put in his mouth so we can wrestle. After a few minutes I release him and scratch him behind the ears.

"Easy, big guy," I say. "I love you. That's right. You're a good boy."

His tail starts to churn in circles like an eggbeater as I take a swig off my beer then head to the couch. I don't want to do anything but flip through the channels and drink. *To hell with beer*, I decide. *I want a siren.* I pour a Stoli and cranberry then go through my room to the garage. I put the ball into the side cup of the foosball table and let it drop. I twist a control handle hard and the three-man pole pops the ball into the goal. I shoot a couple more shots then it's time to make another siren and then go for a cruise with Adolf on the residential highway.

The window is rolled down and Adolf is hanging his head out, getting a blast of air. The Smiths are playing and I drive around till my siren is gone and then head back. Skip and Jorge are home, socked away in their rooms, so I go to the living room and turn on Carson, keeping my drink fresh so I'll be good and loose for Letterman. Adolf is under my arm, a drink is in my hand, and life is good tonight.

As I stare at the screen, though, I keep thinking that I'm actually going to jail. The thought just won't leave my head. I watch Letterman until I get tired then head to bed with Adolf in tow. I turn on the air conditioner and the comforting hum of the compressor accompanies the cold air flowing out of the vents as I climb under the covers. The foil on the windows will keep the sun out of my eyes in the morning, but it can't keep out the thoughts of jail from going inside my head and keeping me awake.

I don't remember falling asleep but I must have because my head isn't pounding when I awake in the morning. I eat a light breakfast and then head to the boxing gym to clear the cobwebs. As I open the gym door I'm greeted by the pounding cadence of the speed bags. One of the trainers sees me from across the room and walks over.

"Hey, Walter," he says. "You wanna spar?"

This particular trainer is a white guy who has a bit of a reputation in the boxing world and one of his hot prospects needs some ring work.

"Sure," I say. "Let's go."

His fighter is a big white guy, close to 300 pounds, with the average boxer's intelligence of negative stupid. He's wearing an old, tattered polo shirt with an alligator on the chest and it's hard to believe that he doesn't have the collar turned up. His black sweat pants come down to mid-shin and make his six feet, two inch frame look even bigger. He's wearing filthy low-top tennis shoes with the shoelaces broken and tied back together.

"Just watch yourself," the big guy says as we climb into the ring. "I was forty-five and zero in the Navy and almost all of them were by KO."

I reply with a non-committal grunt. *We'll see.* The gym equipment and training chatter goes silent as it always does when the big boys get in the ring to play. When the bell rings he comes at me fast then slows cautiously when he gets within striking distance, reluctant to let his hands go. Right there I know that he's all bullshit and just another talker. He throws a looping left hook and I duck under it, feeling the disturbed air pass harmlessly over my head. He's just a poser, not a real fighter; a fat bastard trying to live a fantasy by telling people that he's a warrior and knows how to box. *Fuck you, you fat pussy. Now it's my turn.*

I jack him with a straight right and instantly put him on Queer Street. The guy's hotshot trainer, who's also being the referee, starts the eight-count. When he gets to the end he pushes his boxer from behind to move him into the center of the ring where I await. He stumbles out a few steps but it's clear that he doesn't want to be there anymore. I greet this poser with a five punch combination, teeing off while he covers up behind his big gloves and headgear. *45-0 my ass.* He wants to quit but I swat him a few more times as he backpedals into the ropes. I pound his ample gut with body shots until the bell rings.

I look over at Mr. Big Time Trainer. "Thanks for the work."

He turns around with his fighter without saying a word and they leave the ring. His fighter was just a phony; a typical bullshit artist who quits when you turn up the temperature. So what else is new? I finish my workout on the heavy bag, pack my hand wraps and gloves in my bag, and jump on my bike. I've still got some leftover adrenalin from the sparring session so I hit the throttle, sending the RPM needle spinning around the dial, then pop the clutch. The front tire comes off the asphalt as I speed home.

Adolf is waiting at the front door and strains to get out as I come in. He's letting me know he wants to go for a run and his tail beats like crazy as he dashes to the closet door where I keep his leash. I put his harness on and we go across the lawn to the sidewalk, where he breaks into a full sprint as soon as I get on my skateboard. The nylon wheels groan on the asphalt and we make two lefts and then a right. Adolf settles into a gallop down the long straightaway. When we get to the end of the long street he starts to make a right, to follow the usual route that he knows all too well, but I pull him to the left towards my parents' house.

We cross the main avenue into their housing track, go left then right, and pull into the driveway five houses down. Adolf's girlfriend, Ginger, is barking from behind the screen door. She's just a little wiener dog but she thinks she can kick his ass. He seems to like her attitude, though, and wags his tail and romps with her when I open the door.

"Hey, Mom," I say as I walk in.

"Oh, you brought Adolf," she says, walking out from the kitchen. She pauses for a moment, not sure what to say next, "Your dad told me you're going to jail."

"Yeah, it looks that way," I say, "but don't worry. I'll run the jail. Nobody messes with me. I just can't believe that I'm going to jail for a bullshit story. It's all a bunch of lies."

She can tell when I'm lying, of course, being my mom, and I can tell that she believes me. I guess Dad filled her in on the trial.

"You know what, Mom?" I say. "I was wondering if you knew anyone who works at the jail." She has worked for the county employee retirement system for ages, so she has juice with many of the county sheriffs.

"I don't know everyone there, Walter," she says with a sly smile. "Just the main supervisors who are getting ready to retire in a year or two. They all come to me for retirement information. I'll let them know that you're coming in." She has a concerned expression on her face.

"Don't worry, Mom," I reassure her again. "I'll be okay. You should be worrying about the other guys."

She nods and then lets herself laugh. "I suppose you're right."

She's a strong woman and if anyone ever tried to hurt her I would kill them in a split second.

We chat for a few minutes more then I say goodbye, go outside to my skateboard with my four-wheel drive

Adolf engine, and let him drag me home in no time where I plop down on the couch. It's late afternoon and I'm deflated, staring at the red and blue light bulbs on the chrome ceiling fan. I turn it on and it reminds me of the lights on cop cars. As the blades turn and the wind blows down on me I think to myself, *Screw the world. I'll be in jail in a few weeks.* I roll off the couch and lay on the carpet, more mentally than physically tired. The phone rings but I don't want to talk to anyone. For some reason, though, I feel like I should grab it so I get up and pick it up in the kitchen just before the answering machine turns on.

"Hello, Walter," John Witless says. "I've been thinking that I don't like this verdict at all."

"Imagine how I feel about it," I say glumly.

"I think you have a good chance of winning an appeal," Wittless continues. "The jury found you guilty of simple assault but at the same time not guilty of assault with a deadly weapon. That's inconsistent. You're either guilty of assault or you're not. They can't let you off on one and convict you of the other."

"Yeah," I say. "But I don't think that matters now. I'm going to jail anyway."

"I think I can fix that," Wittless says. "I can keep you out of jail for as long as the appeal is pending and all I want is another $1,000."

I shake my head as I listen to this scumbag. I know he's working me, but I'm a warrior and I might as well fight until the very end.

"You're on, John," I say. "I'll pay you as soon as I get it."

If Wittless gets me out of this then he's welcome to the grand. But if he doesn't then he still owes me for

202

screwing up my trial and I just won't pay. He'll be lucky if I don't put him on the list. I hang up the phone, go back to the living room, and stare up at the spinning ceiling fan lights. Maybe there's still hope.

I pick up the phone and call Trike. "Hey, man," I say when he picks up. "You don't need to do what we talked about."

"Are you sure?" Trike asks.

"Yeah," I reply, "My attorney is appealing the case so I'm out till it's resolved."

"I'll get him anyway," Trike says. "He still deserves it."

"No," I insist. "Just chill. I'm going to beat this and I can't risk jacking it up."

"Okay, Walt," Trike says. "But call me if you change your mind. I gotta run to Home Depot and get a refund on the clothes hangar pole I bought."

We share a laugh and as I hang up it feels like a huge weight has been taken off my chest. I feel that there's a light at the end of the tunnel. At least I don't feel completely powerless. Wittless is an idiot but I have to grab at the only life preserver I've got. At the very least maybe I won't have to do 180 days. This unexpected twist of fate had to appear in my life for some reason and it's time to celebrate. I get Adolf and we jump into the truck and cruise the residential highway. I've got a siren flowing and Adolf is tired from dragging me around all day and doesn't want to do anything but hang with me. When the ice clanks together at the bottom of my empty siren I go back home and call Fred with the news.

"Great to hear, Walt," Fred says when I finish. "I've got a couple of bids for you tomorrow afternoon."

After hearing from Wittless and getting some more work for tomorrow, drinks and TV seems so much better than last night due to all the bullshit that has been weighing me down. For the first time in days I sleep restfully, curled up next to Adolf and lulled to sleep by the buzz of the air conditioner.

In the morning I wake up alert and clear and can't wait to get to the gym and hit a hard workout before going to work in the afternoon. As I walk in after cruising over on my bike, the sounds and smells of the sweaty room hit me like a brick wall. But there's also the ever-present undercurrent of the older trainers and washed-up pugs who almost made it but didn't. They're stuck in the world of shoulda-woulda-coulda but life has passed them by. They seem to not notice it since boxing is their life, but to an outside observer it's as clear as a bell. I feel good and want to bang a little but I can't talk anyone into sparring with me so I bust a heavy-bag workout. I pop it hard and the mounting chain rattles loudly with every punch. Now that I've got this problem off my shoulders I feel better and it shows in my training. I've got a spring back in my step and I'm happy to be happy.

After the workout, a shower, and lunch I head over to Fred's office in the truck to pick up the bids and drive to the potential job sites. I sell one out of three then go back to the office to turn it in. All the bids are pretty much the same thing for me but Fred is happy so I guess I'm doing something right. I head back home, pick up Adolf, and we head out for a little cruise.

We're on Warner Blvd. and as I turn south the ocean comes into view. It's a beautiful day and the sun glistens off the smooth, glassy water. I make a right on PCH like

I did when I was driving to work at the liquor store last year but those days are thankfully over. As I pass the water tower house I look over at Adolf and grab the loose skin behind his neck. "That's gonna be yours someday, pal," I say.

Yeah, right; like I could ever make enough money to buy that place selling garage doors. I pick up a twelver and cruise down the winding back streets of Sea Lion Beach, where I pass the church and park behind the store. I'm pretty sure Brian is working so I put Adolf on his leash and walk around the building to the front. Adolf pulls me like I'm a sled and he's a sled dog. He's either trying to be the alpha male or he knows that he's going to get a piece of beef jerky.

His tail starts thrashing back and forth when we walk in the front door and I let him off the leash. Adolf rushes in and puts his front paws on the counter as if ready to place an order.

"Adolf!" Brian says, slapping him on the shoulder. "What's up, my main dog?" He gives him a piece of jerky from the countertop jar and then gives me a surprised look. "You seem to be in a good mood considering all the bullshit."

"My attorney is going to appeal," I explain. "He thinks there's a good chance we'll get it overturned. I don't have to turn myself in anymore. I think I'm in the clear."

"Cool, man," Brian says. "Looks like you dodged another bullet."

I grab a twelver, get back in the truck, and crack my first soldier. It's a beautiful day, I've got my dog beside me, and I'm not going to jail. I head back out to continue my cruise, make a left instead of a right, and turn back onto Main Street. My head is on a swivel as I look at all the faces on the street, hoping to see just one scumbag that's on my list. I drive slowly out of town on PCH, past the water tower house, and pull into public beach parking, I crack open another soldier then check out the surf. The waves are small and there are no surfers or boogie boarders out, just some people sitting around on the sand. I make another freshy then head back to the highway, heading south past the pier and over the bridge that separates Happening Beach from Newport.

Dusk is starting to settle in and I turn away from the freedom of the ocean and inland towards the human masses of urban sprawl. The beach cities used to be isolated but now they're part of one giant city. I hit the freeway and zoom back to the house. When I open the door Adolf runs past me and jumps on Skip and I follow him in.

"It's been a good day, Skip," I say. "John is appealing the verdict so I'm not going to jail; at least not right away."

"What if you get that guy again?" Skip asks. "You going to?" He knows me pretty well by now.

"Nah," I say. "No reason to now. This bullshit isn't going to stick."

Jorge walks in the front door and I'm surprised to see him. It's unusual for all of us to be home at the same time. I live with these guys but I never see them. They're perfect roommates. It's like I live alone. I tell Jorge what's going on and he reaches out to shake my hand.

"Right on, Bro," Jorge says. "I hope you win your appeal."

I grab a soldier from the fridge and sit on the couch with my feet on the coffee table. I drink the rest of the night, watch Letterman, and then crash. There's no alarm clock to wake up to but I get up early anyway and head to the safe haven of the boxing gym. I do my usual workout and then head off to the weight room. I'm hitting a groove, working out hard and being a good boy. I haven't gone out lately looking for asshats who are begging for a beating and feel a need for some excitement. I'm not meant to lead a normal life.

Maybe I can open my own garage door store. I can work for Fred and move up and learn the business. What the hell am I thinking? That will never happen. But I've got to do something now that all the bullshit with La Mentiroso is over for now.

Even though I hate the thought, maybe I should become a pro boxer. Just bite the bullet, eat the promoters' rip-off bullshit, and make a name for myself. Start at $200 a fight then plot my next move. That seems to make the most sense for now: take it easy on the party scene during my appeal and train hard to become a pro. It's a goal, at least, even if I don't really believe it myself. I have no idea what my life is leading up to. What really worries me is that it might not be anything at all.

# Chapter 19
## The Dark Road Calls

With my appeal filed, the summer sun sets, autumn turns to winter, and the months fly by. I find myself approaching a year since my trial and my life consists of peddling garage doors, training at the boxing gym and lifting weights. I'm bored out of my mind but I've been avoiding the hot spots because one bad move during my appeal will get me the entire sentence and then some. I've been as quiet as a church mouse. I'm at home one night with my mind a total blank from my enforced tedium when the phone rings and it's my friend Rod.

"Hey, Hot Rod," I say. "What's up?"

"Where you been?" Hot Rod asks. "I haven't seen you in ages. Let's go out and tear it up."

I think about turning him down like I have everyone else who's called, but this is just what I need right now. "Sure, man. Pick me up."

I grab a squad of soldiers from the fridge and get reacquainted with a few of them quickly. When the doorbell rings I'm through the squad and already working my way to platoon strength. I turn the knob and see Hot Rod standing there, all gassed up, with Poppa

Chulo behind him wearing the silly grin he gets when he's buzzed.

"Walt!" Hot Rod screams with laughter.

Adolf lunges forward like he's greeting a long-lost brother and I hold him back from slobbering all over Hot Rod's party clothes. I've gone way past watching my P's and Q's for many long months and am now into my R's and S's. I've been staying way inside the wire but I'm ready to kill myself from sheer monotony. It's time to party. They walk in and I grab Poppa Chulo's neck in a collar tie and laugh as he tries to get out. Tonight is going to be fun. We pre-tune in the garage while playing foosball and Poppa Chulo kills me three games to none.

"Let's go to the Dead Grunion or Cafe Pistol and see some babes," I say.

"I got a better idea," Hot Rod says. "Let's go to the new Golden Bear."

"I saw the Red Hot Chili Peppers there," I say. "It was a riot."

"That much fun, huh?" Hot Rod says.

"I mean there was a real riot," I say. "The cops shut down the entire street."

Poppa Chulo and Hot Rod start playing one last game of foosball and I sit on a chair to wait them out.

---

When I saw the Peppers at the Bear it was back when Fred wasn't Mr. Businessman and was doing Bolivian marching powder like it was going out of style and listening to *Ride the White Pony* non-stop. We had gone to Cagney's first and drank like crazy. Our other buddy, Fee, was on booze and Fred was all tweaked up. Strangely, I was the only one that was halfway normal but by the time we got to the Golden Bear I was trashed, too. Dogman, the bouncer, took us to the front because he was Fred's regular customer, as Fred's side job then was selling happy dust.

Fred was never tough but he was always an instigator and would start shit. Then he was good for maybe one sucker punch before backing away from what he started and letting the rest of us finish it. He was, and still is, a small time rip-off; but he had a talent for trouble.

We were up front listening to the Peppers warm-up and having a good time when a chair went flying over our heads. It wasn't aimed at us so we ignored it and continued to party. For no reason, Fred decided to flip off the bass player. The lead singer for the warm-up band was a black guy and he was standing on stage helping the Peppers tune their guitars. I remember because this was back in the day when black guys in Happening Beach were a rare sight. So the lead singer decided to be a hero and came down off the stage to confront Fred, who smiled at him, raises his arms peacefully, and then clocked him with a cheap shot when the singer dropped his hands.

The other band members jumped in and the entire audience erupted, of course, with everyone punching everyone else. The bouncers swarmed in and the cops were called to stop what turned into a small riot, hauling 20 or 30 people off to jail. I popped a bunch of the band members who came down and the Pepper's show was completely hosed. We flew out the back door that had the signatures on it of all the bands that had played there and ended up in the alley running for our lives from the cops.

---

I tell Hot Rod the story as he and Poppa Chulo finish their game

"It isn't like that anymore, Walt," he says. "That must have been before it burned down mysteriously and they got insurance money to rebuild it. It's a regular nightclub now in a new building."

I'm curious to see it so we leave the house and roll down there and he's right. The only thing that's the same is the name. The place has no character at all. We get ID'd and go through the front door and the place is only half full at best. I've got my Stoli and cranberry rolling, Poppa Chulo is out of his mind on beer, and Hot Rod is slamming whiskey. *Holy hell*, I think. *This isn't the Golden Bear, it's another Dead Grunion.* It's dark and the dance floor is sluggish and there are no girls worth standing around for so we move to the back of the club which is deserted.

There are a few high-top tables with bar stools against the mirrored wall so we park at one and drink. As it gets later more guys start to come in and circle what girls there are like a bunch of buzzards over a carcass. By now Poppa Chulo is in full rip-roaring mode and out of the corner of my eye I catch sight of this Bozo I recognize: a pretty-boy heavyweight from the boxing gym who thinks he's tough. When I first started sparring he tried to take my head off; something that should have been easy since I didn't know what I was doing, but he was too weak and hit like a girl. The whole time in the ring with him I remember thinking that if I could get my hands on him outside the gym I'd show him how it was done. Now here he is and it's a perfect time for payback except I have an appeal going on. But I can't let him get away so I nudge Poppa Chulo and tip my head towards him.

"See that pretty boy?" I ask. "He's a boxer named Penny. I'd love to hurt him but I can't. He tried to knock me out when I first started."

"Yeah," says Poppa Chulo. "I know him from the college gym. He's a little kickboxing cockroach who likes to bully people. I'll get him if you want so you don't mess-up your appeal."

"Great," I say. Poppa Chulo is always good for a throw down. "But don't stand up with him. Take him to the ground and then pound the hell out of him."

"No problem, Walt," Poppa Chulo says. "I know what to do."

I walk over to the table where Penny is sitting with his pretty-boy friends and a couple of semi-hot girls. "Hey, Penny," I say.

"Hey, sport," says Penny. He turns to his friends. "I know this guy from the gym. I gave him a few hard boxing lessons."

They all laugh, seemingly at my expense, but I hold my temper. If they only knew what was coming. "You see that little guy over there?" I point towards Poppa Chulo. "He's been popping off about you and talking shit. Just thought you should know."

Now he's on the spot with his friends. He was acting like a tough guy with me and now has no choice but to be a tough guy or lose face.

He takes a long look at Poppa Chulo and sees that he outweighs him by at least fifty pounds. "I'd kill that little greaser," Penny says impressively, more to his friends than to himself.

"I know you would," I say. "But this isn't the boxing ring. He wants to go outside with you."

Penny nods ominously at his friends and the girls seem to be impressed. "Okay. Tell that monkey I'll see him in the parking lot."

I walk back over to Poppa Chulo. "It's on," I say. "Just watch for kicks and shoot in from the start. Don't give him any distance."

We march towards the exit with Poppa Chulo two strides in front of me and Hot Rod two steps behind. This is going to be good. Poppa Chulo is going to give this bitch a good street beating. As we exit the new Golden Bear I wish the old one was still open but good times from the past are unlikely to return. We're about two yards from the front door when all of sudden the battle parade grinds to an abrupt halt.

"I'm not feeling it, Walt," Poppa Chulo says. "I'm too drunk. It's not going to be good."

Poppa Chulo has to really be drunk to not want to fight but it's his call all the way. "I got your back," I say. "No problem. I'll tell him that you don't want to do it."

We walk out the front doors and the night fog has set in and the parking lot lights have a gloom around them. Penny is standing with his drunk idiot friends who have an average weight of 180 pounds and they're shrouded in haze. I recognize a few of them as roofers who work together on construction jobs with Penny. They're on the sidewalk next to an overhang covering the new Golden Bear entrance and are circled around Penny at the far end. I can tell right away that it was going to turn into me and Poppa Chulo fighting this group of six idiots. Once Poppa Chulo started kicking ass I would have walked into the circle of morons and beat them like little children; but it isn't going to happen now. I've got my finger on the trigger, though, just in case something happens when Poppa Chulo backs outs. Sometimes the jackals will rush in when the lion turns his back.

"He got sick in the club," I say as we walk up. "He's too drunk to fight."

Penny was afraid to fight, which is why he brought all his friends to help him. Now I see a look of relief come over his face. He's just a stupid kickboxer after all. We turn to go and a dumb drunk I've had my eye on the whole time, so I don't get sucker punched, pops off.

"Screw you, Foxx," the drunk says. "You're just stirring it up. They don't want to fight each other. You're just causing trouble because you want to see a brawl."

Oh, man. Now I'm getting more steamed at this drunk than I was at Penny. But I can't ruin my appeal.

"You're a piece of work, Foxx," the drunk continues. "I should kick your ass right now."

My blood is boiling because I can't stand the thought of a 200 pound drunk popping off to me. He has a pencil neck attached to bird shoulders and is begging for a beating. I could use him for a mop but I can't do it. I look him in the eye and can tell that he has never been where he is talking about going. If he touches me he will be very sorry. He can't hold his liquor and thinks this is a game to me like it is to him. Like the rest of the idiots in this modern world he thinks he can talk shit to anyone he wants and nothing will happen. He has no idea how close I am to giving him what he is begging for.

"Let's go, Poppa Chulo," I say.

"Why?" Poppa Chulo slurs drunkenly. "I wanna party some more."

"Let's go," I repeat. "You're not going to fight so let's get out of here."

We cross the street and go into the parking garage and with each step my blood pressure surges until it feels like my head is going to pop off. I can't believe that idiot was popping off to me. At least I was a good boy and didn't mess up my appeal in front of a bunch of witnesses. Even though it's against my nature to walk away I did it. That was the hardest thing I've had to do in a long time but I can't go to jail. But I can't let a scumbag like that pop off to me either. *To hell with it. I can't let him off. I have to risk it.*

"Come on, Poppa Chulo," I say. "Let's go back and get those losers."

Hot Rod is worthless in a scrape. He's been standing in the back the whole time but I don't expect anything else from him. It has always been just me and Poppa Chulo and now we're going to give a schoolyard beating to Penny the kickboxing bitch and his harem of hangers-on.

"Stay here, Hot Rod," I say. "Come on, Poppa Chulo. I'm going to beat Penny's ass. Just watch my six and keep the idiots away. Then after that I'm going to get that dumbass with the big mouth. It's going to be a double feature."

We hurry back to the Golden Bear but they're gone. We return to the parking garage and I feel depressed when we get inside Hot Rod's car. The jingle of his keys as he puts them into the ignition sounds like a death march to me. He turns the starter over and the motor roars to life.

"Let's drive around and find those morons," I say. "I want to bash them."

I just took a boatload of shit from these idiots who couldn't hold a candle to me. They're just lucky they crossed my path at the right time. Too bad for me they weren't at the wrong place at my right time.

"Dammit, Poppa Chulo," I say. "I wish you would have killed that moron. He's a soft heavyweight and you could have squeezed his weak ass like a bug. He boxes but he will never amount to anything. He's as weak as a girl and he can't wrestle. Once you take him down on the ground he's done."

"I know, Walt," Poppa Chulo says. "I'm just too drunk to fight anyone."

"Forget it," I say. "Drive by the front of the Golden Bear, Hot Rod." We pass it but they are nowhere to be seen. "Turn right," I say next. "Maybe they parked on the side street."

"You just should have got him from the get-to," Hot Rod says.

"I know," I say. "I was worried about my appeal. But that drunken idiot with Penny pushed me over the edge. He's gonna get it good."

We make a few more rights and then some lefts but they're nowhere to be found. I've never eaten that much crow in my life. I'll see them in the gym sometime and even up the scales.

"Take me home," I finally say.

I hate this feeling of being powerless. My hands are tied and my balls are cut off. As Hot Rod pulls into my driveway I think that I can't live like this. Those scumbags dodged a bullet and will have no idea how lucky they were when they get up tomorrow morning to put on a roof. I stumble inside in too bad of a mood to even say goodbye. Thankfully, I've had enough to drink that when I throw myself on the bed the hypnotic hum of the air conditioner puts the thoughts of killing these guys to the back of my mind and I fall asleep almost instantly.

I awake in the morning with no memories of any dreams at all and my eyelids feeling like a thousand pounds. I'm tired and it takes a long shower to wake me up. I open the shower door and look at myself in the mirror, unable to see anything until I rub the fog from the glass. As I stare at myself I think how messed up my life is.

I'm nothing but a steer anymore. I used to be a bull but now my balls have been removed by a DA geek and a lying coward. Now I have to eat shit from fools who put roofs on peoples' houses. All I have to look forward to in life is selling garage doors to people so I can someday be a rip-off like Fred. My life sucks. What am I going to do? Play the 9 to 5 grind-game like everyone else? It's easy but it's not for me. I can see myself going to prison if people like last night keep antagonizing me. It's just a matter of time.

The mirror fogs up again and I turn the cold water knob so the water pouring into the sink clears it. I brush the teeth that are still left in my mouth. I lost my top front teeth in a car accident on my nineteenth birthday and have had several crowns and bridges since then. My mouth is a wreck but I don't really think about it and it does make brushing and flossing go fast.

*Time to go peddle some doors*, I think as I leave the bathroom. The money is good but I don't want to be another Fred. Oh, hell no. I can't be a rip-off. I'd rather end up in prison than be like that. It's just a payday and it's far below what I know I can do. Running a garage door business is like being a used car salesman. It's paying the bills for now but it's not for me. I've got to wear nice clothes and talk bullshit that I don't care about just to kiss ass for money. How long can I turn my head and look the other way for something I don't have a passion for? Everyone tells me this is real life and that I need to play the game but I know I can't do that forever.

I will never kiss ass for money. I'll be happy as long as I've got food, booze, a roof over my head, and can hold onto who I am. I know I'm walking a fine line when it comes to losing my freedom but I can't deal with people on this side of the wall. There is no way to make a living at what I love to do because street fighting doesn't exist as a profession. So I have to color between the lines without breaking the boundaries. *To hell with it all.*

I head out to the gym to work out, hoping to snap out of the mental funk I've talked myself into. When I walk through the front door I see all the losers working out who couldn't punch their way out of a wet paper bag. They all tell themselves they're super bad and are going to be the next Muhammad Ali and swap bullshit stories to build themselves up: "One time I punched a dude that cut in front of me in the lunch line in high school and I was suspended for two days," they'll say. "Now I'm ready to beat Mike Tyson."

I look the gym over but there's no Penny and no drunken idiot sidekick. This sport is about hitting people and I want to hit Penny and his moron friend. I slap the heavy bag around half-heartedly for a while then leave the gym, go home and shower, then put on a bullshit nice shirt and jeans to go with my bullshit nice haircut and fake smile.

I hit the road and a guy honks his horn as I'm getting onto the freeway, but I can't pull over and kick his ass even though he's begging for a beating. *In a bar a couple months ago I would have killed you with my bare hands, you idiot.* This is getting beyond frustrating. I arrive at my first appointment and ring the doorbell which resonates inside the house. I give my spiel, bid the garage door, and close the sale. Why do people trust me and like me? I'm not really a garage door salesman it's just a job I'm doing. Can't they see the danger in my eyes? Forget them. Is this really my purpose and calling in life? I leave and drive to my second appointment and close another sale, which depresses me. I'm not sure I like being good at this. I'm heading towards becoming a clone of Fred.

With my work done for the day I head back towards the house where I know Adolf will be happy to see me, at least. I wish I was a dog and lived by nothing but my pure animal instincts. I could run with the best. I'd show the top dogs how to run. *You're not getting to the food bowl before me, Rover.*

I get to the house and there's my boy, Adolf. He jumps up as I open the front door and I grab his front paws and hip toss him to his back which pisses him off. I follow him to the floor and lightly grab the skin on his neck and he shows his teeth and growls at me. I start to laugh as I keep him pinned.

"Hey, dog," I laugh. "I'm the leader of this pack. What's up with the growls? I won't hurt you."

I kiss his wet nose and he starts to wag his tail and tries to lick my face. I let him go and grab a beer and turn on the TV. After a few programs and a few beers I head to bed. I know that I can't keep enduring this boring life much longer. I have to start living life on my own terms.

That same thought is still in my head when the alarm clock rings the next morning. I lay in bed dreading another day of peddling garage doors and wondering if this is now my life. I know I can't do this much longer. Every day I go to work, hit the boxing gym, lift weights and then grapple fish in the wrestling room. I've got absolutely nothing to look forward to. Sure, I could run Fred's new second shop. He's offered and I'd make more money but what kind of life is that for me? I'm a warrior without a battle and when the fog fades from the mirror of my life I still have to look into it. Will I like what I see?

Since my trial I've turned and walked away from so many posers that I would have hurt in a split second less than a year ago. All the fun that I've missed out on is driving me crazy. But I'm on thin ice and facing real time if I get more charges filed against me while my appeal is pending. On the surface I've been assimilated into society and am playing by the rules but I'm just pretending to be something I'm not. I might as well wear a suit and tie and be a lawyer or teach school. I'm not a real man right now.

I've gone through summer, winter and now spring since the trial. I'm clearing $1, 000 a week, which is good money, and I've steered clear of trouble for the most part. But the whole time I've been a bear locked in a cage. Just let some scumbag insert the right key and twist it to make the tumblers fall and I'll push the door open and kill him so fast I'll be eating his heart by the time he takes his last breath.

Every morning the alarm clock blares again and I obey it without a thought. I'm getting used to it and that's a bad sign. Is the alarm clock going to rule my life from now on, just like everyone else? I get up and get dressed and then do some more bids and sell some more doors. *I wouldn't buy a door from me so why do they?* It must because they don't know that inside the nice-guy facade is a scary monster just waiting to be unleashed.

I get home from doing bids one day, grab my gym bag, climb on the Interceptor, and ride hard to the gym, the duct tape on the seat slapping against my leg in the hurricane force wind. It's April in Southern California and it's hot. As I walk into the boxing gym I realize that it has lost its shine to me. It has no purpose and I'm wasting my time. Boxing is all political with crooks running the sport and there's no money in wrestling even as a coach. My only passion, street fighting, will just land me in jail or prison.

I change into my gear, wrap my hands, pick out a heavy bag in the corner, and start hammering it with real emotion. *Screw you.* I hit it with a combination. *I'm not a loser.* I double-up with two rights. *I'm not a garage door lifer. No! I just work for them. They can only dream about being me.* Sweat drips down my forearms as I finish six rounds on the bag and get ready to leave.

It's so easy to get lulled into a life that you don't want to lead. I'm eating crow now but I'm making enough money to do what I want. I'm training but not fighting so it looks like I'm turning into a gym rat. Someday I'll transform into a sad old guy with a weathered, puffy face, flat nose, and broken dreams. I already have no teeth from the car accident and a punchy disposition could be just around the corner. I'm surrounded by losers from that same cookie cutter mold and it looks like I'm on the road to becoming one. I have to figure my life out.

I go home, walk in the front door to drop off my bag, and then go to the mailbox and grab the tied bundle that the postman leaves. I pull off the Penny Saver with the rest of the junk mail and sort through what's left. Near the top is an official-looking letter from the County of Orange addressed to me. I'm excited because I never get mail and it must mean my trial nightmare is now over.

I go back inside, brush Adolf aside, and sit down at the coffee table. I stick my finger inside the corner of the envelope and it makes a ripping sound as it opens. On top is the letterhead of the District Attorney and I unfold it and read. In large print towards the middle of the page I see: *YOUR APPEAL IS DENIED.* I read further and see that the date for re-sentencing is two weeks from yesterday. My stomach twists into a knot as I think about what I now face. All of a sudden my boring and predictable life that I hated just an hour ago now seems both desirable and yet totally beyond my reach. I thought regular life sucked, but I was wrong. Now I'm really behind the eight ball!

## Chapter 20
## Behind the Eight Ball

Why is my life so messed up? I've been walking the straight and narrow for a long time now and they still turn down my appeal. I throw the envelope to the ground and the disturbed air fans against my legs just like the air that's flowing out of my lungs. I've been trying to be good and just like that it turns bad. I'm in this position because of a lie but regardless of that, things are not going to change. I'm here and I'll deal with it. Adolf is looking at me somberly as if he knows why I'm upset.

I pick up the phone and call Wittless. "What the hell is this, John?" I ask, telling him about the letter.

"Well, I kept you out of jail for a year," Wittless answers. "That's what you wanted, right?"

"John," I say, "you told me you would get it overturned."

"I said there was a good chance," Wittless says. "I think they'll reduce the sentence now that so much time has passed. Maybe you won't get any jail time at all. Just play it cool."

"Alright, John," I say, forcing myself to remain calm.

I hang the receiver up in the cradle and static electricity zaps my finger. *What else?* I think. *It isn't enough that the carpet has been pulled out from underneath me, it has to shock me too. It's time to bite the bullet, or at least the half bullet.* I take a deep breath, walk to the fridge, grab a friend, tap the top, and then open it and take a swig in one practiced motion. I'm stuck in a legal web and they're trying to bury me. They can do whatever they want but I'm not going down peacefully.

*No more Mr. Good Guy bullshit.* I tried it and it did me no good so I'm done. That shit doesn't fly with me anymore. I pick up the phone and dial Poppa Chulo.

"I lost my appeal," I say. "Let's pound some drinks."

A little bit later Poppa Chulo shows up and we kill a twelver.

"You wanna go to a club?" Poppa Chulo asks.

"Not tonight," I say. "If I ran into somebody like Penny or his dumb friend they would go to the morgue."

"I can't believe this shit, Walt," Poppa Chulo says. "I thought they were going to cut you some slack."

"Forget it," I reply. "What's done is done."

Poppa Chulo takes off and I crack another beer, staring at the chrome ceiling fan as my thoughts churn like the whirling blades. Adolf has his head on the top of my leg and his eyes are closed but he doesn't seem to be asleep, he just looks peaceful. If he could only hear the noise in my head he would be howling to the moon. I watch the tube for the rest of the night before getting up to go to bed. Adolf jumps up and trots to the bedroom behind me and jumps in next to me. I turn on the air conditioner thinking that it's going to be a long night, but to my surprise I go out like a light.

I get out of bed early and head to the gym with Adolf in tow. I feel a need to hit something hard. The gym is slow and no one is there so I pummel the heavy bag as Adolf lies on the painted cement floor. Afterwards I jump into my truck with Adolf and head to Wong Beach State to check on my diploma status. Traffic is heavy as I drive down the street and Adolf is sitting up blocking the right side mirror. I move him out of my way to try to get onto the on-ramp and almost hit a car. *My bad.* I gesture to the woman driver apologetically with a wave of my hand.

Instead of driving on, though, she pulls in front of me and flips me off. I raise both my hands in another apologetic gesture and then point to myself to show her it was my fault. Now the passenger window opens and a guy sticks his head out and glares at me. Then he puts his arm out of the window and flips me off by waving his arm back and forth. At first I was sorry but now the passenger has gone too far. It's on with this idiot.

The car slows down, blocking me behind him, and pulls to the side of the on-ramp as I follow nice and slow. Adolf is jumping up and down on the bench seat and howling as if to say, *Let me kill him, dad.* He's like a screaming hyena. *No, Adolf,* I think. *I've got it.* The air conditioner is blowing out of the vents as I step into the heat. The guy is already out of his door and is short and stocky, maybe five feet, eight inches and 200 pounds. He has on a tee-shirt and long shorts that come down past his knees.

He sees me get out and charges me on a dead run like a wild bull. I slam the truck door shut so Adolf can't get out as he is now barking and jumping like a wild dingo. I feel like a matador standing in the center of a ring awaiting the bull. It's like I'm holding a red blanket. *Oh,*

225

*yes, let's not forget the sword,* I think, as I cock my right arm back. The hyena screaming is echoing out of my truck cab as I watch the bull approach me. I keep track of the driver out of the corner of my eye as well. Even though it's a woman I want to make sure she doesn't jump me also. If it's two-on-one I'll have to change my fight strategy.

The woman jumps out of the driver's door, yelling for the wild bull to stop. The idiot doesn't listen so I take a few steps forward and lift up my sword and chop this asshole right between the horns. *Ole', motherfucker.* My straight right punch hits him dead between the eyes and he stops in his tracks. I take a quick step to the right and crack him on the ear, putting him on Queer Street, then I step away to give him a chance to retreat. The woman is screaming for the guy to get back in the car. She's shaking in fear for her man.

Her screams just seem to energize him, however, and he comes back to life and charges me again, taking my mercy as a sign of weakness. I sidestep his charge and land a three-punch combo: a right to the ribs, left uppercut, and right hook. I pull all the punches and don't blast him hard, not wanting to hurt him as he has definitely gotten in way over his head. He staggers back to the trunk of his car, shakes his head, and comes at me again, ignoring the woman's screams to stop. But it's too late now. The bull is going to get slain by the matador.

I throw hard this time and he's rocked and knows it. Up to this point I kept wishing the guy would chill and pulled my punches to keep his poor woman from freaking out; but no more. I can't give him anymore gifts. It's time to have some fun. I blast him again hard and he staggers back one step and then another. His hands fall and his eyes are empty. *Oh, yeah. He's gone.* I shoot a double leg and the impact of the ground wakes him up and life comes back to his eyes. He has a worried look on his face but is still defiant.

"Get the hell off me," he yells.

"No way," I grunt back. "You're my bitch now." I squeeze his ribs so he can barely breathe. "I'll tell you what to do."

The woman is still screaming and Adolf is louder than ever in the truck.

"I'm going to let you up now," I continue. "If you don't want to get messed up more than you already are then get the hell out of here." He doesn't say a word but his eyes are filled with fear.

I get off him and take a few steps back. He doesn't charge me this time so he has learned his lesson. His face is bloodied and his woman is wiping at it with a tissue. I head back to my truck where Adolf is still growling like a mad dog. There are three cars parked on the side of the freeway watching the show. As I get to the hood of my truck I watch him out of the corner of my eye for any cheap shots. When he thinks my back is turned he pushes his woman aside and charges forward. *Okay, here we go again. This time it's not my problem. The bull is coming at the matador again and the red blanket is going to be soaked in his blood.*

I spin around to meet his charge and blast this short scumbag with full phasers and a spread of photon torpedoes. No more play time. My four punch combination lands perfectly and dazes him. He's still standing but he's gone. Blood is pouring down his shirt and his face is a crimson mask. I hit him with a hard body shot to the short ribs and he staggers to the left. I grab his hair and shorts and throw him on the trunk of his car. He seems like he's out but I know he's a cheap shot artist and am ready when he suddenly tries to punch me. Time to play *Little Drummer Boy* with my drumstick, except this drumstick has been bench pressing over 600 pounds.

I ball up my fist and prepare to give this dumbass bull what he has been asking for. I raise my arm and chop down on his nose. It explodes like a rotten tomato and blood flies everywhere. I hit him enough times to make sure he won't get up to try to cheap shot me again while I'm walking back to my truck. When he is lying still on the trunk I turn and look at the woman to make sure she isn't getting any ideas. But she just cowers away.

I turn and walk back to my truck and the air conditioner blows the heat from outside away as I get in. Adolf is glad I'm back and licks the blood off my hand as I work the stick shift. As I let the clutch out and move forward I can see the cars on the side of the freeway start to move. As they leave the scene so does my anger. When I pass the dumbass, he rolls off the trunk and falls to the pavement, his woman huddled over him. I gave him plenty of chances but some beggars just aren't happy until you give them what they want.

I get onto the freeway before the cops show up and drive to campus and park at the administration building, cursing because I forgot that I have to pay two bucks to park there. As I stroll up to the line at the window I see that I've still got the bull's blood smeared on my forearms. He should have just walked away when I gave him the chance. I have no idea why he wanted to keep the ball in the air. Maybe he wanted to impress his woman. *Yeah, like that worked out so well.* I get to the window and find out that I have enough credits to graduate but that I still need to take a math class.

I leave the school campus and drive the route I've traveled many times before. I pass the liquor store and am glad that I'm not working there anymore. I keep racking up more unfinished business to take care of. I've got to go to jail soon and now I find out I have to take a math class. It seems I will never get my life on track. First of all, though, I've got to get the bull's blood off my arms.

*What a total moron*, I think. He must have been mad at something else and tried to take it out on me and got stretched for his trouble. I walk through the front door of the house and make a cheeseburger with a sesame seed bun. Meat juice drips down over the cheese as I grab some chips and a diet Pepsi: good cheap food. I slam the barbeque lid down and take the food to the dinner table. The grease flows out of the cheeseburger and down my chin as I tear into it.

My thoughts are going a hundred miles an hour. What am I going to do? I can do the six months but the lying scumbag that put me there is getting off scot-free and it's not right. Now I regret not taking up Trike on his offer.

I finish my lunch. I've laid down the blanket and now it's time to put out the picnic and get right. No beer today; I need a siren. I grab a red cup and pour a rooster with Stoli near the top and a splash of cranberry for color. I'm off to the races, telling myself to deal with everything as it comes and to not suffer future pain. I drain the bottomless siren for a good while until I start to feel right and then decide it's time to find some fun. I've been a good boy and I've seen where that has gotten me.

I call up Poppa Chulo and he's hanging with Rolando so I tell them to come over so we can party. I turn up the ceiling fan until it starts buzzing just like my head. The Smiths are playing so loudly on the stereo that I barely hear the doorbell ring. Adolf clues me in when he looks at me and then races out of the bedroom and through the living room and starts barking at the front door. As I walk down the hallway he jumps up and down, frantic to either eat the visitors or greet them; I can't tell which. When I open the door and Poppa Chulo and Rolando come in it turns into a definite greet situation as they endure his jumping excitement.

"Drinks or beers?" I ask, as we head towards the garage for some foosball. They grab beers from the fridge on the way out and start slamming the drinks as we slam the balls with the little soccer men with plentiful laughs.

"You should have seen this idiot I trashed on the freeway today," I say. "I accidentally cut him off and tried to apologize but he kept coming at me and I finally gave him what he begged for. The idiot made a wish and I answered it. Anyway, he got it. Then I went to school and found I still need a math class to graduate, but I have to do my six months first because of that lying scumbag from Sea Lion Beach."

After Poppa Chulo scores on me I smack a ball into the goalie hole from the back line and it hits so hard that it vibrates the whole table. Just thinking about that La Mantiroso idiot has me seething with anger. *Forget foosball,* I think. "Let's go get that moron," I say. "Let's get him good."

"Okay, Walt," Poppa Chulo says. "I owe you one from the other night with Penny."

Rolando shrugs his shoulders and nods. "He has it coming."

We leave the house and pile into Rolando's girlfriend's black Japanese sedan that he's driving tonight. I climb in back while Poppa Chulo takes shotgun. As Rolando drives towards Sea Lion Beach I'm thinking that this drunken day has now turned into payback day. For some reason *Thou shall not bare false witness* pops into my head and makes me feel like an avenging angel.

"Listen, guys," I say. "This has to be done right. I still have my sentencing coming up so you guys need to beat on him. He doesn't need to be killed or anything, just punch him up good."

"Right, Walt," Rolando says. "He's going to get a proper ass-kicking."

"Okay, cool," I say. "When we get to his house let me scope it out first then I'll come up with a plan."

We wind down the streets, approaching where he lives. It's after 2:00 A.M. and nobody is out. Rolando drives by his house but doesn't slow down so we don't look suspicious and attract attention. On the other side of the street is the 20-yard-wide greenbelt that runs for over a mile. Under my direction, Rolando circles to the other side of the greenbelt and parks in a dark spot well away from any streetlights, directly across from the target location.

The crickets are chirping, it's dark and foggy, and the grass is wet with dew. We get out of the car and they walk across the greenbelt while I wait behind so he can't see me. The dense fog is perfect for what is about to go down, with the porch lights providing just a faint glowing halo that spreads throughout the gloom.

It looks eerie but it's all karmic payback for his bad deeds. Lies always catch up to you. He should have taken what he begged for and left it at that. Physical pain is nothing compared to a loss of honor. Don't try to get revenge by lying. Own up to your bad deeds and take the beating you deserve. If not, then it's going to come back on you even worse. It's time for Jerome to face justice.

Rolando and Poppa Chulo disappear into the dark fog and I hear them knock on the door. It's a quiet night and I can hear them clearly as I wait at the car, ready to jump in the driver's seat when the deed is done. I'm waiting to hear the screams of the rabbit as the coyotes tear him apart. The front door opens and I hear a voice that I last heard a year ago at my trial.

"Who the hell are you?" Jerome asks roughly.

"We hit a car in front of the church," Rolando says. "Can we use your phone?"

"Yeah," Jerome says grudgingly. "I guess it's okay."

As I lean against the black sedan with my arms crossed in front of me, I hear a scream. *Yes, Jerome. You've been sentenced to a beating in your house for lying. I wish I could give you more. Your evil karma has caught up to you.*

"Help! Help!" I faintly hear, but it sounds like sweet music to my ears. *The lions of the coliseum have come to eat you and GUESS WHO SENT THEM?* I hear the shuffle and banging of furniture. I want to be smashing this scumbag's face so bad but all I can do is enjoy it from 100 yards away. All of a sudden it gets silent. Even the crickets stop chirping. A smile comes to my face. It's over and Jerome has learned his second lesson.

"No! Stop it!" Another voice comes faintly from the house.

I recognize it as belonging to Jerome's fat girlfriend who cried on the stand about something that never happened. I hear a thud and then it's silent again. I know what has gone down and I can't help but laugh out loud in the night. Two faint forms jog towards me across the greenbelt and Poppa Chulo and Rolando appear out of the fog. They jump in the back seat as I settle behind the wheel and turn the ignition. The sound of a beating drum comes over the stereo as the Doors' song, *The Unknown Soldier*, starts to play.

*Where's your daddy now, Jerome?* I think. I smile at the thought of how powerless Detective Dad will feel when he finds out. That's what happens when you're a grown man who hides behind mommy and daddy and lets them fight your battles. I glance in the rearview mirror and see Rolando and Poppa Chulo sitting in back.

"Lay down flat," I say. "Stay out of sight."

If the cops happen to drive by they'll be looking for two people, not one. I don't haul ass because that would attract attention but rather drive just below the speed limit, with the true heroes of justice lying in back. I drive out of town to the last stoplight in Sea Lion Beach, take a right, and make the long familiar drive through the Navel Weapons Yard. When we emerge on the other side we know that we're in the clear and the car erupts with laughter as Poppa Chulo and Rolando pop up from the back seat.

"Oh, man," I say. "That was beautiful. Tell me what happened."

"When he let us in he turned to walk down the hallway," says Rolando. "That's when I blasted him in the back of the head. He went down and started to scramble around, all squirrely. Poppa Chulo mounted

233

him and started jacking him while I kicked him in the ribs. Then the bedroom door opened and this fat chick comes running out. She was screaming at the top of her lungs and trying to hit me so a drilled her with a straight right and dropped her like a sack of potatoes. Poppa Chulo kept hitting Jerome the whole time and I finally had to pull him off."

"That's great," I say. "They both had it coming."

As I drive back to my house I think that it would be better if nobody saw them for a while and I give them $180 in getaway money so they can leave right then. "Go down to TJ for a few days," I say.

"We'll pay you back when we're back in town," says Rolando.

"Don't worry about it," I say. "Just have some fun."

I stop at my house and get out and Rolando takes the driver's seat and Poppa Chulo gets shotgun. I'm happy that I got some payback but it isn't enough for the six months I'm looking at. But it will make the time less bitter. I think of something and run after them down the driveway.

"Don't worry about the cops," I say, as they pull to a stop. "They won't pry a word out of me."

"Like you had to tell us that," Rolando says. "We're outta here."

As they pull away I start to pirouette in the driveway, turning around in the night with my fists straight up in the air like I just beat Mike Tyson for the heavyweight championship of the world.

## Chapter 21
### Lockdown Countdown

I walk up to the front door and Adolf is there with his usual greeting. He runs towards my bedroom, eager to jump in bed, but I head towards the kitchen and he follows me. *No, we're not going to sleep,* I think. *Let's have a drink and wait for the cops. Yeah, Adolf, the cops are coming.* This thought keeps bouncing around in my head as I pour a drink then sit down with the stereo playing. I wrestle with Adolf and have another couple of drinks.

There are no cops yet so I turn on the air conditioner and fall asleep in my clothes so I won't have to get dressed when they show. I pass out and sleep straight through the night and don't wake until 1:00 P.M. the next day. I peek outside, half-expecting to see a SWAT team in the driveway but there's not even a crosswalk guard. I change into my workout gear and go for a four-mile run. With every stride I wonder where the cops are. Why are they playing around with me? I go to the weight room, get a good lift, and then go home to again find no cops, no messages, and no notes.

Maybe Jerome learned his lesson the second time. The first shift is over and the swing shift cops will be coming on. If they haven't showed up by now then they aren't coming. The coast is clear but just in case I stay home all night, not venturing out and getting ready for my sentencing tomorrow.

I awake in the morning, cop-free still, and get ready for my date with destiny. *Oh, Lord. Where is life taking me? I could be going to jail today.* I drive to the courthouse, climb up the cement steps, and make a left towards Division 1 and stop outside the double doors. Wittless is waiting for me on a bench and he looks worried.

"Walt, come over here," he says. "We need to talk."

I sit down next to him. "What is it?"

"What did you do, Walt?" he asks. "What were you thinking?"

"What are you talking about, John?" I ask.

"The DA called me and told me that you had something to do with the victim getting assaulted at his house," Wittless says breathlessly. "Not only was he severely beaten but his girlfriend had her jaw broken."

I look around the sterile atmosphere of the hallway and allow myself a faint smile. "It sounds like karma finally caught up with Jerome," I say.

"Walt, this could mean serious trouble for you," Wittless warns.

"Look, John," I say. "I didn't lay a hand on him or his girlfriend. I guess he pissed someone off and thought Detective Dad would bail him out again."

"The DA said that if he finds out that you had something to do with this that he'll send you to prison,"

Wittless says. "You could end up in San Quinton doing five-to-ten."

"Let him try," I say. "I didn't touch Jerome."

"Well," Wittless admits doubtfully, "they did say that you weren't one of the attackers but that doesn't mean you don't know who did it. The DA said that if you could give him some leads on who might be responsible that he would cut you a deal and recommend community service with a small fine."

I'd been expecting this so I pause for a long moment and then look Wittless square in the eyes. "Fuck that. Let them give me the whole half bullet."

I walk into Division 1 like I've got nothing to lose, which I actually don't, and stare at the old blueblood judge eye-to-eye. *You're what you think I am*, I muse. *You read books about life while I live it.* I give her a I-would-kill-you-if I-could look. She has no more power over me because she can't give me any more time. I'm getting screwed by her royal highness the judge, a dumbass detective dad who misidentified me as a drug dealer, and a rookie geek DA who bought into this fantasy to further his career even though he had to know it was bullshit.

The DA walks in dressed in another cheap suit. He drops his eyes when he sees me staring at him, like he's afraid looks could kill. *I'll survive my half bullet six-month tour,* I think. *You haven't broken me.* Seeing him makes me know for sure that I made the right decision about not going to law school. The entire system is corrupt and bullshit. The judge slams her gavel and then looks around the courtroom before settling her eyes on me.

"Mr. Foxx," the judge says. "Your appeal has been denied. With the serious events that have come to light recently and with your refusal to cooperate with the court, I have no choice but keep the original sentence and give you the six month maximum term. I only wish it was within my power to give you more. You have five weeks to get your affairs in order before turning yourself in."

Wittless turns to me and looks me in the eye and I think he's going to apologize for not doing more and for fucking up my trial in the first place. "Are you going to be able to pay me by then?" Wittless asks.

"I'll come by your office tomorrow," I say, holding my tongue.

I drift back to my truck like I'm on a sailing ship in the middle of the doldrums off the coast of South America. I'm floating around with an albatross around my neck and a bull's-eye on my back. I've got five weeks to get my life right before going away on a long vacation. I get into my truck and drive away in a slow motion daze like I'm stoned. After having only driven one stoplight I feel like I've driven to the moon and back.

*Let's go, fuckers,* I think. *In five weeks I'll do my six months but you won't ever get over on me. You won't beat me down. Time is nothing. Only I have the power to give you power over me and you're not getting it. You can only have it for this short time of my life. So don't get big heads. In six months I'll be back and if you're abusive while I'm in then you'll pay.*

I can feel my heart beat in my throat as I drive down Beach Blvd. and before I know it I'm home and parked in my driveway. I walk in the front door like a zombie and go straight to the fridge to grab a friend. I fall on the couch and Adolf comes up and nuzzles me. *Well, at least I've got you, Adolf,* I think. *But I've got to go away in five weeks and I know you won't understand.*

I kill the friend in two gulps and wonder what's going on in my brain. At first I say that I don't want to do six months and then I turn on a dime and say let's get it done. It's just my nature to roll with the punches, I guess, and to play the hand that's dealt. The ceiling fan beats down on me and I drink on the couch all night before going to sleep. I get up in the morning with a definite mission in mind and climb on my bike to go see Wittless. As I fly down the cul-de-sac I sink into the duct-taped seat and before I know it I'm back in the middle of Tijuana, USA. I can't believe this is the United States. Rents are lower in this area so it figures Wittless' office would be here.

I park in front of his building, go up the elevator, and tell the receptionist I'm there to see him. I take a seat to wait and pick up the magazine with Mike Tyson on the cover that's still there after a year. Before I can finish the first paragraph I'm called into his office. I walk through the front part of the office where a bunch of women are shuffling papers and go down the hall to where John rents his cubbyhole from the real law firm. Behind Wittless, through the big picture window, I can see all the cars passing by on the freeway and wonder where so many people can be going and what kind of lives they lead.

Well, Walt," Wittless leans forward, "I managed to keep you out of jail for a year, but the DA wants you bad. There was no chance to get you a lesser sentence once Jerome and his girlfriend got beaten up and you wouldn't cooperate. If they find any evidence you're involved it would mean state prison. You'd be smart to cooperate now."

I'm silent for at least thirty seconds, just staring out the window; then I turn to Wittless and look him dead in the eyes. John's face turns from casual confidence to scared intimidation in a heartbeat. I know that look well. He can tell I'm not playing. He knows I don't care and could do anything at that moment.

"Look, John," I say softly. "You can tell the DA that everybody involved in this case has fucked me and that includes you, the judge, him, Jerome, his dad and his girlfriend. What happened to Jerome is what he begged for. He started the fight and hit me first but he didn't want to man up and face the consequences. You see, John, I'm not like the rest of you. If they push this and I go to state prison for five or ten years for Jerome getting beaten up the other night I will kill everyone involved when I get out. I'll start with the lying victim, then his girlfriend, then his detective dad, then the DA geek, and then the judge. Then I will make right the poor representation I received in my defense. Got it, John?"

Wittless lets out his breath sharply and his mouth moves but he doesn't speak. It's like a bad voice dub in a late-night kung-fu flick. Finally words come out.

"You're starting to scare me, Walt," he says, stumbling over the words. "The DA is gunning for you. I don't know what's going to happen."

"Well, I do," I say. "Trust me. I'll kill everyone involved."

Wittless slides back in his chair, away from his desk and from me. "I don't think we should talk again. You're really scaring me."

I get up and go to the door, pause for a moment, and look back at Wittless. "I'll be seeing you around, John."

I slam his office door shut and go down the elevator to the lobby. The system says I have to take a detour in my life: a half-bullet, six month detour. It's not a big deal. It's just a bump in the road. But they better hope it doesn't turn into more for their sakes. I walk out the front door, glad to be back in the fresh air, and walk towards my bike, hoping I can survive the bad drivers that fill the roads of the United States of Mexico.

Out of the corner of my eye I see a pay phone and decide on the spur of the moment to call Barry, my regular attorney. I look up his number from his card in my wallet and dial it.

"Hello, Barry?" I ask when he picks up. "I'm in Santa Ana, just down the freeway from you. I need to talk."

"Okay, Walter," Barry says. "See you when you get here. I'll be in the office all day."

As I approach the Interceptor I notice that the back tire is flat. *Perfect.* It's down to the rim but from experience I know that I can still ride it if I'm careful and go slow in turns. I go down the freeway in the slow lane until I get to the off-ramp for Newport Beach. I park in front of the lobby and go up the elevator. This is his building, but from the ground floor directory I can see he's in a suite now instead of an office. I walk in the door to his suite and give the receptionist my name. While I wait I look over the pastel floral wallpaper and overly feminine lamps and paintings. I could give him some decorating advice. He needs a heavy bag or two to man up the place. But I'm not here to give but rather to receive.

241

I think dark thoughts as I wait. My whole world is blowing up in front of me with the threats of new charges for Jerome's most recent beating. I know Wittless is not on my side and will help the DA anyway he can. I wonder if I'm going to have to get my gun and shoot John. My thoughts are interrupted by the receptionist directing me into the back and telling me to go two doors down the hallway on the right.

"Have a seat, Walter," Barry says personably when I walk in. "What brings you here?"

We're in a conference room and the long wooden table is surrounded by fourteen expensive-looking leather and chrome chairs. Barry comes around the table and sits next to me, not like Wittless who tries to keep as much distance between us as possible. This small act helps me relax and makes me feel like Barry is on my side.

"The usual, Barry," I say with a smile, surprising myself with how casual I sound. "Just wanted to lay some things out for you and see what you think."

I decide to let Barry know everything, except this time to not tell him anything that would keep him from representing me in the future if I need him.

"Wittless jacked me at the trial," I say. "He didn't ask questions that could have cleared me. When I went into re-sentencing after my appeal the DA told John the victim got beat up in his house and his girlfriend's jaw was broken. Wittless told the DA that I would give him information for a lighter sentence and when I refused they gave me the maximum. Now, Wittless says the DA wants to send me to prison."

"Okay, Walter," Barry says. "I understand. Did you assault La Mantiroso or his girlfriend the second time."

"No," I say.

"Did you directly witness anyone assaulting them?" Barry asks in his best trial voice."

"No," I say, which is totally true, because I was in the car the whole time.

"Is there any trail that connects you to what happened or are there any witnesses who can place you at or near the scene?" he asks.

"No," I say again.

This is why I like Barry; he doesn't use prison as a hammer to scare me but just cuts straight to the bottom line. He's been a straight shooter all the years that I've employed him professionally.

"So you have nothing to say about what happened," Barry continues. "Right?"

"Yes, that's correct," I say, taking his lead. "I have no comment."

"Then you have nothing to worry about," Barry finishes. "If anything further develops then give me a call."

I get up and he walks me down the hallway and out the door. "That Wittless is a piece of shit," I say.

"A lot of us are, unfortunately," Barry shrugs and smiles.

I feel better as I go down the elevator, now that I know I won't get dicked over by threats of prison. Now I know exactly what to say and what not to say if questioned. As I exit the building through the lobby I look at all the suit-wearing geeks going into the building. I get onto the Interceptor thinking I'm glad that isn't me.

I don't know what I'm going to do with my life when I get out of jail, but I'm not going to prison and I'm not wearing a suit just because someone tells me to. I stare up at the sun and wonder what's coming next for me.

Every day seems to bring something worse. My thoughts hurt as bad as the sun in my eyes. I take a deep breath, push the start button, and pull out of the parking lot at a low rpm. I make a left then merge to the freeway on-ramp and go from zero to 100 in seconds despite the nearly flat tire. I'm back to the safety of my house in a blur.

The front door squeaks as it opens and Adolf runs up. Skip is home but goes to his room to avoid contact with me, probably afraid I'll be in a bad mood. *What is going to happen will happen*, I think. If anyone thinks they're a shot-caller they'll soon learn that life can't be directed. Shit happens and then you deal with it; we're all just along for the ride.

After the morning I've had I need a rooster bad and I reach for the Stoli, pouring it into a glass. I drop a drinking straw into the cranberry bottle so it fills up to the top, then I use it as a dropper to add the perfect amount to the Stoli. I'm starting earlier than normal but after the day I've had I need it.

The phone rings and I don't want to talk to anyone so I don't answer. I've got to do six months and I don't feel particularly sociable. I ignore it and the phone eventually stops ringing. Two hours pass on the couch. I have a couple more roosters and the phone starts to ring again. *Nope, I'm not answering.* It stops but a minute later starts up again.

"It's not for me," I say aloud. "Right, Adolf?"

He hears his name but just kicks his legs on the couch where he's lying down. It's nighttime by now and I'm getting really drunk and I don't want to see anyone, I just want to feel sorry for myself. I get up to make another rooster and the wall phone rings again as I go past it. I pause beside it, willing myself to ignore it. I'm drunk and highly open to suggestions and could end up doing another run with Poppa Chulo and Rolando, who are back from Mexico now. *Okay, I'm drunk. So what?* I pick up the phone.

"Hello?" I say.

"Is Jorge there?" A female voice asks. It's Shelly, a girl that Jorge dates from time to time.

"No, Shelly," I say. "I haven't seen him."

"What are you doing?" she asks.

"Just partying with Adolf," I reply, "and drinking while I can."

"Do you want to go party with me?" Shelly asks. "I'm really bored and I want to go out."

*What did she just say?* I think. "Well, Jorge isn't here."

"Yeah, I heard what you said, Walt. He's never there. But do *you* want to go out. I'll drive."

"Well, okay," I say, going into a brain freeze. "I'm partying by myself so a change of scenery might do me good."

"I'll be over in a few minutes," she says and hangs up.

*What is this about?* She's hot but I don't really know her. Maybe she has some friends I can meet. I'm feeling self-destructive and wondering how my situation can get any worse. Give me six months or give me six years: I'm drunk and I don't care what happens. I'm out to have as much fun as I can before I turn myself in. Life as I know it is going to come to an abrupt stop soon. I'm lost and adrift on the ocean and don't know how to read the stars to get back home. The last thing I need to do is party with one of Jorge's girlfriends. I'll go to a strip club and be gone before she gets here. I grab my stuff, make a freshy, and head out the front door.

## Chapter 22
## A Crazy Run

I open the door and Shelly is standing on the front porch, about to reach for the knob. "Oh, wow," I say, stumbling for words. "I was just going out to the strip club. I didn't think you were coming."

"Can I go?" she asks. "We can take my car."

"Okay," I say. "I'm not sure I can drive anyway."

I take a swig off my rooster and we climb into her little car. It's a small, black, Honda CRX that's low to the ground. I'm really drunk so I'm actually glad she showed up when she did. This fits the pattern of what I've been through the past year. I have no control of what is happening in my life and have nothing I'm trying to achieve. I'm just along for the ride, although I now know that ride ends in jail. I envy those who have a strong goal like becoming a doctor or training to be an astronaut and going to Mars. College is just about done and I have no dreams in life to pursue. *Forget those thoughts,* I tell myself. *Just get drunk.*

"Where are we going?" Shelly asks.

"You're asking the wrong person about the right way to go," I say.

"What?"

"Oh, nothing," I say. "I was thinking about something else. Just go to the 405 and head north."

Music blares from her radio and I get lost in my thoughts as she drives to the freeway. Now that college is almost over can I really say that I'm smarter than people who don't have a degree? Not really. College just shows that you have the discipline to finish something. It isn't really about intelligence. For me it was just a way to buy time to figure out what I wanted to do in life. I didn't do it for the bullshit that other people buy into like being able to get a good job, wear a suit, have a family, and start the endless cycle all over again for your kids. *No. That's not for me!*

"What's not for you, Walt?" Shelly asks.

"Uh, nothing," I say, realizing I'd spoken out loud. "I'm just drunk."

My life is like a period at the end of a sentence. I'm not going to be a teacher, a wrestling coach, a suit-wearing lawyer like that geek DA, or even a pro boxer getting ripped off by scumbag promoters. No, I'm going to jail. I'm a 28-year-old teenager and what I want to do in life doesn't exist. There is no place for warriors in the modern world. I should be living centuries ago, sitting on a wooden bench in a Viking longboat, pulling on a 20-foot oar with a bunch of other warriors and sailing to distant lands to conquer them. The flash of oncoming headlights pulls me out of my trance and back to reality.

"Hey, Shelly," I say. "Get onto the 605 North."

As she changes freeways I consider the Pandora's Box of misery my life has become and kill my rooster to kill the thoughts about my situation. I've got five weeks to live and I don't care what happens until then. Nothing matters anymore.

I look over at Shelly as she navigates through traffic. She's been nothing but a booty call for Jorge the whole three years we've been roommates. Now I'm in her car going to a strip club with her. She changes lanes and the reflective road bumpers vibrate the car just like this moment is vibrating the core of my personal integrity.

Shelly isn't Jorge's girlfriend by any means, but he has been seeing her on and off for a while. But I only have five weeks left in my life and then I'm gone with no guarantee I'll ever make it out; especially if the DA has his way. If I only have five weeks left to live, I decide I'm going to be selfish.

Shelly parks up front at the strip club that's in a seedy neighborhood. I've been coming here with the boys for a while now and the talent is top shelf. There's crazy ass inside these doors and I've run through all the girls and know everyone who works here. There's no one here that I would say likes me, or I them for that matter, but it's a good place to get drunk and have some scenery while you throw down drinks.

I walk up to the window where Jimmy, the doorman, is sitting behind a glass partition. "What's up," I say. "This is Shelly, my designated driver for tonight."

"That's cool," Jimmy nods. "Have a good time."

Jimmy is 68 and nearly bald with cheater glasses on the end of his nose. He wears an old Arrow button-down shirt and gray polyester slacks. He smiles as he brushes his bad comb-over from his eyes. I would bet that he has screwed all the girls that work in this shithole. *Run down the hill, young bull*, I can imagine him saying to me.

"I'm going in for six months in a few weeks," I tell him as I leave the booth and head inside.

"Well in that case," he yells after me, "have a really good time."

I look back at him and smile; it's looking forward that makes me frown. I go to the runway and pull out the 1960's kitchen chair and belly up with Shelly beside me. My roommate's sometime girlfriend is sitting next to me in a strip club and I wonder what exactly I'm doing. I'm drunk but I still know what's up. She wants to sleep with me. Even though I only have five weeks left to live, for some reason I'm still holding onto my personal code of integrity. It's hard to do when you're sober, much less drunk.

I stare at the mirrored disco ball as it diverts light across the room. Several strippers come and go and I have another drink. A new song starts and a stripper named Amber with size D assets comes out and gets everyone's attention. My head bobs up and down as her breasts bounce around and I start to lose my balance on the chair, grabbing the stage to keep from falling.

"Let's get out of here, Shelly," I say. "I'm really messed up."

I lean on her as we walk out the door just to keep from falling over. As we pass Jimmy he takes it for affection and winks at me.

"Have fun, Walt," he says.

*Yeah, why the hell not?* I think. The heavy steel door slams shut behind us as I stagger to her car and fall into the passenger seat. She closes the door for me then gets in and heads for the freeway. As we speed down the 605 I stare out the windshield as the heater clears the frost.

The hum of the tires puts me in a trance. My eyes are open but I'm asleep inside.

"We can't go back to your place," Shelly says, breaking the silence. "Jorge will be there. I don't think he really cares but it would just be weird."

*Oh, man*, I think. *It wasn't my imagination. It really is on.* "Stop at the hotel at the last exit before the house," I say. "I've only got five weeks."

"What?" she asks.

"Nothing," I say. "Just get off there."

She exits the freeway when we get near the house and pulls into the parking lot. It isn't a great hotel but it's clean and cheap. I throw some bills to the clerk and we get a key and go into the room. It's hot and I go to turn on the air conditioner but it's broken. *Forget it. I'm too drunk and in too deep to ask for another room.* I fall on the bed and watch as she slowly takes off her clothes. She pulls me to the edge of the bed and I grab her smooth inner thigh and squeeze hard. My hand is four inches from her crotch and she is ready as I get my own private version of the Chinese water torture on my wrist. We fall together in a jumble on the bed, my face buried in the scent of her hair. We melt together as my head spins and our bodies twist.

Morning light streams through the window as I wake to the groan of the air conditioner, which has somehow come on in the night. I feel a body next to me and instinctively put my hand out to shake Adolf before realizing it isn't him.

"Wake-up, Shelly," I say. "It's checkout time."

The sun is beaming through the window and into my eyes. I hate waking up to sunlight as much as I hate the alarm clock. I'm a night person and don't live by the rules of normal people. I still have a residue buzz going and need to get home. We look at the disheveled state we're both in and start to laugh. It's cool there's no weirdness between us.

"That was a crazy night," she says as we get dressed.

"Ya think?" I answer.

We get out of the room and climb into her CRX and it seems even lower than it did last night. My head is still spinning like a top as we get onto the freeway. I've bitten the forbidden apple of a friend's booty call. Even if he doesn't care it's still not in my code of conduct. I suddenly get a feeling of awkward shyness that I don't think I've ever felt before. I shouldn't have done that but I was drunk and she was more than willing so things happened. It's an observation not an excuse. We both had fun and it's done so there's nothing to do but live with it.

By the time we meander through the mid-morning traffic to my house it's around noon. When I open the door it's like a rush of air is pushing me out of the car. There's a weird pause between us before I finally speak.

"I'll see you later," I smile. "Call me if you want to party."

She smiles back at me. "I will. You're a lot of fun, you know."

I squint against the sun and bend over to look through the open passenger window. "I'll be here."

I turn and stumble up the driveway. My residual buzz coupled with the beating sun is making me feel more than a little discombobulated. I stub my toe on Adolf's heavy steel chain that I hook him up to when I can't watch him. *Shit! That hurt!* I make it to the front door and go inside slowly, wondering if anyone saw Shelly drop me off, and am relieved to find no one home.

I suddenly remember that it's Mother's Day and Skip and Jorge are both at their parent's houses. *Thank God for small favors.* Adolf runs up and I pet him behind his ears. He looks up and focuses on my face.

"Hey, boy," I say. "I wish you could understand what I want to tell you. I know you want to know."

I know that we don't need to speak, though. Everything that needs to be communicated is done with our eyes: human to animal, and animal to human. We're best friends and don't need words.

I grab the phone in the living room and call my mom and wish her happy Mother's Day. Then I turn on the ceiling fan, collapse onto the couch, and fall asleep instantly. I awake a couple of hours later and find that Adolf has climbed next to me and put his head on my shoulder. I turn my head down and lightly bite his ear until he starts to growl. I laugh and rub his head and pass out again with my feet hanging off the end of the couch.

The next thing I know Adolf is barking. He runs through the kitchen and down the hallway to the front door. *What the hell?* I realize the doorbell is ringing so I get up and go to the front door, pushing Adolf out of the way. It's only been four hours since I got home and when I open the door I'm surprised to see Shelly.

"Hey, Walt," she says pertly. "You said to come by if I want to party, so here I am."

"Okay," I say rather stupidly. "Hold on a second."

I hold Adolf by the collar to keep him from jumping on her and she walks in and I shut the door behind her. As I walk into the living room in front of her I crack a smile. *Screw it. It's already done. Just have fun while you can.*

"I'll be right back," I say as she sits on the couch.

I turn down the hallway, go into the bathroom in my room, and splash cold water on my puffy face. I look at the mirror as the water rolls down my eyebrows and beard and laugh at how close to the edge I'm walking. I change tee-shirts and walk back with an energized stride. *Oh, yeah, it's time to party.* I turn the corner, head straight for the fridge, grab two soldiers and crack one. The bottles vibrate against each other like a Mozart symphony. I power down the first beer at the fridge and grab a third for the road. As I close the front door I see Adolf looking at me worriedly, wondering where I'm going.

I go back to the front and we leave the house and go out to her car. The CRX rumbles as she fires it up. The adventure of the unknown is bouncing around inside my head.

"I brought you a beer," I say.

"That's cool," she answers.

"I didn't think you were coming back," I say.

We make it to the end of the cul-de-sac and she turns left. So far today there's been no Jorge or Skip to weigh me down, just my jail countdown of four weeks and six days staring me in the face. As we drive away from the house I look out the window and up at the sun and raise my hand to block the brightness. I feel like I could reach out and touch it. I'm suddenly in a relaxed state that is not really me. I know nothing is going to last but I'm going to run hard before I turn myself in.

I live with a code of conduct and I'm not letting go of my personal integrity; I'm just not thinking beyond the next five weeks. Right now that's my entire life and what happens now just happens. It's a temporary escape from the sharp blade that has already been released and started its journey down to cut off my head. I've reached up and grabbed the sun and now I let it go, turning my face away from the bright sky.

I haven't done anything wrong but I'm letting Shelly and this crazy turn of events lead me in whatever direction it wants to go. We go to a strip mall to get some booze at a liquor store then make some travelers and cruise down the coast. Shelly shows me a new watch that her mother just bought her. It's a nice day and since it's a holiday a lot of people are on the road. We end up at a restaurant for drinks. The dinner crowd hasn't arrived yet so the crowd is light and we have the bar mostly to ourselves. We start to chat about nothing and end up drinking and hanging out for over four hours. I'm surprised at how fast the time passes.

"So what are you thinking of doing," Shelly asks, "now that you're done with college."

"Right now I'm just out to have a little fun," I say honestly. "I have to go to jail in five weeks so I don't want to make any plans until I get out. I'll think about the future in six months."

She doesn't seem the least bit concerned by this but just nods sagely. "I know the feeling. I just graduated with my Masters and I don't want to start working for a while. I want to take a little time off and relax and party."

After a few more drinks we leave and start back up the coast and Shelly lifts her arm to check the time and her watch isn't there.

"Oh, no," she says. "Where's the watch my mother bought me?"

I look in the glove box and around the floor but don't see it. "You must have left it in the bar."

She turns around and we go back and she goes in to ask about it and comes out empty-handed a few minutes later.

"It had to be in there," I say.

"Yeah, somebody must have picked it up," she says, really bummed out. "I don't know what to tell my mom. She was so happy to give it to me."

"Let's go get another one at the mall," I say, feeling bad for her.

"Really?" she says, smiling broadly. "That would be great."

We go into all the department stores in the mall but can't find the exact match. We find the same model in a different color and I get it for her.

"I'm not sure about this," Shelly says sadly. "It's not the same."

"It'll work," I answer, wanting her to feel better. "Nobody will notice the color is a little different."

"Well, okay," she says, obviously relieved. "This is really sweet of you."

She drops me off as the night unravels and I hit the bed, tired from all the drinking. I wake the next morning to the ever-present hum of the air conditioner in my room. The foil on the windows is loose and waving, sending flickering light into my face. I stare at the ceiling and think what a crazy run the last couple of days have been.

# Chapter 23
## Out with a Bang

I get up the next morning and make it to the bathroom and stare at the water in the toilet bowl. My brain cells crackle and buzz with the memories of the last two days. I go over my drunken selfish indulgence and refuse to blame myself for what went down. I'm not a one-man band and she was definitely part of the duet. It's not like Jorge is going out with her, anyway. He's probably glad I took her off his hands. As the toilet water flushes and refills, I try my best to flush the guilt from my body. I hit the shower, let Adolf out, and fall back in bed for a while before getting dressed and heading to the living room.

I'm on borrowed time so I decide I'm not working today and fire up the barbeque then eat and watch TV with Adolf. I start to power down roosters and late afternoon comes quickly. The door opens as the sun starts to dip outside and Jorge walks in from work.

"Hey, Jorge," I say. "What's up?"

"Nothing, man," he replies. He's got on jeans, a floral print spooner and topsider shoes. He grabs a soldier and sits down to party with me. I know I need to tell him for my own piece of mind. He has a tone of voice like everything is cool but I know he can sense something is up. I party like always and we go full throttle.

"Let's go to the bar by the freeway," I say, feeling cooped up from being in the house all day.

"Sounds like fun," Jorge replies.

"Hey, big dog," I yell to Adolf as we walk out the door. "See you later."

We get into Jorge's truck and I see that it's in perfect condition. Jorge fires up the motor and drives down the street in slow motion. He's an extremely mellow, kick-back guy and his driving mirrors his personality. As we drive sedately along my brain is screaming at me to tell him what happened with Shelly. But I just sit on my hands as we navigate through suburbia to the parking lot that sits between two bars.

"Don't park next to that other bar," I say as he starts to pull into a spot. "Go into the parking garage. I almost killed a bunch of people in there and I don't think they've forgotten yet."

He laughs and nods and pulls up two ramps to the second level. The sound of the nearby freeway hums into the parking spaces like the sound of my bedroom air conditioner. We get out and walk down the cement ramp.

"Let's have some fun," I say.

We walk out of the garage and as we approach the single-story building the disco beat from inside the bar starts to vibrate inside my chest. The glass on the outer walls is all fogged and I can't tell what's going on inside. We stop at the front door and start to pull out our IDs but the fat bouncers look us up and down and wave us in. Inside, the lights are down and the music is pumping. We walk to a table in the far corner and I sit with my back against the wall. Jorge walks to the bar, orders two drinks, then walks back and hands me a double Stoli with a cranberry back.

"Thanks, bro," I say.

"No problem," Jorge replies. "We haven't partied in a long time."

"I've gotta take advantage of it while I can," I say. "I've got to go to jail in a few weeks."

"Yeah," Jorge says. "Skip told me. That's messed up."

"I'll deal with it," I say. "But I got something else to tell you."

"Yeah? What's that?

"I was partying by myself the other day and Shelly called up looking for you," I say. "She was bored and came over and we went to a strip club and had some drinks and shit."

"Oh, that," Jorge says. "I already heard."

"Man, I'm really sorry," I say.

"It's not a big deal to me," Jorge says. "I go out with a lot of girls, not just her. She parties with who she wants."

"I'm so relieved," I say with conviction. "I was going out of my mind."

"Nothing to be sorry about, Walt," Jorge says. "Everything's fine. But it's cool that you told me."

"Well, I still feel a little bad," I say. "I'm going to jail and I'm not thinking right."

"It would be no big deal even if you weren't going to jail," Jorge laughs. "She's not my girlfriend. Hell, I've even dated some of her friends. Let's get drunk and forget about it."

We tap our glasses together and I take a long pull. Here I was tore up about going out with Shelly and telling myself that it was a drunken mistake and Jorge is totally cool with it. I feel like a ton of bricks have been lifted off my back.

As we set our glasses down from our toast, a scrawny 180 pound twerp shoulders his way between us, blows out a big mouthful of smoke, and then puts his cigarette out on our table top. I don't react because I'm so glad that Jorge didn't care about Shelly. But Jorge stares at the guy hard as he walks away.

"Did you see that tragically hip geek disrespect us?" he asks.

"Yeah," I nod. "He did, didn't he?"

I look at the long-haired, big-nosed guy in glasses who got in our space, and see he's standing with a group of black guys, like he's their leader. He sees Jorge staring at us and looks us over with an arrogant gaze, like we should be intimidated by him. *If anyone should be scared*, I think, *it should be you guys. This is Orange County not Los Angeles; if you want to play in Happening Beach I'm here for you.*

The guy looks over at me and puts his arms out with his palms up and mouths, *What's up?* That's two strikes for him and I'm not going to wait for the third. Jorge and I walk to their table and I get right in front of this skinny moron.

"Who do you think you are," I say, "coming here and disrespecting us? This isn't your town. You might want to leave on your own two feet before you have to be dragged out."

The white guy steps back and leans over and whispers something to the biggest black guy in the group. The black guy steps up to my face and looks me in the eyes.

"What's your problem?" I ask.

"You," he says. Then with a quick motion he brings his fist up from his waist and punches me in the side of the head.

The punch doesn't stun me because it was all arm, so I bear hug him, put my leg behind his, and take him down to the floor. He tries to scramble up but I grab his head with both my hands and smash it into the booth seat he was standing in front of. His eyes start to roll back in his head and I look up and see the white twerp run away as Jorge starts throwing down on the other two black guys, hitting each of them with lefts and rights.

My guy starts to struggle again so I smash my fist into his face. He raises the glass he's still holding and I smash it with a punch as well, shattering it and making him drop it. All the fight has left his eyes now and blood is streaming down his face from a cut on his cheek.

"Go act tough somewhere else," I say under my breath, as I pop him a few more times. He's getting his ass handed to him just because of a little twerp who thought he was protected by some wannabe gangsters. I've locked horns with the genuinely scary hard-cases from South Central before and these guys are not them. I'm on him like a magnet on steel and keep popping him until the bouncers show up in force and tear me off.

When the black guy gets to his feet his face is closing around both eyes and he's breathing hard with his face downcast and leaning against the table. I check my right hand and see it's cut open from the glass and will need stitches. I wrap it with a cloth napkin and rush outside to back-up Jorge, who has followed the rest of their crew outside. I look into the eyes of the guy who sucker-punched me and see that he isn't a warrior. He got duped into thinking he was going to scare people by the little twerp and got a beating for his idiocy. The club crowd has filtered outside now and the little twerp has taken up a defensive posture away from the front door.

"Come on, you fuckers," I yell at them, standing next to Jorge. "You want to get down then let's go!"

As they back-pedal away the cops show up in two squad cars and everything comes to a halt. We stand around while they talk to the bouncers and then they come over to me and Jorge.

"The bouncers say those guys attacked you in the club," one of the cops says to me. He looks down at my hand and sees blood oozing out of the cloth. "You're going to need to go to the emergency room. You want us to arrest them and file assault charges?"

"No," I say. "I'm good."

"Alright," the cop nods. "Go get your hand taken care of."

Jorge drives me to the hospital but I have a good buzz going so it's not that bad. I'm in and out quickly with five stitches to close the cut and we get home and I crawl in bed with Adolf happily beside me.

It seemed like I had barely closed by eyes when the ringing of the phone jars me awake. *Who's calling me in the middle of the damn night?* Adolf jumps down and his toenails click on the floor as he stops by the door in a clear sign he has to go. I turn the knob to let him into the backyard and sunlight streams into the room. The painkiller they gave me for the stitches must have really knocked me out, I realize. I see that the clock reads 10:30 A.M. and I try to lie down and sleep but the phone rings again.

I walk down the hallway past Skip's and Jorge's rooms and see their doors are both open and they're

262

gone. I glance out the window and observe Adolf laying on the grass and taking in the sun as I reach for the phone. I'm hoping that it's Skip or Fred with some bids to do, but instead I hear Shelly's voice after I say hello.

"You sound sleepy," says Shelly. "What did you do last night?"

"Nothing," I yawn, looking at my bandaged hand. "Just normal stuff."

Outside on the grass, Adolf has arisen and is drinking from his water bowl. He shakes himself and then curls up in a ball and closes his eyes with not a care in the world. *Oh, to live his life,*

"What's normal?" Shelly laughs.

"I went out with Jorge last night and got some drinks," I say. I open and close my hand and the stitches stretch as my hand gets tight from extending my fingers.

"Did you guys have fun?" Shelly asks.

"I always have fun," I say.

"Yeah, I noticed," Shelly giggles. "Do you want to party today?"

"I'm always up for that," I answer.

"Great. I'll pick you up at 1:00."

As the receiver hits the cradle I go into the kitchen to make some toast and see Adolf's head pop up. He's got infallible kitchen radar. He slowly looks back over the length of his body, wondering if there's any food to be had. I wolf down the toast then shower and get ready to leave. I thought I had dealt with this situation last night when I told Jorge it was a one-night thing. Now she's calling me again and it's starting all over again. Neither one of us has anything to do for a few weeks so it's definitely nice to have someone to party with. At least Jorge doesn't seem to care. Maybe I should have ignored the phone and gone outside in the backyard with Adolf: two dogs having their day. I grab a sandwich and wait in the living room until Shelly shows up.

We exchange a perfunctory hug and head out and pile into her CRX. It seems dirtier today and smells like fast food. As Shelly turns the steering wheel to back out of the driveway the strap from the leather steering wheel cover falls across the top of her smooth athletic legs and I get interested again.

"What do you want to do?" I ask.

"I'm on vacation," she laughs. "Let's get drunk."

"Twist my arm a little harder," I smile.

*Jorge was cool with it so why the hell not?* I tell myself. She turns on the radio and we head downtown and make an afternoon tour of the bars that stretches into the evening. The night turns into one big blur of drinks and music and I vaguely remember hailing a cab to get home, where I stumble into bed and close my eyes to instant oblivion.

Before I know it the alarm is going off in the morning and I smash it with my hand to turn it off, sending a sharp stab of pain up my arm from the stitches. *Damn, that hurt! Will I ever not have to wake up to that alarm clock?* I stare at the red numbers on the clock and think how my mom would tell me that it's just something I'll have to get used to. I roll over in bed and suddenly realize, with a sinking feeling in my stomach, that Shelly is lying next to me. *Once can be forgiven*, I think, *but twice? What does my code of conduct say about this?*

"We need to get out of here," I tell Shelly. "Jorge is still here."

"Shit. You're right," she says.

In a mad scramble we throw on our clothes.

264

"Go outside through the bedroom door and along the side of the house," I say. "I'll pick you up down the street."

I walk outside through the living room and close the door behind me. As I get in my truck I see Jorge looking out the bathroom window, most likely watching me to see if I'm alone. The sun is out and the air is quiet as I put the truck in reverse and hear the groaning of gears. *I shouldn't be sneaking around like this*, I tell myself. *I'll have to confess to Jorge again.* I creep down the cul-de-sac and see Shelly waiting just around the corner in her cute, short flowered skirt and red blouse. She runs into the street and hops in and we drive off. I turn on the air conditioner and the cold air blows refreshingly over my hung-over and throbbing head.

"How did we get home last night?" I ask. "A cab?"

"Yeah," Shelly answers. "You were really out of it. My car's at Happening Harbor."

I drive over there and stop next to her CRX at the far end of the Dead Grunion parking lot, wondering if she is having any second thoughts about us.

"Thanks for a fun night," she says, grabbing her purse. "I'll call you later." She pecks me on the cheek and goes to her car.

*I guess she answered that question*, I think as I drive off. She seems fine with everything, Jorge included. I still have a residue buzz going and go into a hypnotic state, dreaming about my air conditioned room and warm bed. By the time I get back to the house the cars are gone from the driveway and everyone has left.

When I open the front door my personal greeter is waiting for me with tail wagging as he welcomes me back to the pack. As I make it to the bedroom and close the door I laugh out loud about the absurdity of my life. I hit the sheets like a skydiver falling from 10,000 feet without a parachute and am instantly asleep.

I awake four hours later hugging Adolf as if he were Shelly; or maybe it's the other way around when she's here. It's already afternoon but that's no surprise to me considering how hard I've been running. *But why not?* I'm going away soon and all this will be a distant memory then. I decide to shake out the cobwebs and to go to the gym, grab a lift, and then hit a run. I force myself out of the familiar security of the warm bed, humming air conditioner, and Adolf's peaceful snores and go to the bathroom and take a shower then get dressed.

Primed and ready I climb on my bike with the straps of my workout bag hanging around my neck like a yolk on an ox. I pull up to the gym after a quick ride and the familiar melodic beat of the speed bags fills the air. I didn't realize how much I missed the gym with all this bullshit going on in my life. One of the trainers comes up to me and asks where I've been and I tell him I have to go to jail in a few weeks and have been busy getting my life in order.

"Well, it never hurts to get a good sweat in," he says. That's probably the same advice he gives to everyone regardless of what their problem is.

As I wrap my hands I watch a new batch of wannabe bad-asses hitting the bag and jumping rope. I can see they have no fire, though. They think learning technique is the key to being a badass but they are just lying to themselves. *If I just learn this*, they tell themselves, *I will kick ass.* I want to go up and tell them it's not what you know but rather who you are. It isn't how much you can do but rather how much you're willing to do. There's a universe of difference between can and will.

I go through my workout and leave the gym and the new batch of losers behind. I pack up my gear and push out through the steel doors and the bright sunlight makes me squint. The cool air feels good after a hot workout and I'm glad I rode my bike as I swing my leg over the duct-taped seat. I laugh when I come across wannabes who have no idea how I would love to kick the shit out of them. I can't, though, because I live in a society that punishes warriors and rewards posers.

I shift to first and pop the clutch and head towards the liquor store, my head on a swivel looking for a certain Mr. La Mentiroso in hopes of seeing the remains of his most recent beating. I park in the liquor store lot and go inside where Marty is working. We have a beer from the big fridge in back and he's bummed that I'm going to jail soon.

"Yeah, it sucks," I say, "but I'll be okay."

We rap for a while longer then he slides me a twelver and I go out to my bike and pack it between my torso and workout bag. I cruise down the path I took home that night Jerome decided to start something with me and come to the old stone church. I turn right and drive by the front door of his house but it's quiet. I was hoping that he or his girlfriend would see me drive by and it would freak them out, but no luck. So I speed up and make it out of town on PCH and get home quickly.

I open the front door to Adolf and he's there with his usual greeting. After I shower I get busy with the twelver in the living room. I inspect the stitches and they're on the side of my hand so the boxing workout didn't hurt them. As the sun goes down I play with Adolf and grab his snout but all he does is lick my stitches. I'm halfway through the twelver when the front window lights up from the headlights on Jorge's truck. Adolf runs to the front door as I inspect all the empties on the coffee table. I've really been getting down.

Jorge throws his stuff on the wooden dining room table that's marked up from too many games of quarters and walks into the living room. "Hey, man," he says. "How's the hand?"

"It's fine," I say. "I boxed with it today."

"Right on," he replies. "Let's party a little and then go out to a strip club."

I slow down a little while Jorge pre-tunes and catches up with me.

"What club?" I ask. "The one off the 605?"

"No, man," he says. "Let's go to the new one they opened in OC. Some of the same girls work there."

"Fine with me," I say. "Same place, different location."

Jorge offers to drive so we get in his truck and have some travelers on the way there. The new club is located in a converted grocery store and is nice inside compared to the shithole we usually go to. We sit and order three or four roosters and watch the girls. By now we're really blasted and we go upstairs and Jorge has a few lap dances. I watch the dancers on the stage from over the rail and we drink almost until closing time. I'm glad Jorge is driving on the way back but we have no problems and its lights out in my bed within minutes of getting home.

When I wake up in my cave the next morning Adolf is snuggled next to me and the sun is sneaking through gaps in the window foil. My head is pounding as usual and

I'm relieved that Jorge seems to not care about the Shelly situation. He didn't bring it up once so he really must not give a damn. I feel better about it but still wonder a little, but decide I'm not going to worry about it anymore.

I get up and stumble down the hallway and Adolf jumps off the bed and races past me. As I turn the corner I hear the flaps on his doggie door flutter as he goes out to the backyard. When I get to the kitchen I look out the window and see Adolf on his stretch of grass taking in the sun, thawing out from the cave's cold temperature. As I go through the fridge and rustle up breakfast I give Skip a call at Fred's office.

"Hey, man," I say. "Are there any bids for me?"

"Not today, Walt," Skip answers.

"I need to make some money before I go in," I say.

"I understand," Skip says. "I'll let Fred know and to give you call as soon as something comes up."

"Okay," I say. "Thanks."

I hang up and grab a Diet Pepsi from the fridge and turn on the TV. I don't even have time to finish it before the phone rings. I rush over to pick it up hoping its Fred with some work but instead it's Shelly.

"How are you?" she asks.

"I'm fine," I say. "Just trying to find some work before I go in."

"What did you do last night?" Shelly asks.

"I went out with Jorge again," I say.

"I told him what happened between us the other night," she tells me.

"Really?" I say. "I did too."

"Yeah," she says. "He was fine with it."

"I know," I say. "No reason to hide from him like we did the other day. I just didn't want to throw it in his face before I told him."

"That's cool," she says. "Why don't you come over to my place? I've been to yours and mine might be more relaxed."

I consider her offer and realize that it isn't like I have anything else to do. "Okay," I say. "I'll cruise up."

She gives me directions and I putter around and get ready and it's early afternoon before I start driving in my truck. The vibration from the grooves in the freeway vibrates the stitches in my hand through the steering wheel and actually feels good. I get to her exit and drive down the main artery to the South Bay. This place is much different than Orange County. The buildings are old and made of cement and look like they were built in the '50s. All around me are outdated store signs, old-style stop signs, and homeless people pushing shopping carts. The closer I get to the beach, though, the better the buildings get and I can feel the vibe change for the better.

I wind down a one-way street on a hill that runs parallel to the beach and start feeling more at home. It's not Happening Beach but at least it's near the ocean. I find her apartment building without getting lost and park at a meter on the street. I've finished a whole siren on the ride up and I'm feeling good. I put some change in the meter, pour a freshy, and head up the old creaking wooden steps. The building is an old house that has been converted into apartments and her unit is on the top floor. I knock on the door and her very attractive roommate answers and lets me in.

"Hi," she says in a friendly voice, "You must be Walt. Have a seat. She'll be out in a second."

The furniture is from the '70s and I sit on the threadbare couch and take a sip of my siren. As her roommate walks to her bedroom her butt hangs out of her short skirt, matching the ample cleavage that is pushing up through her skimpy top. A few minutes later Shelly comes out in her regular garb of a sheer blouse, floral print mini-skirt, and high heels. I'm relatively sober today and for the first time I check out Shelly without the beer goggles on.

She's about five feet, four inches tall and maybe 125 pounds with a hard athletic body. Her brown hair is shoulder length and matches her brown eyes and bronze skin. She is definitely a cutie but I usually go for girls a little taller so she isn't really my normal cup of tea. But she's fun to hang out with and that's all we're both looking for at this point. I'm going to jail in just a few short weeks so right now it's all about letting the good times roll.

We spend the whole day together just hanging out at the mall and window shopping and then at night go to a bunch of bars on the South Bay pier in her neck of the woods. We eat a late night breakfast at a diner and then crawl up the stairs and crash, which is definitely better than sneaking around my house. I awake in her bed in the morning to the vibration of my pager and reach to the nightstand and fumble for it. The cool ocean air is blowing down the alley and into her window which is open about six inches. The page is from Skip and I see a telephone at the foot of her bed and reach down and grab it.

"Hey, Skip," I say, when he picks up. "What's up?"
"I have a bid that just came in if you want it," he says.
"Sure," I say. "Thanks."

He gives me the information and I put the phone down. "I've got to go to work," I tell Shelly.

"Can I go with you?" she asks. "I'm not doing anything else."

"Why not?" I answer. "It'll be good to have company on the road."

I drive to the house with Shelly and luckily Jorge is not there. I take a shower then we drive to South Orange County and park in front of the house that wants a quote. There's a bunch of bikes in the driveway so they have to have a lot of kids. A man in is late fifties answers the door.

"Hi," I say. "I'm here to give you a price on a garage door."

He's a friendly type and we banter back and forth as I tell him the different options. He orders the door on the spot, gives me a deposit check, and we shake hands.

He walks me down the driveway, sees Shelly's head poking out of the truck's passenger window, and pokes me in the ribs.

"I wish I was your age again," he says, pointing at Shelly. "I'd arm wrestle you for her. Must be nice to be you."

I share a laugh with him and walk away to the truck, grabbing the door handle to get in. The old guy was pretty cool. I smell of booze, I'm not working much, I have a lot of free time, and there's a hot girl waiting in the truck for me. My life is not what it seems to an outside observer, though, and I think about how I'll be going to jail soon. Being me right now isn't all that great. I get in, turn the key and we drive off.

"I saw that man pointing at me," Shelly says. "What did he say?"

"Nothing," I reply. "He just thought you were hot."

"That's nice," she giggles. "What do you want to do now?"

"Let's just have fun," I say, thinking about the little amount of time I have left. "Let's go get drunk."

# Chapter 24
**Gates of Smell**

The next few weeks are a whirlwind of bids in the morning and a blur of bars in the afternoon and evening until I pass out. I get to know the South Bay almost as well as Happening Harbor due to Shelly being there and us crashing at her place. But every week that goes by brings me closer to my own personal D-Day; the day my life as I know it will come to an end.

It's Thursday and I make it to my house and walk in the front door. My house doesn't have the feeling of being a sanctuary that it used to have. There's a different feeling. I've been on a vacation from reality for a while now and I can see the wall that I'm going to crash into looming before me. It's so close I can almost reach out and touch it. I'm not afraid of the wall but I don't want to crash into it head first either.

Jorge has moved out and so has Skip and the house is depressingly empty. Only my stuff is around. It's like I'm sitting in a school classroom looking for the other kids but nobody's inside but me. Adolf's paws echo louder than ever on the tile floor. I walk into my cave, turn on the air conditioner and fall on the bed. Adolf jumps up and takes a nap with me, not knowing that our days here together are coming to a close. I keep waking up thinking that I should be going to jail. *Yeah, I am*, I remind myself, *but not today*.

I finally give up trying to sleep and fall out of bed and call a storage place. I make arrangements to store the things I've collected over my life as I travel to my new adventure. I'm depressed but I force myself to keep doing all the mundane details that need to be taken care of. It's my last weekend of freedom and I know Shelly wants to go out and do the same old drill, but now it's different.

I get off the phone and Adolf is in the kitchen waiting for me. All my stuff is in boxes and only the fridge is still here with the couch and old TV. My spartan bedroom looks fittingly like a jail cell but for the next few days I'll have everything I need. I keep drinking as the day goes on until I get a strong buzz going. A sharp bellow like thunder comes from outside and echoes in the silent house. Adolf whimpers a little and crowds closer to me on the couch.

"You know I don't want to leave you, Adolf," I say, grabbing his snout and tilting his head up at me. "It's not my choice. I wish you could understand, buddy."

I put my nose on the cold black button on his face and we look eye to eye. For just a second I know he understands me. A flash of light comes through the front window and he jumps down and rushes to the front door barking. I get up and look out and see the two neighbor kids, a six-year-old boy and an eight-year-old girl, lighting off fireworks in the street. As their dad looks on they run around with sparklers from a Red Devil box sitting on their lawn.

They wave their arms in circles as their father sets off a cone that shoots red and white flames into the air. I start to laugh and put my drink down and start to clap in time to Adolf's barking. I'm the only one who can hear but it still cheers me up somehow. Independence Day is just around the corner for the country but lock-up day is just around the corner for me. After 20 minutes of sparkers, pinwheels, Smokey Joes and the occasional illegal bottle rocket the show is over and I go back into the kitchen and make a freshy. *To hell with it.* These are my last days of freedom and I decide I'll drink and lay low at the house with Shelly.

She comes over a couple of hours later with an overnight bag and plans to stay over. We get up and party all day Friday and Saturday. Sunday is the Fourth of July and we go watch the local parade. I see a lot of people I know, many of whom I've beaten up at one time or another. I'm not having a good time knowing what is coming so we go back to the house when it starts getting dark and drink ourselves to sleep.

Beep! Beep! Beep!

*Holy hell!* I swat at the alarm clock when morning rolls around to shut it off. Even on my last day of freedom I have to put up with that stupid-ass thing. I swear to myself that someday I'm not going to have to wake-up to that sound. I'll get up when I want to, not when I have to. My mom's voice comes into my head: *Walter, just calm down. It's just something you have to do.* I slam the snooze button again, get up in the dark of the foiled-covered window, and open the bathroom door.

The sunlight from the small ventilation window burns my eyes and snaps me awake instantly. As I get ready for the day I make a mental plan. First I'll take all my stuff to storage and then I'll relax for the rest of the day before I turn myself in. Shelly is a trooper and hangs out with me. After a quick breakfast I start taking one truckload after another to my storage unit as I move a shitload of stuff. I thought I could do it before lunch but 9:00 A.M. turns to 4:00 P.M. in a flash. When we're finished we sit in my truck in the driveway of the completely empty house.

"I have to go now, Walt," Shelly says quietly.

"Yeah, me too," I respond. "The last few weeks have been a crazy time. Thanks for everything."

"It's been a blast, Walt," Shelly says. "Good luck with everything."

There's nothing else to be said so she gets out and walks down the driveway to the street where her car is parked. The driveway is like a pier leading to a navy ship that is leaving to sail around the world. She climbs into her black CRX and it floats away down the cul-de-sac then into the open sea. We both know that when it's time for the ship to return to port, though, that nobody will be waiting.

It was a good vacation from the reality of where I'll be in a few hours but it's over now. Everything is over now. I walk through the front door and into the deserted house. Three years ago I walked into this same room when the three of us found this place and now look how it all ended. Adolf has a panicked look on his face as if he was afraid no one would ever be coming back to get him. I give him a reassuring squeeze on the ribs and his tail wags.

I jump in the shower and take a deep breath as the hot water runs over my head. *Forget it. I'll kick these 180 days out, no problem.* I soap up and rinse off the sweat and grime from moving. It goes down the drain just like my life and I stop the water and dry off. I put on a fresh pair of jeans and a spooner and stuff my dirty clothes and towels into a plastic bag.

"C'mon, Adolf. Let's go."

We walk down the hallway like we've done a thousand times before, but this time it's different because we're never coming back. Adolf knows something is wrong and keeps looking at me to make sure everything is alright. I call him outside with me and lock the door for the last time. As I begin my last walk down the driveway I start to laugh. I've had a lot of fun in this house over the past three years but good things never last; only shit sticks.

Adolf jumps in the door and scampers to the passenger side, excited to be going for a cruise. I roll the window down so he can hang his head out and then pull out of the driveway and go down the cul-de-sac. I pass the old, retired drunk that always hangs out in his driveway on a folding lawn chair. He watches me go past with no idea this is the last time he'll see me. I wonder if he'll miss having somebody to call the cops on.

I make the short drive to my parent's house, park in the driveway, and take Adolf inside. My mom is on vacation in Iowa seeing relatives so I call her long distance.

"I'm dropping Adolf at the house," I say, after my cousin gets her on the line. "Did you call your friend at the jail?"

"Yes," she answers. "He said he'll do what he can."

"Thanks," I answer. I can tell from her voice that she's stressed out. "Don't worry about me, Mom. I'll be fine. I'll see you when I get out."

"Okay, Walter," she says. "I love you."

"I love you, too," I reply.

I hang up the phone and wait for Coby to come by. He's supposed to pick me up but he's always late. He pulls to the front 10 minutes after he's supposed to and we get in and speed away. He drives like he's 16 years old, racing everywhere. We pull up to the front of the jail 15 minutes early and he parks the car on the street.

"You've got a little bit of time," he says. "Wanna smoke a joint?"

"No," I say. "Better not. I'll see you when I get out."

"When's that?" he asks.

"One hundred and eighty days, dumbass," I answer. "You've got to cut back on that shit."

"Good idea," he says, starting to roll a hooter for himself right in front of the jail. "Don't kick too much ass in there."

I get out and walk to the ten-foot-wide sliding glass door that automatically opens up to welcome me into the belly of the beast. As I walk in I hear a screech of tires and turn to see Coby, burning joint hanging from his lips, peel out in front of the jail and speed off. The guard at the front door turns and looks at me but I just raise both hands, palms up, and shrug before continuing to the front desk.

"I'm here to turn myself in," I say to the deputy behind the desk. "I'm supposed to be here at six."

He points me to a row of plastic chairs without looking up. "Wait there."

I'm tired from moving my stuff to storage and slouch down in one of the seats, sticking my legs out to stretch them. The radio behind the desk keeps going off and I've got nothing to look at. I give the deputy a once over and see that he's a typical cop. He's got a blonde flat top and looks like he lifts weights. The way he looks at the parade of losers walking by tells me he's sick of dealing with scumbags.

The plastic chairs are not comfortable. They are screwed to the floor and the backs barely recline. I push back as far as I can and cross my arms and look at the ceiling. I start to laugh to myself as I think about how I ended up here and where my life is at. I close my eyes because the bright mercury vapor ceiling lamps are burning too brightly to look at. That reminds of my friend, Marcus, telling me to wear my sunglasses while driving my motorcycle so they didn't get burned by the hot air. Marcus was a great guy who died young and it's strange that I remember that particular comment so clearly.

I laugh aloud thinking of how Marcus climbed into the back of that Bronco when we had the fight with the PJ Boys at Happening Harbor, which was a collection of five islands where the spoiled rich kids lived. Marcus and I used to drink at a park on the richest island, surrounded by crazy mansions while he dangled a fishing line into the water. He would drink his bat-juice-with-the-pink-bonnet mixed with coke and smoke cloves, not really caring if he caught anything. The rest of the crew would drink whatever their poison was and time would just slip by. I still have trouble talking about the night he checked out. Sometimes you just want the bad things to be as far away from you as possible but that's something I'll never forget.

---

What a weekend it was. I was at a bar in Westminster and Tim and I pulled into Brandon's Irish Pub parking lot, on the outskirts of a big retail mall. The bar was packed and all the weekend warriors were well lit. Tim parked his green Volkswagen Rabbit at the far end of the lot and we started our march to the front double-doors. We had just cleared the hood of the Rabbit when these four pretty boys wearing nice clothes and alcoholic bravery popped off to us because we walked in front of their car as they were leaving. There was an open lane they could have turned into ten feet to the left, so I knew they were just looking for trouble – and I'm always looking for fun.

"Move your ass," the tallest and biggest one slurred from the front passenger seat. "This isn't a sidewalk."

"What are you?" I shot back. "A crosswalk guard?"

"Screw you, smartass!" He shouted out.

*Oh, really?* I thought. *You want to go there?* Without a word I turned and stared at him, my hands closed up into balls of destruction, ready to fire on this suit-wearing fool.

He got out of the car with his three buddies and squared up drunkenly, his suit disheveled and wrinkled. It looked like he'd been on a two-day bender and hadn't changed clothes all weekend. They fell out of the double doors of a bar that they should have stayed behind and now their drunken buzz has put them in the crosshairs of what they are begging for. They didn't realize it yet but they didn't want what they were asking for and would be sorry when they got it.

Brandon's Irish Pub used to be an old tire garage for a May Company store. It's two stories tall and constructed of six-inch white, stone bricks stacked as tall as the liquid courage that's poured inside. For some drunken reason these fools thought they were tough just because they were outside of a bar. It's funny how our paths had crossed.

I let the tall one get close, waited until he threw a sloppy looping right, then stepped inside it and hit him with a short uppercut to the stomach, not wanting to risk breaking my hand on his face. The punch lifted him off his feet and he went down in a heap, puking beer onto the ground. One of his friends decided to unwisely step up and I'd had enough so I blasted him with a left hook that crunched into his jaw and dropped him cold. I could tell it was probably broken. Meanwhile, Tim had tackled the third one and was straddled on him, speed-bagging his face with lefts and rights.

"He's had enough!" I screamed at Tim, pulling him off the rich, clean-cut snob, now covered in blood and with eyes rolled back into his head.

The final one scampered back, yelling towards the bar for somebody to call the cops, instantly forgetting they were the ones who started it. I decided this poser also needed a lesson in parking lot etiquette and stepped forward but someone was quick on the phone and I already heard the blare of sirens in the distance.

"Let's go, Tim!" I yelled.

He jumped up and we piled into his Rabbit and headed out to beat the arrival of the flashing red lights.

"Take me home, Tim," I said, as the mall disappeared in the rear view mirror. "I don't want the cops looking for me at another bar. Someone might have gotten your license plate number. Maybe you should sleep at my house."

"I'm not worried about it," he said.

"Just to be on the safe side take the residential highway home."

"Quit worrying, Walt," he said. "I'm fine."

I pulled myself out of bed early the next morning and headed over to Tim's house where I saw his retired stepdad outside watering the lawn.

"Hey, Ted," I said. "Is Tim up?"

"Nope, Walter," he shook his head. "You did it again. The cops came and took him to jail at 6:00 AM. The bail bondsman wants one thousand and five dollars to get him out. His mom and I will kick in five dollars but you should cover the thousand."

I couldn't believe what he just said but I bit my tongue. If the old fool didn't already have one foot in the grave I would have blasted him right then and there. I told him I'd get in touch with a friend whose dad is an attorney and drove back home. I called my friend's dad in Happening Harbor and he told me there's nothing he could do until Monday morning, since it happened on a Friday night, but that he'd call the court on Monday as a favor to me.

"Is there anything I can do until then?" I asked.

"Yeah," he answered. "Get out of town and get an alibi in case somebody recognized you."

"Okay, thanks," I said, hanging up.

I thought for a moment and remembered that Marcus and some of the crew were out in the desert at his dad's golf condo that weekend. I made a call and the phone was picked up.

"Hey, Marcus," I said. "It's Walt. What's up?"

"Nothing much," Marcus said, "just hanging out in the desert. You should come out."

"I was thinking the same thing," I said. "Tim and I hammered some yuppie jackasses last night and Tim got picked up by the cops and Kevin's dad told me to get out of town."

"You don't need a reason, Walt," Marcus said. "You're always welcome."

"Cool," I replied, feeling some relief. "I'll see you in a couple of hours."

"As long as you're coming out can you pick up an eight-ball from Fred for me?" Marcus asked. "Dick stayed up all last night and got into my stash when I was in my room."

"No problem, Marcus," I said. "See ya in a couple."

"Be sure to wear your sunglasses if you're riding your motorcycle out," Marcus added. "It's crazy hot here and your eyes will burn out of your head if you don't protect them."

"Gotcha," I replied.

I went out and strapped an old, plastic milk crate that my dad had taken from the back of Dairy Doors late at night to use as garage storage containers and packed it full of clean clothes. I climbed on and kicked the gears shifter down, got on the freeway, and popped the gearshift lever up with the top of my foot. The hot leather of my white basketball high-tops burned through the gears as I hit the freeway and made the two-hour ride to Marcus's Dad's golfing condo in an hour-and-a-half. I could have made it faster but I didn't want to get pulled over given what I was delivering. I pulled up to the country club's massive gate, flipping my sunglasses up and squinting against the bright sun.

A rent-a-cop came out from an air-conditioned guard booth just behind the fence. "This is private property," he said severely.

"I'm Walter Foxx and I'm here to see Marcus Howard," I said to him.

He glanced down at the clipboard he was carrying and then nodded. "Oh, okay. You're on the list. They said they're waiting for you."

"Yeah, I'm sure they are," I smiled, thinking of the eight-ball I was carrying.

The massive, black, wrought iron gate slowly opened and I twisted the throttle on the handlebars, shooting away and making the front tire light under my hands. As I blazed down the road that cuts between the fairways I burst into a bellowing laugh. *The cops aren't here and there are no other problems that can find me*! I parked my bike in a visitor space, walked to the front-yard gate of Marcus's condo, and pushed the entry buzzer.

"Who's there?" Marcus's voice came from the speaker.

"It's me," I said, "with a special delivery."

"That was fast, Walter," Marcus laughed. "Get your ass in here."

The gate popped open and I pushed it forward with my foot and carried my milk crate full of clean clothes and other items down the walkway towards the front door. One each side of the walkway grew green bushes with purple flowers that were wilting in the heat. *Probably hard to keep things alive out there*, I thought.

Marcus opened the door before I even knocked and motioned me in. "How was the ride out, Walt?" he asked. "Hot as hell?"

"Actually, it was relaxing," I replied, "especially since I'm not in jail. If we had driven my car last night then Tim would be here instead of me. Thanks for the sunglasses tip; the canyon pass was a blast furnace."

An air-conditioner hit me with a cool blast of air as I walked in and Marcus shut the door behind me. I reached into the front pocket of my shirt and gave Marcus the magazine page folded into a bindle that I got from Fred. He took it and walked hurriedly down the hallway to the master suite just as Dick and the rest of the crew came out of their rooms. We started to party and slam down drinks at the kitchen breakfast bar that adjoined the dining area. After a couple of hours of drinking and messing around on the putting green outside the back door, Marcus came out of his bedroom.

Marcus was a big non-athletic guy with a full head of hair on a high forehead who was 6'3" tall and 250 lbs. plus. He was wearing a red flowered spooner and board shorts and brown topsiders with the steel outlets popping out. He was overweight but didn't give a damn and had a contagious way of putting a smile on everyone's face. He walked down the dark hallway with his usual big smile on his face and in his normal good mood.

"What's up, guys?" he said. "Let's party!"

I was in the kitchen so I opened the freezer, grabbed some ice and put it into two glasses. A bottle of bat-juice-with-the-pink-bonnet was sitting on top of the ice maker next to a bottle of Stoli; so I poured a pink lady with coke for him and a Stoli-cranberry for me and took them to the living room where Marcus was sitting. It was late afternoon and the sun was setting through the backyard sliding glass door. Marcus was facing the door and his teeth got whiter and his smile brighter as the sun crept lower. Marcus finished his drink, unfolded his arms, and reached behind his back and pulled out a compact, gray metal, automatic pistol.

"Check out my new prize possession," he announced loudly so everyone could hear. "It's a P226 with fourteen in the clip and one in the breech. I shot it yesterday and it's got a sweet action with barely any kick."

A cold freeze came over the room. It got as quite as a freezer in a butcher shop with the compressors pumping and the cow carcasses swinging in the cold, damp air.

"Put it away, Marcus," Dick asked.

This was old hat for Marcus as he loved showing off his guns and had done it many times before but it always made everyone nervous. Marcus was all yakked up and he chattered away and pointed it around the room. His eyes got big as he took a drag off his Djarum clove cigarette. The smell and his laughter filled the room.

"I'll take out the clip if it makes you ladies nervous," he laughed, popping the magazine out of the P226's handle. "Let's get out of here and have some fun."

He went to his room and came out a few minutes later having changed into a black spooner. "Let's go to the nightclub at that fancy new Hyatt that just opened up."

"Sounds good to me," Dick said.

We all agreed and piled into a big Suburban that one of the guys had driven out and went to the Desert Sunset club. It was completely cherry with giant, two-story tall TV screens and huge speakers everywhere that sent thudding bass vibrating up from the floor into the soles of everyone's shoes! Outside of the two story windows was a manmade lake with electric boats taking high-rollers to restaurants where they could eat away from everybody they think they're better than.

*This was a place I could never get to unless I knew Marcus,* I thought morosely. I came here on a $500 motorcycle wearing surf-shop clearance-rack clothes with a milk crate strapped on the back. Despite all that I think how lucky I am to be here and not be in jail like poor Tim. The whole club was empty with no girls at all and so we got the best table in the club, close to the bar and the DJ. The crew that was there liked to have a good time and Marcus was setting the pace, going full throttle and burning hard, doing small bumps off a credit card. He wiped his nose and walked to the bathroom, returning a few minutes later.

"There's no waiting line to get a stall," he said to me. "You want a little bump?"

"No, Marcus," I said. "Thanks but I'm good."

It's almost closing time when a couple of young punks from the Harbor come strolling in. They were just little bitches spending their daddy's money but Marcus recognized them.

"Hey, kids," Marcus said, ribbing them a little. "You want to go back to my dad's place at the country club with us and party?"

"Sounds good," the taller of the two replied. "We'll follow you."

We all filtered out of the empty club and made it back across town and through the big, black gates of the country club. From there it was only a short drive down the fairway road to Marcus' roost on the 18th hole. Marcus opened the tall sliding door that looked out over the green and turned on the stereo which funneled out hardcore punk rock noise. The rich Harbor punks were in the living room smoking cloves and dressed in spooners and board shorts. Marcus was smiling constantly and was lit up good. He had been twisting the throttle hard and there was no sleep in his future.

All of sudden Marcus got up and walked down the dark hallway to the master suite. As the heavy door closed behind him the room quieted as the life of the party had left. After a few minutes his door opened and Marcus reappeared and came back out to the living room and sat in the big leather recliner that he always used. He looked over at the Harbor kids and then glanced at me and cracked a sly smile. Then he leaned forward and reached into his back waistband, drawing out the little P226 semi-automatic pistol. The magazine was not in the handle of the gun and he treated it as a big joke but just having it waved around made everyone flinch.

"Whoa, Marcus," I said. "Take it easy."

Marcus stood up and pointed the gun at the little Harbor punks to introduce them to his new toy. They obviously had never had a gun pointed at them before and their eyes grew big and their faces tightened with fear. They couldn't possibly understand how to react to the barrel of a gun because they hadn't lived life yet. Marcus took the aim off of the little boys who thought they knew how to get down but were now wetting their pants. He pointed the handgun around the room and then out the window. As the handgun passed in front of everyone's faces the mood of the party changed and everybody got a little nervous. It was funny when it was pointed at the Harbor punks but not so funny when it was pointed at you.

Marcus shook his head and rolled his eyes in exasperation, obviously wondering how anyone could be nervous around an unloaded pistol. To apparently show everyone there was nothing to worry about he smiled brightly, stretched his arm out, and pointed the gun at his head. We could all see there was no magazine in the gun but it still made everyone wince, which made Marcus smile even more at his joke. Just to prove his point he laughed and squeezed the trigger.

There was a loud pop and an explosion of red as the gun fired and Marcus fell lifeless to the living room carpet. *Holy Shit*! There was still one in the pipe that Marcus never cleared. As he died so did my belief that I would live forever and that bad things would never happen to good people. My childish faith died right there. Party while you can and live every day like it's your last because you never know.

---

"Foxx, get up," a voice says harshly.

I jerk my eyes open and with a startled glance at the clock see that I've been in the seat for over two hours. Standing up actually sounds good and I stretch as I uncoil from the chair. The building is so clean from the inmates constantly cleaning it that you could eat off the floor. But it's still a jail and in this case cleanliness is definitely not next to godliness. A big steel door rattles open at the far end of the lobby and another deputy walks out.

"This way, Foxx," he says.

I go slowly across the room to the steel door and walk in. I'm in a covered outdoor walkway that feels like being in grade school. It's 50 yards long and every 10 paces there's a blue metal column that holds up a corrugated steel roof. It has 45 degree bends in it and looks like the folds of an accordion bellow. The sun is just going down and my heart is pounding with apprehension. *Is this the fork in my life that will take me down a path I don't want to travel?* If I hurt somebody inside then I'll be in here forever sitting in a cell and living with scumbags.

*Now that I've walked through the gates of hell*, I think to myself, *will I ever see heaven again?* Heaven to me is a bar, a pool table, a rooster, and somebody to fight. *Does that make God a bartender?* I smile at the thought and walk towards the far end of the hallway as a motor groans and the steel door shuts behind me.

## Chapter 25
## Belly of the Beast

A deputy walks out from a side door. "This way," he says, with a look of bored indifference on his face.

I walk into the cell he directs me to and it shuts behind me, locking with a loud clunk. Two steel benches hang on the side walls and on the far end is a glass wall with another door that opens to a counter staffed by several deputies. The wall is made of thick glass and I can't hear anything they say. I'm alone in the holding cell so I sit on one of the steel benches and watch the deputies at the counter do paperwork. The cell smells like shit, with a disinfectant odor masking a sour but noticeable hint of unwashed bodies and day-old puke. *This is more like the gates of smell than the gates of hell*, I think. After a few minutes the rear door vibrates and slowly slides open.

"Foxx," the P.A. speaker blares, "come to counter seven."

I walk out of the holding cell and look through the thick glass behind the counter into what has to be the nerve center of the jail. It's a big office jammed with desks with green-uniformed deputies carrying manila folders, walking between them like ants with breadcrumbs. There are at least 20 bank-like teller slots in the glass and I stop at my counter in front of a female deputy who's reading my file.

"Mr. Foxx," she says. "You're here for assault and have been sentenced to six months."

"That's right," I say.

"Have you ever tried to kill yourself?" she asks.

"Nope," I reply. "Just others."

"Very funny," she says without looking up. "Are you feeling depressed or suicidal now?"

"Nope."

"Okay. Go and wait in that cell across the walkway."

I look around and see another empty cell with an open door facing the counter. I walk in and see that the bench on this one is solid concrete from the floor up. I hear the now-familiar clunking noise and the glass door slides shut. The cell is big and looks like it could hold 20 people or more but I'm the only one in it. Next to my cell is a line of 13 others and they all have glass fronts facing the deputies' office.

As the hours go by one dirtbag after another comes in, talks to the female deputy and is sent to a cell further down the line from where I'm at. I soon get tired of dirtbag-watching and close my eyes. After a while I hear a clunk and the glass door slides open. I look up and see a white guy in his early twenties walk in. He has brown hair and eyes and looks scared to death. He sits down at the far end of the bench and bends over at the waist with his elbows on his knees, looking at the floor. He has on a collared dress shirt, nice jeans and running shoes and looks like a college student.

"Hey," I say, looking to break my boredom. "What are you in for?"

"DUI," he says slowly, looking up cautiously. "You?"

"I got in a fight," I say.

I can tell it's his first time behind bars and he's scared so I talk to him and he seems to relax a little. More dirtbags come in and talk to the female deputy behind the glass counter and are sent to other cells. The night drags on slowly and the hours seem like days. The door clunks open again after a while and an older Mexican guy walks in. He's 5'8" or so, wearing nice clothes, and is scared also. These guys are both cherries, I realize, and nervous as hell. We all chat a little and I confirm that it's their first time in jail and both for DUI. They are terrified to be here.

More raggedy-ass dirtbags come in and are sent to other cells down the line. I finally realize that I'm in the cherry cell. Being in the clean-cut pussy holding tank is fine with me. Outside the glass I see three tatted guys with jail-yard muscles come by, sweeping the floor. Two of them have brooms and one is pushing a wheeled trashcan. They are dressed in prisoner garb and are wearing yellow plastic bracelets. *Typical jail losers*, I think.

I glance over at the cherry boys and they are looking at the janitor prisoners with fear written on their faces. One of the janitors makes eye contact with me and I glare at him. He stares at me for a moment and then a thin, cruel smile crosses his lips.

"Hey, I remember you," he says loudly, his voice muffled through the glass. "We're gonna get you, sucker!"

"Is he talking to you?" the college boy asks.

294

"He'll be sorry if he is," I say.

I walk to the glass wall and with a sudden movement punch the door. The loudmouth scumbag jumps back away from the wall and I point at him.

"You're dead!" I bark. "I'll teach you to not mess with me!"

The smile leaves his face replaced with a big O as his mouth gapes open. The scumbag now looks like one of the cherries sitting next to me, with fear in his eyes. He grabs the trash can and looks down and the three of them hurry away, their wannabe macho bullshit having turned into scared schoolgirl whimpers. I back sit down and the cell is quiet for a while.

"Do you know them?" the college kid asks.

"Nope," I say.

"Wow," the college kid says, his eyes getting big.

"They were just trying to punk us," I say. "They're lucky that glass was there."

The two cherries edge next to each other in the holding cell that smells like shit and puke, as if there were strength in numbers.

"Where do you think we'll end up?" the college kid asks.

"I'm hoping for the Honor Farm," I say.

"What's that?"

"It's an outdoor work area in south Orange County. No cells, just barracks, and you're not locked up like in this bullshit place. My mom works with the Sheriff's Department, administering the savings accounts for the head guys getting ready to retire. She made some calls for me. It's not one hundred percent sure but I've got my fingers crossed."

More time passes and it seems like I've been in this cell forever. Finally the door slides open again and a deputy walks in.

"Everybody out," he says.

We walk behind him in the direction the dirtbags have been going and into another cell. There are three guys in the cell and they all have dirty clothes, shoes with no laces, messed-up hair, and unshaven faces. I sit on the bench away from the dirtbags. The two cherries from my first cell are getting even more scared. I can see it in their faces. They sit near me but still hang together. After an hour the door slides open again and the same deputy walks in.

"Okay, guys," he says. "Let's move along."

All of us get up and file out and he points us to a cell deeper into the jail complex. We walk along the hallway that runs in front of the glass cells and stop at the last one, which is filled with nearly 20 dirtbags all dressed in rags like the three guys from the last cell. The college kid, the older Mexican guy, and I are the only ones who look presentable. The rest of these guys are scumbags and the cell smells like shit from their body odor. I sit in the corner and the cherries squeeze in next to me. Everybody has their backs against the wall and I'm watching just in case one of these losers tries something.

A little white skinhead gets up and walks across the middle of the cell towards the toilet. It's blocked off from the rest of the cell by a four-foot-tall cinderblock wall. As he walks everybody stares at the floor in the usual jailhouse protocol of everybody minding their own business. I watch out of the corner of my eye because the dirtbag is taking too long to do his business. He is not taking a shit but has cheeked a rig; probably a syringe of heroin that he's shooting up before flushing it down the toilet.

The two cherries have a look of pure terror on their faces as he comes out and goes by them to his spot on the bench. The cell door slides open after just a short while and everyone empties out to the walkway between the cells and the office area. We move to yet another glass cell and from this vantage point I can see that the office area the deputies are in is a huge rectangle. The game of musical cells has moved me down one of the long sides and I'm now in a cell on the shorter bottom side. The counters in front of this cell are different from those on the long side. They're compact booths with dividers separating each window, with a deputy sitting on a tall stool behind each.

Three names are called and the corresponding dirtbags go out of the cell door and talk to a deputy. When they come back and sit down, my name is called in the next group and I go out and walk to an open counter.

"Mr. Foxx," a black deputy says, "how are you doing?"

"Alright, considering," I say.

"You got any problems I can help you with?" he asks.

"Nope. I just want to get this over with," I reply.

He reaches through the opening and puts a white plastic bracelet on my wrist with my name and booking number on it. It's labeled "low security."

"Does this mean I'll go to the Farm?" I ask hopefully.

"I don't see how," he says, taking a few moments to look through my paperwork. "Somebody must have made a mistake. You're a high security risk. Only people with non-violent offenses go there."

"I figured as much," I say, disappointed. "Thanks, anyway."

I walk back into the holding cell frustrated. I can survive in here but I'd rather not. I'm not afraid to be here but rather afraid what I might do to some scumbag if they get in my face. Two more hours pass as the deputies work their way through the rest of the scumbags. Finally the processing ends and a deputy appears at the cell door.

"Everybody with a white band get up and walk on the red line to the next cell," he says.

The two cherries and I leave the main group and follow the line to a long rectangular cell with a steel bar at one end with mesh bags hanging from it. Behind the bags is a steel fence with a window in the middle with a deputy behind it.

"Grab a bag and line up at the window," the deputy who took us there yells.

We arrange ourselves near the back and he passes out orange jumpsuits, white undershirts, boxer shorts, and red rubber flip-flops. As he's doing that two female deputies walk in.

"Take off your tops," he orders, "and put them in the bag." When everyone has done that he speaks again. "Now take off your shoes."

With a pause between each order he works his way through all our clothes until we're standing jaybird naked in front of the steel fence. The two female deputies with him are acting like they are not looking at us, but I wonder how this works. I bet the female inmates don't have male deputies present during their processing.

"Now turn around, put your feet apart, spread your butt cheeks, and cough," he says.

I hear some half-hearted hacks from the college boy and a couple of nervous laughs from the Mexican guy and then he tells us to stand back up.

"You all look clean," he snickers. "Now put on the jumpsuits we just gave you, get in line, and turn in your personal effects at the window."

We shuffle forward in single file and I get to the window and hand my bag through the slot and read off my booking number, which another deputy attaches to my bag.

"Okay," he says when everyone has turned in their bags, "continue following the red line to your new cell."

We march on and I see that I'm now working my way up the other long side of the rectangle. It leads us to another long, narrow cell with a glass door at the end. As I walk towards it I realize that I'm finally inside the jail itself. Through the final remaining door I can see a walkway that leads to a turret that looks like a dark castle keep on the other side. A deputy is sitting in a steel mesh cage inside it that has small windows and a steel door.

Each side of the turret has walkways that lead away, each a potential path to the new adventure I'm embarking on. Once I go through one of those I most likely won't be coming out for years. I can easily see my 180 days in county jail becoming a decade in state prison.

The rest of the inmates we were with earlier walk in and I can see they have on yellow bands, which probably classifies them as higher security risks. The dirtbag who shot himself up earlier is with them and is stumbling noticeably. As they walk in the two cherries move closer to me until they're sitting in my hip pocket.

"You still think you're going to the Farm?" the college kid asks.

"I don't know," I shrug, not feeling like talking. "Maybe not."

Another hour of waiting passes and the scumbag that shot up is now in the Land of Nod. He head is bobbing up and down and he's slobbering down his jumpsuit. He leans his head between his legs and falls forward, slamming his head onto the cold cement floor. Everybody in the room knows what's up except the deputies and maybe the two cherries. He gets off the floor and drool comes out of his mouth in a constant drip.

*I've got to get out of this cement box*, I think, looking at the two glass doors at opposite ends of the cell. One is where I came from and the other is where I'm going and between them is a boatload of shit. I wonder what new treats are ahead beyond the deputy in the glass turret. I see him look at the slobbering scumbag and pick up a phone. A few moments later the entrance door opens and two deputies come in and walk to the scumbag, who is now slumped over on the bench.

"Hey," the deputy says. "What did you do?"

The scumbag tries to get up but can't rise to his feet, so the two deputies hook him under the arms and drag him out the door.

"Shit," the other one says. "He's OD'd on something. Better get an ambulance."

Their voices fade out as the door closes and they move further down the hallway. I glace at the cherries and can see that they are both freaked out. I just laugh to myself about that stupid moron. Who in their right mind would do that to themselves? The deputy in the cage seems unconcerned and is reading with the help of a long-necked desk lamp.

A new deputy walks out of the dark walkway behind the turret with an armful of files. He looks through them and separates them into two stacks, one of which is far larger than the other. He separates a file from the smaller stack and examines it.

"What in the hell is this?" he raises his voice to the deputy in the cage, loudly enough for me to hear. "This can't be right. I'm not sending Foxx to the Farm. Did you read his file? Get him a yellow band. I'm putting him into the high risk group."

"This came from on top," the turret deputy says. "You can't change his assignment on your own."

"Screw the sheriff," he says, "and screw you. Foxx is staying in the main lockup."

The turret deputy mutters a few curses, shakes his head, and picks up the phone. I look down at the cement floor and see the drool from the scumbag still splattered on the floor and wonder if that dude is still even alive. *Darwin in action*, I think. From a clock inside the cage I can see that it's been nine hours or so since I first checked in. The door in the cage opens and the deputy walks out with the folders in his hand. *Time to see what lies beyond the gates of smell*, I think.

"When you hear your name go out the far door into the main lockup," he says.

One by one he rattles out names as he works his way through the folders, sending each inmate to the far door in turn. He calls my name last and I walk to stand with the yellow band scumbags leaving the two cherries standing alone at the far end of the room.

"How about us?" the college kid asks.

The entrance to the cell opens and the deputy who was holding my file walks in. "Consider yourselves lucky. Go back and get your regular clothes and change into them," he says. "You two are going to the Farm."

"What about the big guy?" the college kid asks, pointing at me. "He was with us."

"He should be doing five years, not a hundred and eighty days," the deputy laughs. "There has to be some kind of mix-up. He's going in with the gangbangers and skinheads."

I resist the urge to scream at the idiot deputy or even to rush across the cell and bash his smiling face in. The DA has hard-on for me and if I smash some dirtbag he'll press for the full sentence and then some. He might even try me on felony assault charges and get me sent to state prison. The blueblood judge would be fully on his side. I glumly realize that the chances of me making it though my first week in the main jail without pummeling some lowlife are slim to none. I'm truly in the belly of the beast.

The adventures of no-holds-barred fighter Walter Foxx continue in *Street Warrior* and *Cage Fighter*, books two and three of David "Tank" Abbott's *Befor There Were Rules* trilogy.

**Full Circle Press, Inc.**
Presents

David **"TANK"** Abbott's

*BEFOR THERE WERE RULES* Trilogy

Book One
**BAR BRAWLER**

Book Two
**STREET WARRIOR**

Book Three
**CAGE FIGHTER**

Tank Abbott, the "Huntington Beach Bad Boy" and the world's most famous brawler, had over 200 street fights before bursting onto the MMA scene in 1995 when he shocked the world by defeating larger opponents with crushing ferocity inside the cage to become a household name. He later went on to star in the most watched "Friends" episode of all time before becoming a fixture at Ted Turner's World Championship Wrestling where he quickly became one of its most recognizable personalities. He later returned to the cage with his trademark intensity, leaving an indelible and enduring legacy.

His seminal three-novel work chronicles the adventures of fictional character Walter Foxx, who is at the crossroads of his life and who navigates the harsh worlds of bar brawling and street fighting with the goal of living his dream and following his passion and someday becoming a no-holds-barred fighter. Written from the ultimate insider's perspective, Tank Abbott takes readers from the parking lot to the cage with a realism and honesty about mixed martial arts never before told or exposed – until now!

**Available from Amazon.com**
**Also available on Kindle, or iPad and Android through the Kindle app**

Made in United States
Troutdale, OR
07/24/2024